PURLS AND POISON

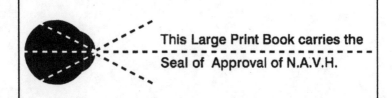

A BLACK SHEEP & COMPANY MYSTERY

PURLS AND POISON

ANNE CANADEO

WHEELER PUBLISHING
A part of Gale, a Cengage Company

Farmington Hills, Mich • San Francisco • New York • Waterville, Maine
Meriden, Conn • Mason, Ohio • Chicago

LIBRARY OF CONGRESS CIP DATA ON FILE.
CATALOGUING IN PUBLICATION FOR THIS BOOK
IS AVAILABLE FROM THE LIBRARY OF CONGRESS

ISBN-13: 978-1-4328-5487-4 (softcover)

Published in 2019 by arrangement with Kensington Books, an imprint
of Kensington Publishing Corp.

Printed in Mexico
1 2 3 4 5 6 7 23 22 21 20 19

*To the wonderful Nancy Yost —
all things a literary agent should be, and
so much more.*

We would often be sorry
if our wishes were gratified.

— Aesop

CHAPTER 1

That scheming little minx! The woman has no conscience. No soul! She's a bald-faced liar and a cold-blooded thief.

Suzanne knew she was speeding, edging fifty in a twenty-m.p.h. zone, but she couldn't help it. Luckily, the ride from her office to Maggie's knitting shop was barely a mile down Main Street and the Plum Harbor police were not the most vigilant group in uniform.

Her foot pressed the gas pedal, her brain churning with murderous scenarios.

I've always just sucked it up. Doing a tap dance to stay ahead of her schemes. This time, she's pushed me too far.

Lost in a silent diatribe, she nearly flew right by the Black Sheep & Company shop. The sight of familiar cars parked along the street told her she was the last to arrive. She usually warned her friends when she'd be late for their weekly get together, but the thoughtful touch had slipped her mind entirely. She knew everyone would understand when they heard her story.

A parking spot came into view; Suzanne hit the brakes and aimed the huge SUV. As the vehicle came to a jerking stop, the rear fender jutted into the street and a front tire was wedged against the curb. Suzanne barely noticed and didn't care.

Without pausing for her requisite hair and lipstick check, she hopped to the sidewalk and headed for the shop, trailing her huge leather purse and knitting tote behind her.

The Victorian house, turned into a retail space, had been neglected when Lucy's friend Maggie had rescued it years ago. As usual, Maggie's artistic eye had spotted the possibilities — the ample wraparound porch that was a perfect perch for knitters in the warmer months, the faded shutters and gingerbread trim that needed only a dash of paint to restore their former glory. It was "a jewel box" now, or so Suzanne might say in a real estate listing. Not that Maggie was likely to retire and sell anytime soon.

Maggie had left her position as an art teacher at Plum Harbor High School to follow her bliss and turn her passion for needlework into a full-time career. She had recently lost her husband, and needed a complete change to pull her from her well of grief.

Using her retirement nest egg, she'd bought the building and set up a knitting shop as cozy and inviting as her living room. Comfy love seats and armchairs were carefully arranged among displays of yarn and stitching supplies. A knitting nook near the front door provided another, quiet working space, and a large room in the back served as the perfect spot for classes and demonstrations.

The apartment above was soon rented to Phoebe Meyers, who worked in the shop and was sort of a surrogate daughter for Maggie, whose own daughter Julia was away at college most of the year. Phoebe had recently graduated from a local college with a degree in fine art and Maggie had promoted her to assistant manager.

Suzanne marched up the brick walk, barely noticing the flower beds on either side, freshened for fall with bright mums and purple cabbage plants, and more autumn flowers that spilled from boxes along the porch rail.

In the shop's front window, a grinning scarecrow in a hand-stitched vest stood guard over a field of pumpkins and skeins of yarn. Just above, scarves, socks, and baby sweaters hung from a tree branch, and a few curious blackbirds looked on.

She noticed none of it. Even the sign above the door, BLACK SHEEP & COMPANY, had no effect. The sight usually elicited a wave of pure calm in expectation of chatting and stitching all evening with her very best friends.

All she wanted to do tonight was vent her heart out and soak up some sisterhood sympathy. And sip some wine. Not necessarily in that order.

She stepped inside and saw the group in the back room, seated around the big oak table. It looked like they were just about to start dinner. An appetizing scent greeted her and she remembered she'd skipped a real lunch, resorting to the dwindling stash of diet drinks she kept in the office fridge. She could have sworn she'd left a full pack there just the other day, but her co-workers were not above food pilfering. That was the least of her problems today.

Maggie walked out of the storeroom that doubled as a kitchen, a bowl of green salad in her hands.

"There you are. We weren't sure if you were coming. We just sat down to eat. Everyone was so hungry. Come, take a seat."

"Working late on a hot deal?" Lucy's tone

was teasing but also admiring, Suzanne thought.

She glanced at Lucy and felt fixed to the spot. Maggie and the others — Lucy, Dana, and Phoebe — stared back, waiting for her reply.

"Not exactly . . . More like having a nervous breakdown."

"Are you all right?" Maggie drew closer and touched her arm. "Did something happen at work?"

Suzanne nodded, chin trembling. She thought she might cry, but valiantly fought the urge. "Not something. *Someone.* You know who I mean. The name that shall not be spoken?"

Everyone knew the famous quote from the Harry Potter novels about the evil Lord Voldemort, didn't they? Even so, Suzanne was sure the meaning was clear.

Dana smiled and shook her head. "Liza Devereaux again? Or should I say the Dark Lord-ess . . . ? Is that even a word?"

"Any way you say it, that woman is pure poison. She was put on this earth to drive me mad. And she finally succeeded." Suzanne felt her blood pressure shoot up all over again. "I'd like to string her up by the strap of that Prada handbag. I'd like to wrap that strand of pearls around her scrawny little throat. . . ."

"Suzanne, calm down." Maggie put an arm around Suzanne's shoulder and gently guided her into a chair. "What in the world has gotten you in such a state?"

Suzanne took a breath and glanced around at the group. They looked back at her with surprise and concern. As if she'd lost her mind.

"I sound crazy, right? Maybe I am. Dana, tell me honestly. I can take it." She turned to Dana Haeger, the group's resident psychologist, half asking, half dreading a professional diagnosis. "How would you rate my sanity, on a scale of one to ten?"

Dana's expression was pure sympathy. "I'd say you were extremely distressed. Just slow down and take a breath. How can we help you?"

She did take a breath, as Dana advised. But she felt tears well up on the exhale. Lucy sat the closest; she leaned over and patted Suzanne's hand. Then handed her a glass of Chardonnay.

"Here you go. I'll get your dinner. Calm down and tell us what your mortal foe did now."

Not good to drink on an empty stomach, Suzanne reminded herself. But she took a healthy sip anyway and tried to focus.

"Stole another sale right out from under my nose, that's what. It would have been my biggest commission this year. Maybe of my entire career!"

Dana sat at the far end of the table, most of her dish filled with salad, Suzanne noticed. "Liza is that super-sharp salesperson at your office, right? Your big rival?"

"To put it mildly. A rival is another mom in your kid's grade school class who bakes cuter cupcakes. Liza is a vicious predator, ready to pounce at any moment. A deeply despised nemesis. A painful thorn in my backside . . ."

"I think the expression is simply a thorn in one's side," Maggie corrected in a mild tone.

"I just call 'em the way I see 'em." Suzanne shrugged.

Lucy returned with a dish of pasta that smelled and looked very tasty. She set it down in front of Suzanne along with a fork and napkin.

"Bless you." Suzanne spread the paper napkin across her lap, then tucked another under her chin to protect her black cashmere poncho. She'd been careful all day not to drag the fringe through things. Not the most practical garment she'd ever purchased, though it did hide a myriad of figure flaws, and quite stylishly. Style was way more important than convenience, or even comfort, she'd always thought.

"Carbs are calming. Nature's tranquilizer," Lucy advised.

"Dig in and tell us what went down," Phoebe urged.

Suzanne took a small, fortifying bite. "It started Sunday. I was running an open house in Harbor Hills, the two-acre zone near the country club? A jaw-dropping colonial — five bedrooms, three and a half baths, gourmet kitchen, stadium-sized family room, and a gorgeous stone fireplace that —"

"— A highly saleable property, with a high price tag to match?" Maggie selected a piece of garlic bread and passed the basket to Suzanne.

"Yes, and yes. And mine, mine, mine. Exclusively. That is, until *she* showed up." Suzanne felt the pressure in her head build. She knew what people meant about seeing red, and it wasn't just the sauce on the pasta. Which was delicious. She had to compliment the chef. Maggie, she suspected.

"Liza Devereaux is a killer shark hiding behind Chanel sunglasses. She can smell a juicy listing from one hundred miles away. I

16

should have expected a sneak attack. But everything was going so smoothly, I dropped my guard."

"So Liza crashed your open house?" Phoebe prodded her.

"More like wiggled in, wearing one of her little pencil skirts and super high heels. And all that bouncy, fake hair. A great look . . . if you're a size zero."

Just picturing her mortal enemy on the fatal day made Suzanne's breath catch. Suzanne was a fashionista to her friends, but Liza had a certain classic, country club look that always won first prize on the office runway. Her rival's sleek figure — practically skeletal, Suzanne thought — just made it worse. She'd often heard it said, "You can't be too thin or too rich." Liza definitely had the former down and was very close to achieving the latter.

Suzanne paused for a crunchy bite of garlic bread as her friends waited to hear more.

"She claimed that Harry, our boss, heard there was a lot of traffic and sent her to help. As if *I* ever need help. And certainly, not hers. It was so obvious. She wasn't getting any action on her listings that day and slunk around to poach." Suzanne took another sip of wine and continued. "Before

I could check the story, Liza comes waltz-ing into the kitchen with Juanita and Bob Briggs. I've been cultivating those two for months. I showed them every pricey house for sale within fifty miles. A few weeks ago, they told me that they needed a break from looking. They promised to get in touch once they knew what was going on."

"That sounds reasonable," Dana said.

"Sure, I get it. But I never heard back and didn't want to be pushy. It's a fine line. Anyway, there they are. As large as life and prequalified over a million. The hunt was obviously on again, but I missed the memo."

She sighed and sipped her wine. "We all say hello, nice and polite. I could see they really liked the house. I knew they would. I'd even sent Juanita an e-mail last week about the property. Maybe she missed it? I don't know." Suzanne shrugged. "I talked them up a little, but Liza had covered the sales points and they had to go." She paused and sighed. "Looking back, I should have chased them out the door, tackled them on the lawn, thrown myself on the hood of their Land Rover. . . ."

"Do you really do that?" Phoebe didn't look surprised, just curious. She'd recently started her own business, a sideline to her job at the shop, and often asked Suzanne for sales and marketing tips.

"Whatever it takes, Phoebe. Never hesitate to make a total fool of yourself if it will close a deal. Did I follow my own Golden Rule? No. Oh golly, do I regret it now."

"Don't be so hard on yourself. They'd already signaled they didn't want to be pressured," Dana pointed out.

"That's what I thought. On Monday, I checked to see if they were interested, but they never called back. On Tuesday, I sent an e-mail. Again, no reply."

Lucy helped herself to some salad. "Uh-oh. I think I know where this is going."

"No place good," Suzanne replied. "This afternoon we had our weekly status meeting. The sales team reports on progress with clients, new listings and closings. That sort of thing. I always dread when it's Liza's turn. I never know what she's got up her sleeve. Today, with this big phony smile, she announced she just got an offer on the Harbor Hills property. *She* got an offer."

"— From your clients, Juanita and Bob," Maggie filled in.

"That is so unfair! Classic pickle jar syndrome. Just classic." Lucy tossed her hands in the air while everyone else exchanged confused glances.

"Classic . . . what?" Dana looked the most

confused.

"It's like a pickle jar with a tight lid?" Lucy explained. "Suzanne twisted and banged, ran it under hot water. Did everything she could to pry it loose. But it didn't budge. Then Liza gives it one tiny turn and it pops right off. And Liza gets the credit, while poor Suzanne did all the work. It's a law of physics or something."

"I know what you mean. Though I doubt you'd find that one in a textbook," Maggie murmured.

"That happens all the time. I just never knew what to call it before," Phoebe said. "Ever notice when a woman is dating some guy for years, and no matter what she does, he won't commit? The next girlfriend comes along and that slacker is running down to the mall, shopping for diamond rings. Pickle jar syndrome, definitely."

"I don't know about physics, or slacker boyfriends, but in real life, pickle jar syndrome stinks," Suzanne said.

Dana had put her dish aside and opened up her knitting tote. "I hope you brought this to the attention of your boss."

"Of course I did. I put in months on these people, gallons of gas and so much smiling, I sprained a dimple."

Maggie started to say something, then

caught herself. "Sounds painful," she said finally.

"Tell me about it. Liza, as phony as her stick-on eye lashes, chats them up for five seconds and waltzes off with my commission? No way, babe." Suzanne shook her head. "Over my dead body. Or *her's.*"

"Now, now . . . I know you're upset but there must be some reasonable way to sort this out." Maggie met her gaze with one of her school teacher looks. Suzanne felt herself simmer down, as if by long-conditioned reflex. "You must have confronted her. What did she say?"

"She brushed me off. The little witch. She claimed the Briggses were fair game. They must have told her I'd shown them some houses, but we hadn't gone out in a while. So she twisted it all around." Suzanne paused and then mimicked Liza's throaty, drawling tone. " 'Suzanne could have driven those people around for a year and never sold them a thing. I have an offer in hand in three days. With all due respect, isn't that what counts?' That's just what she said. In front of everyone. I was mortified."

"That's awful. How humiliating." Lucy's blue eyes were full of sympathy.

"And a total lie. I sell properties left and right and Harry Prentiss knows it." Suzanne heard her voice rising again, but she couldn't help it. "I was so mad . . . I was speechless."

Phoebe had also taken out her knitting. She looked up from her work and met Suzanne's gaze. "No offense. But I don't think we've ever seen you in that mode."

A smidgen of sarcasm, but true. Suzanne had to admit. "Yes, little old me. Tongue-tied, for once in my life. All I could do was lunge across the table and try to grab a hunk of that fake hair. Lyle Croddy, this older guy who covers commercial properties, held me back. It's all extensions. She thinks no one can tell, but it's so obvious."

Maggie looked concerned. "Oh dear. Sounds like a bona fide brawl. I guess nothing was resolved?"

Suzanne shook her head and sighed. She ate a few more bites and put her dish aside. "Our boss was upset. He reprimanded both of us. Me, especially. He wants to meet with us privately first thing tomorrow morning."

"At least you have time to cool off and approach the situation in a calmer, more professional manner," Dana said.

"The *situation*? There was no situation until she stole my clients. I called the Briggses right away. They would have worked with me. They claimed Liza pressured them and said there were a lot of offers and they'd better get one in if they wanted the house. A classic sales tactic. I've pulled that one myself," she confessed. "But she also told them it didn't matter who they'd started with and that she could do a better job negotiating with the owners." Suzanne brushed aside a few strands of her dark hair that had stuck to her cheek. "Another out-and-out lie. She doesn't even know the owners."

"Aren't there rules? Professional guidelines or something? Is she really allowed to do that?" Lucy sounded indignant — as much as her good nature would allow. Suzanne felt grateful for her loyalty.

"If the listing had been sitting on the shelf with no action for weeks, and Liza brought in a client and made the sale, I wouldn't have minded at all. Well, maybe a little," she admitted. "But we would have just split the commission. And something is better than nothing in my book. That scenario is way different than client-napping Juanita and Bob, and then brainwashing them. Turning them totally against me."

"A lot different, when you put it that way," Maggie agreed.

"Exactly. Why should I give her a penny?" Suzanne glanced around at her friends, as

23

she closed her case.

"Your boss has to admit her move was totally out of line," Lucy said.

"Most would. But this has happened before. Harry always takes Liza's side. And gives her a big slice of the pie, whether she deserves it or not. She could set the place on fire and he'd find some way to overlook it. She's his biggest earner, and if that wasn't enough . . . well, I shouldn't be telling you this, but they had a pretty serious fling a while ago."

"That explains it," Lucy said. "And makes defending yourself even harder."

"Is it still going on, this fling situation?" Maggie asked.

"Nope. Finito. Ended on a bad note, I might add. Liza even dumped her husband for Harry. Though I hear the marriage was already shaky. Maybe the affair just tipped it over the edge? People said her ex has a gambling problem and she got tired of bailing him out. No kids, so no worries in that department. Though I also heard the divorce has been pretty messy even without children in the mix."

Suzanne took a breath before delivering the punch line to her captive audience. "Anyway, once Liza was free, everyone expected Harry to leave his wife. But he

24

didn't. So Liza broke it off." She thought back for a moment. "That was about two years ago. Maybe a little more. If you ask me, Harry still hasn't gotten over it."

Dana looked up and slipped off her reading glasses. "Wait, I think I heard something about Harry Prentiss a while back. Jack used to golf with some guys who know him. I think he heard Harry put all his property and his business in his wife's name, to protect his assets. When he had this affair, he was stuck. He couldn't leave his wife without losing everything."

"So I guess men like to gossip as much as women do, though they'd never admit it," Maggie noted.

"And the country club foursomes shared the story as a cautionary tale." Lucy delivered the words with a humorous note.

Suzanne laughed. "Isn't it every businessman's worst nightmare? You can't leave your wife for the other woman without abandoning your entire fortune? But Harry's wife, Claire, doesn't seem like the grabby type you'd imagine in that domestic drama. She's an academic, with a PhD from an Ivy League school. The complete opposite of Harry."

"Does she teach at a college or something?" Phoebe took a few dirty dishes off the table.

"Nope. She runs her own school, a posh academy for baby geniuses. The 'gifted and talented' is how she spins it. My guess is that she's so out of touch in her ivory tower, she had no idea Harry was playing around," Suzanne said with a wave of her fork.

Dana had begun knitting, stitching in her calm, steady way. Like a plough horse, Suzanne liked to say. "Reasonable and bookish or not, with a good lawyer on her side, she probably would have held her ground and fought for her due."

"It happens more than you think," Maggie remarked. "Couples trapped in unhappy relationships because their finances are tangled up. Especially if there's a business."

"It must have been hard for Liza to work in the office after that. I mean, since everyone knew her private business." Phoebe had gone into the kitchen a moment and returned with a tray of peanut butter cookies, which she set in the middle of the table. They looked and smelled home baked. "Personally, I would have slunk away and started over somewhere new."

Phoebe selected a cookie and took a big bite. With her broomstick figure, she could eat the whole plate. Suzanne eyed the sweet treat but didn't reach for one. Even though the cookies were definitely calling her name.

"We're talking about a person with ice water in her veins and a calculator for a heart. But she did leave town. Not long enough for me, I might add. She moved up to Maine, to be near her sister. Was I ever relieved. Don't you guys remember?"

"I do. You were positively euphoric," Maggie recalled.

"Fool's paradise, it turned out to be. She was gone about two years. Long enough to take up knitting and be better than me . . . which doesn't take much, I admit." Suzanne sighed and waited for someone to deny her self-inflicted slight.

Lucy took the bait. "Come on, Suzanne. You're not so bad. You just need to settle down and finish your projects. You're not supposed to triple task when you're knitting. I think you forget."

"That's true. I really have to work on my needle attention span." Suzanne knew that she grew tired of projects too easily. A new pattern caught her eye. Or a brightly colored skein, full of possibilities, begged to be purchased. Knitting was a calming pastime for most. Even suggested as a means to make one more mindful, like meditation. But Suzanne felt little of that benefit and often thought she was too emotional to ever be a really good knitter. Her stitches got too loose, or too tight, depending on what she was talking about. Or even thinking about. Tonight for example, she was so worked up she knew she'd make a complete mess of things.

"Why did Liza come back to town after all that time? Do you know?" Dana asked.

"Her mother had a stroke a few months ago. Liza and her sister wanted to be close by, to take care of her. Mrs. Devereaux had moved into an assisted living community right before she got sick, but never sold her house. A grand, old place on Hickory Hill. Liza and her sister have been living there. I guess they plan to sell it at some point."

"I know that neighborhood. Lots of tall trees. Very pretty," Dana said.

Suzanne fished around her knitting tote and pulled out her project. "I never met her sister. Liza is an expert at keeping her private life and business life totally separate. Except for that slip with Harry, of course."

"She compartmentalizes well," Dana remarked, adding an official tag to Suzanne's observation.

Suzanne rolled her eyes. "If you need to stick a ten-syllable word on it, that's what I mean. I guess."

Lucy had taken out her knitting, too. She

was making a sweater for her husband, Matt. They were newlyweds, married in July, not quite three months ago. Suzanne predicted he'd love her hand-knit creation and wear it proudly. No matter how it turned out. Not so once you were married awhile, she'd learned. She recalled her husband Kevin's bemused expression last Christmas as he unwrapped the vest she'd made him. She couldn't blame him; even she knew the garment was more a demonstration of love than skill. And she'd given him extra credit for not laughing.

"You hear a lot on the office grapevine, don't you?" Lucy said.

"I'd feel guilty about gossiping, but I'm sure everyone talks about me when I'm not around. It works out evenly."

"So she came back to Prestige Properties? Interesting," Maggie said. "If she's such a good salesperson, you'd think she'd have lots of other opportunities."

Suzanne had wondered about that, too, but did see the logic in Liza's choice. "She probably could have had her pick. But why work your way up someplace new? She was, and still is, Queen of the Dump. She just went into exile a while."

Lucy was smoothing the stitches on one of her needles but paused to meet her gaze

29

and smile.

"The bottom line is, Liza Devereaux still has Harry wrapped around her little finger. That's why I know he'll never take my side. And why I'm terrified of talking to them tomorrow. I saw her stop him in the hallway after the staff meeting let out. She asked if they could meet privately before he left for the day. To convince him to fire me, I'm sure. But he was late for a big event, a fund-raiser for his wife's school, I think. She'd just dropped of his tuxedo and was waiting for him." She gazed at her friends, her tone low and nervous. "I heard him tell Liza to come in extra early and they would talk before they met with me."

Phoebe looked alarmed. She took another cookie. "You really think she can persuade him to fire you? She's the one who caused all the trouble."

"I know that . . . and you all know that. But I'm the only one in the office who stands up to her. The rest of the sales staff are a bunch of shivering sheep — no insult to present company, of course."

"None taken," Maggie assured her.

"I know that the rest of the sales team, Anita and Lyle, have some grievances with her. But I'm the only one fishing in the same pond and competing with her for the big sales. Harry doesn't like confrontation. It makes him nervous. He wants everyone to play nice. Or at least, to pretend that we like each other."

"So, what will you say tomorrow at the meeting? Maybe you should practice with us," Dana suggested.

Suzanne finally broke down and took a cookie. She thoughtfully munched on a bite. "Not a bad idea. A little rehearsal might help." She often rehearsed sales pitches in the bathroom mirror. It did help. "Here's how it will go. Harry will want us to share the commission. But I think I should get the whole thing. It's the principle of the matter. I have to stand my ground and show him I'm just as valuable as she is. And I want to show Liza that I won't be silent while she picks my pocket."

"Sounds more like you were mugged," Phoebe murmured.

Dana met Suzanne's gaze and nodded. "It was rough. But are you really willing to lose your job to prove a point? You just said there's a strong possibility that could happen."

"Yeah, it could . . . and I really can't afford to get fired right now. Kevin's business is doing all right, but it's always feast or famine. And the jobs are never completed quite as quickly as he expects," she admitted. "I could find a sales spot at another realtor, I guess."

"But there's a Liza in every office," Lucy pointed out. "Trust me on this."

While living in Boston, Lucy had paid her dues in advertising agencies and publishing houses. But ever since moving to Plum Harbor, she ran her own business as a graphic artist and worked at home. An option Suzanne would have adored, but one that wasn't open to her right now.

Maggie shook her head, her brown and gray curls bouncing. "I know you won't like this, but my advice is to smooth things over with Liza, before the meeting with your boss."

"Easy for you to say. I wouldn't know how to start. If I suddenly go all nice and smarmy, she'd see through me in a minute."

"Just be honest," Lucy advised. "You don't have to pretend that what she did was okay. But you might admit that your reaction was not ideal, and now you're afraid of losing your job. Tell her you can't afford for that to happen. Your family relies on your income. Promise that you'll try to do better in the future and work things out with her."

"And it won't hurt to get a little smarmy.

32

Eat some humble pie? It's very low in carbs, I hear," Maggie teased her.

Dana nodded in agreement. "Turn on that legendary Cavanaugh charm. Get those dimples back in gear. Before she has time to persuade Harry to give you the boot. Doesn't that make the most sense?"

Suzanne sighed and took another cookie. "Perfect sense. I'm just so boiling mad every time I think of her. I can't see straight, no less think sensibly."

"To be expected. Don't decide now. Sleep on it. Things will look clearer in the morning," Dana advised.

Suzanne nearly laughed. "That's what I always tell my kids when they get worked up about something."

"It's sound advice. And we all need to be reminded from time to time. Even a mother of three." Maggie had risen from her seat and was gathering supplies that were set out on the sideboard. She brought two baskets of rolled yarn to the table and placed one on each end.

"For what it's worth, I think Liza Devereaux does have a reasonable and even a sympathetic side. I'm sure you can work something out with her. But I know you don't want to hear that either," Maggie quickly added as Suzanne made a face.

"You're right. I don't. She is sharp, I'll grant her that. She can quickly reason out what's best for Liza. But I've never seen a drop of sympathy. Not when it comes to business."

Maggie shrugged. Suzanne could tell she didn't agree. "She obviously cuts some corners in the office. But I've dealt with her many times in the shop and she's not the worst person in the world. She's always been very pleasant to me and other customers."

Suzanne couldn't hear another word. "Stop right there, Mag. I know she takes lessons here and buys a lot of yarn. I know it's your livelihood and I've never made a thing about it. But it pains me to hear you take her side in this."

Maggie looked surprised and immediately apologetic. "I am not taking her side. Not one bit. I'm just pointing out that she's not a monster. She has some good in her, too."

"Like Dr. Jekyll and Mr. Hyde. Sooner or later, Ms. Liza Hyde will show up for a knitting lesson. Then you'll see that what I said is true. Believe me." Suzanne didn't mean to pout but could feel the corners of her mouth turn down.

"I consider myself warned. In the meantime, I may as well tell you that Liza asked me to do a favor for her . . . and I agreed."

Suzanne had only been half listening, silently fuming at Maggie's sympathies with her sworn enemy. Now she sat up sharply.

"What sort of a favor? A big favor?"

"Not so big. I didn't think so. As you know, Liza's mother moved into an assisted living community recently, and she can't seem to make many friends. Ruth is a lifelong knitter and Liza asked if I could do a little class or demonstration at the community center. She thinks it will help her mother meet some like-minded neighbors."

"Good idea. I would have suggested something like that myself," Dana said.

"I thought it was a good idea, too," Maggie said. "She seems so concerned about her mother adjusting to the move, and her challenges after the stroke. It was hard for me to refuse. They clearly have a close, caring relationship. I think that speaks well of a person. Don't you?" Maggie's voice was quiet as she posed the question.

Suzanne's eyes narrowed. "Al Capone loved his mother. Did that make him a nice guy?"

"Oh, Suzanne . . . you know what I mean. No need to be so dramatic. I'd hardly compare the two," Maggie insisted.

"I think it's a very apt comparison. And

I'm surprised you got so involved . . . knowing how much I dislike her."

Maggie took a stack of printed pages from a folder and placed them in the middle of the table, next to a basket. "You're being petty now. That's not like you. It didn't feel right to refuse her. Besides, I like giving classes and helping people learn to knit, even for free."

"She's not even paying you? Figures . . . sweet-talking little worm. I can't believe you fell for that."

"I didn't fall for anything. You're a dear friend and I love you immensely. But I don't see any reason to be rude because you don't get along with Liza at work." Maggie paused and held Suzanne's gaze. "Life isn't a middle-school playground."

"Oh yes, it is. Very much so," Suzanne insisted. "It's a jungle out there."

She stopped herself. She could see Maggie was losing her patience and she didn't want to say anything she'd regret. She had done enough of that for one day. More than enough.

She did let her emotions get the best of her at times. And override the filter on her mouth — that was for sure.

"What will you do tomorrow, Suzanne? You still didn't say." Lucy yanked out a strand of yarn. She sounded concerned.

"I'll follow your advice and try to make nice with Ms. Hyde." She glanced at Maggie, who looked pleased to hear her decision. "I'll head her off at the pass before she meets with Harry. That makes the most sense. Though my heart isn't in it. Why does just the thought of eating humble pie give me heartburn? I usually love pie."

Maggie laughed and patted her shoulder as she passed behind her chair. Suzanne felt relieved. Their moment of tension was dispelled. "Everyone hates that dish, dear. Even dressed up with whipped cream and a cherry on top. But once in a while . . ." Maggie let her voice trail off.

"There's no avoiding it," Lucy finished. She caught Suzanne's gaze. Suzanne knew when she was beat, and the advice of her friends made good sense. As always.

"I doubt that eating a pile of humble pies will work. But for the sake of my family, I'll try."

"You're doing the right thing. Maybe she'll be so shocked and caught off guard, she'll hand the whole deal back to you." Maggie leaned over and placed several sets of super slim needles on the table.

Suzanne was curious to see what new project their fearless stitching leader would introduce. Her pals had been so patient with her problem, but even she needed distraction now.

"That would be a miracle . . . but stranger things have happened." Suzanne reached for a pale yellow ball of yarn, so soft to the touch, she was tempted to stroke it against her cheek. "Enough about my office intrigue. You've all been very patient and given me some great advice. Time to stop kvetching and start knitting."

"I second the motion." Maggie had taken her seat again, and slipped out a stack of printed pages from her own knitting bag. "With the holidays coming, I thought it would be nice to knit some items we can donate to a charity. Like knitting warm clothes for babies and toddlers, and donate them to a group that will get the clothing to mothers and children in need."

She picked up the pages and passed them to Lucy, who sat on her left. "I planned on using the project and service idea for my demonstration at Brookside, where Ruth lives. I thought it would be nice if we got involved, too."

"That sounds great. What gave you the idea?" Dana asked.

"Liza and her mother. It's their favorite charity. They donate knitting there often."

Maggie gave Suzanne a look, as if to say, "Would a truly heartless person do that?" Then she said, "I hope that doesn't bother you, Suzanne."

Suzanne wanted to object, but knew that would be terribly petty, and aside from that, she actually liked the idea.

"I'm on board. Even a broken clock has the right time twice a day," she murmured.

Phoebe looked up, her dark eyes shining. "There's like ten weeks until Christmas and five of us. So if we only knit two items each a week, we could easily hit one hundred."

"I love the idea, too. But two items a week?" Suzanne looked around at her friends. "I could only do that if I locked myself in the bedroom for the next three months."

Dana had taken a sheet with the pattern and was reading it as she spoke. "Suzanne's right. It's for charity. It should be fun, not stressful. Why don't we just knit at our own pace and see where we get?"

Suzanne felt better about that plan. She had no doubt the speedy knitters, like Phoebe and Maggie, would definitely make up for the slowpokes, like herself and even Lucy.

"I'm glad you're all on board. Here's a good pattern to start with. It's a very simple baby jacket, knit in one piece and then folded over and stitched on the sides." Maggie had a picture handy and showed it to them.

Lucy took the photo to get a closer look. "This is adorable. And it looks easy, too. I'm going to start right now." She rolled up Matt's sweater and pushed it aside.

Suzanne laughed. "Watch out, Lucy. If you come home knitting baby clothes, Matt might ask some questions. Who knows where that discussion will go?"

Lucy blushed. Everyone knew she wanted to have a baby soon. But they'd just gotten married and she didn't want to rush. "You're right. That could get tricky. Maybe I'll just tell him it's a dog sweater."

Lucy seemed perfectly serious, but her friends couldn't help laughing. Suzanne included. Matt was a vet and they were both obsessed with dogs, mainly their two silly dogs Tink and Wally. But any dog could send Lucy into a puddle of oohs and ahhs.

"The reason that's so funny is because he would believe you," Suzanne said. Lucy smiled but didn't argue, and Suzanne realized that she hadn't thought about her awful day in at least . . . five minutes?

Where would she be without knitting night and hanging out with her BFFs?

As Suzanne left the shop with Lucy and Dana, a chilly wind greeted them, tossing tree branches and scuttling dry leaves down Plum Harbor's quiet Main Street. Up above, a silver sliver of moon glowed in a deep blue sky. Suzanne pulled her poncho close and waved good night to her friends as they each ran in a different direction to their cars.

She climbed into her SUV and headed down the street. Knitting night had definitely brought some peace and perspective.

But alone again, worries crept in. Was Kevin still up? It was only a quarter to eleven, but her husband worked hard at his construction jobs. "Early to bed, early to rise" was his motto. He really did need his sleep and Suzanne knew she wouldn't have the heart to wake him when she got in, even to share her awful day. Or warn him that she might get fired tomorrow. *At least one of us should get some rest,* she reasoned.

Right before the turn for her usual route home, the sign for Prestige Properties came into view. Suzanne noticed lights on inside. She expected to see the van for the office cleaning service. They came every Thursday night, without fail. A reason she preferred to invite clients to meet there on a Friday.

But only a white Mercedes SUV stood parked in front of the building tonight. The personalized plates on the back — AMEY-MOXI — told Suzanne all she needed to know. Liza was burning the midnight oil.

Probably making her case for getting me fired. Or trying to figure out what other deals she can steal.

Now, now . . . you have to summon up a better attitude, pronto. Remember what your friends said? Good advice. Get yourself resigned to some heavy duty groveling. Or you might be very sorry. You can catch more black widow spiders with honey than vinegar, right? You've got to sweeten her up, before she talks Harry into giving you the boot.

Suzanne slowed down and pulled up behind Liza's vehicle. Time to get this over with. The pep talk from her pals had psyched Suzanne into doing the right thing. But she knew that by tomorrow, she could wake up feeling mad all over again. It had certainly happened before.

Suzanne shut the ignition, then checked her hair and lipstick in the visor mirror. Not going to win any beauty contests, but looking a little ragged might work on Liza's sympathy. If she had any, as Maggie claimed.

Suzanne slipped out of the driver's seat, took a deep breath, and headed for the realty office.

As Mom always said, "No time like the present."

CHAPTER 2

Large lights illuminated the gold-lettered logo of Prestige Properties, which hung above the storefront window. The glass was covered with glossy photos of houses, apartments, and vacant land for sale. It was a thriving office with lots of juicy listings, and Suzanne would hate to leave it.

The heavy glass door was unlocked and Suzanne swung it open easily. She wondered why Liza wasn't more careful. There was little need to worry in Plum Harbor, but a woman alone, especially at night, needed to be cautious anywhere. Suzanne always told her daughter that.

The reception area was dark and empty. Further back, where the worker bees sat in partitioned cubicles, a soft light glowed, and Suzanne headed toward it.

Suzanne liked to joke about the padded walls in her cubicle. Definitely a plus when things got crazy. Most of the time, she didn't mind not having a "real" office. She did most of her wheeling and dealing in her car, or at home, from her cell phone and tablet, as did the rest of the sales staff. The cubicle was a landing spot, a little nest where she rested and recharged before new adventures. She liked to think of it that way.

She passed her own space, catching a glimpse of the photos that covered one wall. Mostly of her family — dressed in their best at some holiday party; Alexis, in her lacrosse gear, grubby but victorious; her twin boys, Ryan and Jamie, mugging for the camera as they blew out the candles on matching cakes at their last birthday party.

When she felt drained and unmotivated, the smiling faces of the people she loved most in the world never failed to pump her up again.

That's why I work so hard, she reminded herself as she walked by. Not to "best" Liza Devereaux. Or even for cashmere ponchos and other fine things. *I do it for my family and I'll sweet talk, or even beg this woman, in order to keep my job. I'll do what I have to.*

A thin shaft of light stretched into the hallway from Liza's space. Suzanne's steps slowed as she approached. She listened for keyboard clicks or Liza's voice, talking on the phone. She didn't hear a thing.

45

Was she in there? Maybe she was back in the staff kitchen, getting a cup of coffee? Or sipping one of those diet shakes she seemed to live on?

Suzanne paused and delivered her opening lines as she stood near the entrance to Liza's cubicle. "Sorry to bother you so late. But I saw your car outside and wondered if we could talk."

Suzanne stepped into the partitioned space, listening for a reply. . . .

But only heard her own scream of panic.

The desk lamp had fallen to one side, the harsh light shining directly in Suzanne's face, casting long shadows around the small space. She raised her hand to shield her eyes and get a better look at Liza, who was sprawled out on the floor.

Suzanne rushed toward her and crouched down. She quickly checked for a pulse and leaned closer. Was Liza breathing? She couldn't tell for sure.

"This can't be . . . Liza? Please! Can you hear me?" Suzanne slapped Liza's cheek, but there was no reaction. She felt for the pulse in her wrist and then her neck. Then pressed her ear to her rival's chest, desperate to hear a heartbeat.

Nothing.

"Oh, Liza . . . Answer me . . . please! Can

you hear me? Please wake up. What happened to you?"

Suzanne stared down at Liza's motionless body, the blue-tinged skin of her complexion, her blank, staring eyes. The surprised expression, frozen on her face. Suzanne sat back on her heels and felt the room spin. She staggered to her feet and stumbled backward. The soles of her boots rolled on small, round objects, and nearly made her fall.

She looked down and saw pearls, all over the carpeting. From Liza's favorite necklace, she realized. The string had somehow burst and sent the precious beads flying.

Someone could gather them up and have the necklace restrung. It would be as good as new, Suzanne thought. No such easy repair for its owner. No remedy at all . . .

She turned and ran into the hall, heading for the light in the staff kitchen. "Help! Help, somebody! Is anyone here?"

No one answered. She was all alone. She pulled out her cell phone and dialed 911 with trembling hands.

The operator came on immediately. "What is your emergency?"

Suzanne could hardly speak. She felt sick to her stomach, but forced herself to form the words. "Someone's dead. I just found

47

her. A coworker. I checked her pulse and breathing. But she's just lying there. . . . I can't believe it. . . ."

"Slow down, please. Your name and location?"

Suzanne took a deep breath and answered the operator's questions as quickly and clearly as she could. All the while a voice in her mind was saying, *How could this be? How could Liza be dead? I was just screaming my head off at her a few hours ago. I was just complaining about her bitterly to my friends.*

Was she dead all that time I was groaning and gossiping? I feel so awful now.

"The police are on their way," the operator said. "Do you want to stay on the line until they come?"

"I'll be okay. I'll go wait outside for them."

"All right. But don't go far. They'll need to take your statement."

"Yes, of course." Did the operator really think she would call in about a dead body and then just go home and go to sleep?

She wouldn't sleep for months. The chilling image of Liza's face, her rigid expression, her unseeing eyes staring straight into the desk light . . . The pearls scattered all around her body . . .

Suzanne shivered and pulled her poncho

48

closer. She looked out at Main Street, as quiet and picturesque as a movie set. A strange, surreal feeling washed over her. Had she really just found Liza's stiff, lifeless body? That couldn't be. It had to be a dream, a nightmare. She'd wake up any minute now.

Suzanne glanced through the office window, almost expecting Liza to strut out in her Manolo Blahnik heels, the keys to her Mercedes in hand. "I really got you that time, didn't I?" she'd say. Suzanne could even imagine the tight, superior smile as Liza sashayed by.

Suzanne stared out at the street again. Liza was not sashaying out of the office tonight. She wasn't going anywhere.

I'll never be on the receiving end of that smug smile again, Suzanne realized. A hard truth to get her mind around right now.

Suzanne began to cry — deep, wracking sobs that shook her body. She took a wad of tissues from her purse and wiped her eyes, but the tears wouldn't stop.

Despite every mean thing she'd ever said or thought about Liza Devereaux, Suzanne knew her nemesis did not deserve to die. Not at her age. Early forties, probably? Had it been a heart attack? A stroke? Some other sudden health crisis just as swift and deadly?

49

She'd wished Liza ill at every turn, and she felt so ashamed now.

I should have been a bigger person. I shouldn't have let the woman get under my skin the way she had. Sure, Liza had her faults. But didn't everyone? *Wasn't I just as annoying to her?*

Suzanne's rambling thoughts took a dark turn. What if it was a stroke? What if the fight at the staff meeting had killed her? Just pushed her blood pressure through the roof and she burst an artery or something? *What if she had some secret illness that I didn't even know about?*

Suzanne felt so awful. Sure, she'd been angry today. But she'd never wish such an end on anyone. Even her worst enemy.

She thought of calling one of her pals, to share the shocking, dreadful news. Lucy would still be up. She'd mentioned a project with a deadline. But Suzanne realized she wasn't ready to talk about this yet. Not even to her circle.

She did need to call Kevin. It was late and he'd wonder why she wasn't home yet. His cell phone rang and rang, but he finally answered, his voice thick with sleep.

"Hi, honey, it's me." She tried to keep the note of panic from her tone, but it was impossible. "Something awful happened. . . .

It's just so horrible. I'm at the office and I have to wait for the police. Can you come and stay with me? Just tell Alexis I had some car trouble and you need to pick me up in the village. She's probably still up, doing homework."

Their oldest child was a junior in high school and more intense about her schoolwork than Suzanne had ever been. She was usually up after midnight, studying, though Suzanne nagged at her to sleep more. And Alexis was often left in charge of her younger brothers, though she rarely volunteered for the job.

"You're at your office? What are you talking about? It's half past eleven. I thought you were at Maggie's shop tonight."

"I was. But I stopped at the office on my way home and . . ." The effort of trying to explain the events in a calm, logical way was too much. Suzanne broke down. "Oh, Kevin . . . Liza Devereaux is dead. I just found her, lying on the floor. Not breathing or anything. It was awful."

Suzanne's voice dissolved into tears. She could hear her husband's confused but conciliatory words, but couldn't answer.

"Are you kidding? That's horrible. Did you call the police?"

"They should be here any minute. Can

51

you please stay with me? I feel so bad. You know I never liked her. But I never wanted anything like this to happen."

"Of course you didn't. What a thing to say." She could tell from the sounds on the other end of the line that he was out of bed and stumbling around the bedroom, trying to get dressed, she assumed. "Sit tight. I'll be right over."

"Thanks, honey," Suzanne said, though she knew no thanks were really necessary. He'd always been protective of her.

A few moments later, she heard a siren down the street and a blue and white patrol car pulled up in front of the building. Suzanne waved nervously, though she was sure the police had already noticed her.

The two officers, a man and a woman, got out. They looked so young, in their mid-twenties, she guessed. The male officer did the talking, introducing himself as Officer Zericky and his partner as Officer Durbin.

He first checked her name, reading it off a pad in his hand. "You reported a death, Ms. Cavanaugh?"

He looked very serious, and a bit nervous, she thought. *That makes two of us.*

"She's inside . . . on the floor in her cubicle." Suzanne heard her voice quiver.

"Liza Devereaux. She's a coworker of mine."

"Can you show us, please?"

Suzanne swallowed to clear her throat again. She had hoped the police could find poor Liza on their own. But she nodded and led the way back inside the building. "Right through here. The office spaces are in back. That's where she is."

When they reached Liza's cubicle, she stopped and pointed. "In there. I felt for a pulse or a heartbeat . . . but . . . Well, you'll see."

Officer Zericky walked past her and entered the cubicle. Officer Durbin followed. Suzanne stayed in the hallway, but listened in on their conversation as they examined Liza's body, then made a call on a crackling radio.

She heard Officer Zericky speaking. Though most of the conversation was in police jargon, coded with terms and numbers, Suzanne got the drift.

The two officers emerged and led her into the reception area, where Officer Durbin turned on the lights. "I need a brief statement, Ms. Cavanaugh. Detectives will be here soon and they'll want to speak to you, too."

Suzanne nodded. "Of course. I understand."

This was going to be difficult, to review over and over the ghastly moments of finding Liza. But she knew that she couldn't refuse. At least Kevin was coming. She hoped he'd get there soon.

Officer Zericky had his pad out again and began to ask her questions — her full name, address, and contact information. Easy stuff at first.

Then he got into the specifics about finding the body. His questions were brief and Suzanne tried to keep her answers brief, too.

She heard her husband's voice and saw him through the window, just his head, above the gallery of properties for sale. He was talking to the other police officer. He looked as if he'd just rolled out of bed and pulled on a sweatshirt and jeans. But she'd rarely been happier to see him in her life.

He turned and met her glance, then shrugged. Suzanne guessed he wanted to come in, but Officer Durbin had told him to wait outside.

She felt frustrated. "My husband is here. Can I talk to him?" she asked the other police officer.

He looked at his pad, as if he might find

the answer there. "I guess we're done. But you need to speak to the detectives before you can go home," he reminded her again.

"Yes, I know." Suzanne had been through this ordeal before. When she'd found the body of a good friend, floating in a swimming pool. Poor Gloria. Everyone assumed it had been a tragic accident. But as time went on, she and her friends knew that there was more to dear Gloria's demise than met the eye, and they helped find her killer, too.

But there was no mystery to Liza's death. She'd obviously died of a heart attack. Or maybe a stroke.

Suzanne wondered how soon the police would be able to tell and was about to ask Officer Zericky, when a tall man in a dark green barn coat walked through the door. He had an air of authority, even in street clothes. His sharp gaze quickly found Suzanne, dark eyes staring out from below bushy eyebrows.

It was Maggie's boyfriend, Charles Mossbacher, a detective with the Essex County Police Department. Suzanne felt instantly relieved to see a familiar face — serious expression and all.

"Hello, Suzanne. I just saw Kevin outside. You're the one who found the body?"

"Yes, I did. She was a coworker. Liza

Devereaux. It's so awful. Such a shock. She wasn't sick or anything. I mean, not that I knew of. I feel terrible about this, Charles. We never got along, but I never meant to . . . to hurt her. I never imagined she'd end up like *this*. . . ."

Suzanne was rambling. Charles looked confused. "Hold on. You've had a shock. You just sit down and relax a few minutes. You can tell me all about it, very soon."

"Okay, Charles. Whatever you say." Suzanne nodded obediently, then dabbed her nose with a tissue. "Can Kevin wait with me?"

"No problem. Zericky, let the husband in," Charles called out to the uniformed officer. Officer Zericky was talking to a man who had walked in behind Charles. He wore a khaki raincoat and carried a large black suitcase. Charles met his glance and nodded, then turned back to Suzanne.

"The medical examiner is here. I'll come as soon as we're finished."

Suzanne watched him walk away. She hoped that he didn't take too long looking over Liza's office. What was there to see?

But she had died alone and the police had strict rules and procedures to follow when that happened. Suzanne knew they had to close off the area, until they were certain that Liza had died from natural causes.

She looked outside for Kevin and saw Officer Durbin stretching yellow tape around the storefront. POLICE LINE — DO NOT CROSS, the tape read. Until the medical examiner did his job, or maybe even until an autopsy, the police might not be certain of the cause of her death.

Suzanne took a seat on a leather couch in the reception area. She had never sat there. It was odd, seeing the office from a customer's point of view. A large gold plaque on the blond wood reception desk proclaimed the name of Prestige Properties in bold type. Suzanne had never noticed before that it was just painted plastic. The sign looked tacky and a bit worn in the harsh, fluorescent light. Not so bad in daylight . . . did it? She'd have to mention something to Harry.

It was odd, the way your mind wandered in a crisis. Why was she even fretting about that?

She couldn't see Kevin outside and wondered what had happened to him. Officer Zericky stood just outside the door, recording the names of everyone who came in and out. Suddenly her husband appeared and rushed across the space to meet her.

"Suzanne . . . are you all right?" Suzanne stood up and Kevin wrapped her in one of his famous bear hugs — famous in their family. She allowed herself to be enveloped and rested for a moment with her head against his broad shoulder, his beard brushing her cheek.

"I'm okay, I guess. It's been a rough night. A rough day followed by an even rougher night, actually," she mumbled into his shoulder.

He stared down at her, his expression puzzled. "Why did you come back? Did you forget something?"

"I saw Liza's car and I needed to talk to her. Something happened in a meeting today. It's sort of a long story."

Kevin met her gaze. "Did you have another argument with her?"

Suzanne nodded. She felt embarrassed now to admit her bad behavior. As if she was a little girl who had a history of acting out at school.

"It was a doozy. The absolute worst yet. I never actually pulled her hair. Lyle caught me just in time."

Kevin rolled his eyes and groaned, but didn't interrupt.

"I know. You've seen better social skills in a preschool, right? I'm so ashamed," she said sincerely. "I never thought she'd die. I mean, what if I killed her? What if she had a heart condition or high blood pressure, and I got her so upset, she just threw a clot or something?"

Thinking back to that shocking moment, Suzanne felt her emotions carry her away again. Kevin rested his big hands on her shoulders, calming her down.

"It's okay, honey. Who could have ever predicted this? I bet the argument had nothing to do with it."

Suzanne glanced up at him, sure that he was just saying that to make her feel better. He took her hand and led her back to the couch. "Let's sit down. Do you want some coffee or tea?"

"Some tea might be nice. Something herbal, with no caffeine." Suzanne felt chilled to the bone. Probably shock. She was sure she wouldn't sleep a wink, caffeine free or not. A cup of tea might warm her up a bit.

Kevin headed for the coffee station next to the reception desk.

Suzanne silently wished him luck. The machine was finicky; the Alfa Romeo of coffeemakers. She'd always thought one needed an engineering degree to work it. She was sure it had cost Harry a fortune, but he'd told the staff it was important to present the right image to everyone walking into the office — one of luxury and success. He'd say, "It primes them to expect six-figure listings, and want to be part of the 'inner circle.' "

Harry was definitely in that circle, and a good salesman. A master, truly. He never seemed to work at it, either. It came so easily to him. He was rarely out in the field these days, practicing his magic powers, but he'd taught his sales team well, herself included. And Liza, of course, who had enjoyed the benefit of private lessons. Little good they did her now, Suzanne reflected.

Kevin carried the hot drinks back to the couch and they sat side by side, his warmth and sheer size a comfort, as they sipped from their paper cups.

"Harry will be crushed. He absolutely adored her . . . even after she dumped him. Maybe even more," she said in a hushed tone.

"I think he'll be here soon. I heard the police call him." Kevin blew at the foam in his cup. "Were he and Liza still an item?"

"Not for a while. Who really knows?" Suzanne whispered back. "I do know he followed her around the office like a puppy and stared at her in meetings like he was in a trance."

"Maybe you should tell Charles."

Suzanne glanced at him. "Why?"

Kevin shrugged and sipped his coffee. "Maybe he should know what went on here, under the radar."

Suzanne wasn't sure about that. She didn't want to get involved. The less you said to the police the better. Or they would be asking questions all night.

"I hope Charles doesn't take too long. What time is it?" Suzanne squinted at her watch, designed more for fashion than information.

Kevin had his phone in hand. "A quarter to one. I sent a text to Alexis. I told her we'd be home soon."

Suzanne rarely lied to her children. But in this case, she thought it was the best choice. She'd explain what really happened tomorrow, when they were all together and could talk about it as a family. Kids generally took cues from their parents, and if she didn't act rattled and upset, they wouldn't be either. First, she had to get her own head together.

"Maybe you should go home if this takes much longer. I'll be okay."

Kevin looked shocked and even insulted by the suggestion. "I'm not going to leave you here. You just found a dead body. Someone you've known for a long time.

You've had a shock, Suzanne. I don't even think you should drive home. We'll leave your car and get it tomorrow."

Suzanne didn't think that precaution was necessary. She patted his hand. "Let's see how it goes."

They both looked up and saw Charles emerge from the back of the office. He stood talking to Officer Zericky and another officer in plain clothes, who Suzanne guessed was Charles's partner.

An ambulance had pulled up outside, and the attendants had taken out a rolling stretcher but had not brought it back to collect the body. The sight made Suzanne feel sad, the reality of the situation hitting home again.

Charles walked toward them and caught her gaze.

"Good, here he comes. He'll ask you a few questions and we can go," Kevin said.

"Hope so." Suzanne took a last sip of her tea and set the cup aside.

Charles greeted them with a brief smile. "Sorry to keep you waiting, folks. But we can't rush these things. Haste always turns around and bites you later."

"We understand. Suzanne wants to help you as much as she can." Kevin's tone was utterly cooperative, but with an edge of eagerness to get the interview over with.

"I'm sure she does. Why don't you wait for her outside, Kevin? This won't take long."

Kevin nodded at Charles, but looked surprised by the request. He glanced at Suzanne. She was too. Why couldn't he sit with her for the questions? Was Charles afraid he might be a distraction? "Are you all right, honey?"

"I'll be fine. See you in a minute." Suzanne summoned a positive note she did not honestly feel. She glanced back at Charles. "Right?"

He sat down on the other end of the couch and took his pad out. "Absolutely. Some of these questions will be the same that Officer Zericky asked. But please bear with me. I need to be clear on a few points."

If there was one thing she hated it was repeating things she'd already said. Not to mention, things someone had written down word for word.

She brushed aside her annoyance and tried to keep calm. Police had to be painstakingly methodical when someone was found dead. For some reason, she felt she owed it to Liza — and her family — to help figure out what had happened. It was the respectful thing to do.

"So, you told Officer Zericky that you came in to the office because you saw Ms. Devereaux's car and wanted to speak with her?"

"That's right. I had planned to come in early tomorrow. . . . Well, today, I mean," she amended, remembering it was past midnight. "I wanted to talk to her about a business matter. But I saw her car and thought I'd get it over with."

"All right." Charles made a few notes on his pad. The gesture seemed so . . . official. It was jarring. She thought of Charles as a friend.

He's here doing his job, she reminded herself. *Not sent by Maggie as a comforting emissary. Of course he's going to write down things that you say. There's a woman in a cubicle a few yards away, stone cold dead. And you're the one who found her. He has to make a full report.*

"What time did you get here? Did you notice?"

"About eleven? A few minutes before, maybe. I checked the time because I was wondering if Kevin was still up at home. I parked behind her car, that white Mercedes." Suzanne turned and pointed out to the street. "And I came in."

"All right." He made more notes and then

posed more questions, many the same as the uniformed officer had asked.

She again described walking into Liza's cubicle, seeing the lamp knocked over and Liza's body on the floor. How she had tried to revive her, though it seemed hopeless.

"Anything else that you recall?"

Suzanne thought a moment. "Her pearl necklace was broken. She always wore it. She had it on today. But there are pearls all over the floor."

"Yes, we saw that." Charles nodded and wrote some more. "Did you see anyone near the building? Or out on the street when you arrived?"

"No one, honestly. You know how it is in Plum Harbor. We roll up the sidewalks early this time of year."

Summer was a different story. Main Street, the village green, and harbor were filled with people until late at night. Day-trippers who had tied up their boats at the town dock, spilled out of cafes and bars. There was often music in the gazebo, families and couples out for an evening stroll, walking dogs and eating ice cream cones.

Once the cool weather set in and school was in session, the town grew quiet and empty, hunkering down for a winter sleep,

Suzanne often thought.

Charles nodded. "Quiet is a good thing. If you're in my line of work. We don't mind that."

"I'm sure you don't," Suzanne agreed.

"How well did you know her?"

The question was surprising. "Not that well. We've worked together a long time. But we weren't friends." She stopped there, not sure how much to elaborate. "Liza was pretty much all business. I don't think anyone in the office was really friends with her. Except . . . well, no one really."

Charles's expression grew interested. "Except? You were going to say something else, I think."

Suzanne sighed. "I don't want to gossip. But everyone in the office knew that she and Harry Prentiss, our boss, had an affair. I'm pretty sure it's been over for years. But if anyone knew her at all, it would have to be Harry."

Charles looked like he wanted to hear more. "Why did it end? Do you know?"

"I can only tell you what I heard. Who knows if it's true?" Suzanne prefaced. "Rumor has it that she left her husband for Harry, but when the time came, Harry wouldn't leave his wife. So Liza broke things off."

66

She'd never minded gossiping about Liza before. But for some reason, she felt uncomfortable talking about her now.

"When we spoke earlier, you said something like, 'I didn't mean to hurt her. I never imagined she'd end up like this.' What did you mean by that, Suzanne?"

He'd recalled her exact words. Impressive. Had he jotted that down on his pad? She couldn't remember now.

Suzanne swallowed a lump in her throat. She felt her eyes fill with tears and blinked. "It's just that . . . the thing is . . . I had a fight with her in a meeting today. It got really nasty. We've had arguments in the office before . . . but this was bad. I totally lost it. I said some things I never should have said. To anybody. I feel so ashamed now. . . ." She took a breath and wiped her eyes. "That's why I came back tonight. To apologize. And I was just thinking, after I found her . . . what if she got so upset that she had a heart attack? Or a stroke? I never liked her. We were always competing here and she'd pulled some nasty tricks on me over the years," Suzanne explained. "But I never wanted her to die. . . . I mean, not really."

Her voice trailed off to a small squeak. She looked up at Charles again and wondered what he was thinking. It was hard to tell.

"The cause of death is still unknown," he said finally. "But I don't think anyone has ever been accused of murder, or even manslaughter, *simply* because they argued with the victim earlier that day."

Was he laughing at her? Not at all. He was perfectly serious and trying to comfort her, in his way. "It's only natural to have regrets if you left things on a bad note with the deceased," he continued. "And, being the one to find her on top of it — that's a lot to handle."

He glanced at his pad a moment, then snapped it closed. Suzanne was relieved to see that. "We may need to talk again, depending. But that's all for tonight. Thanks for your help, Suzanne."

"Don't mention it." Suzanne stood up and picked up her purse. The ambulance attendants were finally wheeling in the stretcher and she noticed a gray plastic bag on top. The kind with a zipper.

She quickly looked away and turned back to Charles. "So you have no clue at all how she died?"

He slipped his notebook into the breast pocket of his coat. "Hard to say for sure right now. We do have an idea."

"You do?" Suzanne prodded.

"No more questions. You're just as bad as Maggie," he added with the first smile of the night.

"We're all pretty bad that way, Charles," she said, referring to her knitting gang. "I thought you knew that by now."

He shook his head, the smile fading as quickly as it had appeared. "Good night, Suzanne. I'll see you around."

"Not in your official capacity I hope," she nearly replied. Instead, she gave a short wave and headed out to her husband. "See you, Charles. Take care."

As Suzanne left the building, Officer Durbin lifted the crime scene tape so she could slip under. Kevin waited for her on the sidewalk and insisted that he drive her home. Suzanne was too tired to argue.

She saw Harry nearby, dressed in a tuxedo under a long tan topcoat. He stood talking to Charles and his partner. Harry's back was turned and he didn't see her.

Just as well, Suzanne thought. *I'm too tired to talk to anyone else tonight.*

Kevin slung his heavy arm around her shoulder and they walked in step across the street to his truck. "How are you doing, honey? Holding up? Why did that take so long? He must have asked you a million questions."

"Not really, but it felt like it. I told Charles about the argument, and how guilty I feel now. He said that was only normal, since I'd left things on a bad note with her. He seemed to think I'm just in shock from everything."

"Anyone would be, babe." He pulled open the passenger side door for her and Suzanne climbed into the truck.

As she fastened her seat belt, she noticed another van pull up and she quickly recognized the sign for the local news station, painted on the side. She knew that the vans followed the calls on the police radio and a prominent businesswoman, dying alone in her office for no apparent cause, was newsworthy. In this town, at least. She felt relieved that she and Kevin were leaving and wouldn't be stopped by nosy reporters asking more questions.

Kevin got in the driver's side and started the truck. Just in the nick of time, she thought.

"Let's get home and get some sleep. That alarm clock is going to ring awfully early tomorrow," he said.

Suzanne knew that was true. Though she doubted she'd sleep a wink. Not after what she'd just been through.

Liza's frozen expression and unseeing eyes — Suzanne was sure that was all she would see tonight, if she even tried to close her own.

CHAPTER 3

Suzanne heard her phone buzz with text messages and roused herself from a deep sleep. The bedroom was dark and Kevin's side of the bed, empty. She had no idea what time it was. As she fumbled for the phone on the bedside table, the events of last night flooded back.

She didn't want to think of that now, first thing. But she couldn't help it. She lifted the phone and checked the time.

Yikes . . . nine o'clock? That was like sleeping until noon for her.

About ten text messages from friends and clients flashed on the phone's home screen, and one at the bottom from her boss, which she thought best to read first.

I've already reached most of you by phone. I want to confirm that we're closed for business today while police investigate Liza's tragic death.

In case you haven't heard yet, she was

found unresponsive in her office late last night.

The police will be contacting everyone on our staff to take statements. I'm sure you will all cooperate.

Suzanne was relieved to see that Harry hadn't told the entire office she'd found Liza's body. They would know soon enough and she didn't feel like fielding a lot of texts and phone calls from curious coworkers.

I'm sure this news comes as a shock. Liza was a beloved, respected, and valued member of our team and her passing is a great loss.

The office will be open tomorrow, and my door will be open as well, if anyone has questions about the situation. More importantly, I hope we can lend support and care to one another in this sad time. Like a family.

Harry's words struck a chord. She did feel shocked and saddened, no matter what she'd said about Liza. And she had some questions. Lots of questions.

Why had Liza been at the office so late? Did she really work that hard to keep her edge? Suzanne knew that most of the work in real estate sales could be done from home. There was no need to be in a depressing little cubicle to wheel and deal.

As far as Harry's hope that the staff acted like one big "family," Suzanne had her

73

doubts. If she and her coworkers were a family, it was definitely one teeming with dysfunction.

No one there had truly fond feelings for Liza. Except for Harry. And maybe Beth Birney, their office manager, who rarely had a bad word to say, brimming with an indiscriminate fondness for everyone on the staff. Like a cuddly Labrador retriever.

I should definitely be more like Beth. Starting today, Suzanne vowed.

She shuffled into the kitchen in her fuzzy slippers and robe and in a sweeping glance read a history of the morning's activities. A trail of toast crumbs, cereal boxes, open jars of peanut butter and jelly, and sticky knives covered the counters and kitchen island. Random slices of bread had escaped their wrapper, while apples and oranges wandered blindly around the fruit bowl, with no idea how to jump back in.

Kevin had managed to get the boys and Alexis off to school, but hadn't made it out of the house yet himself. He stood at the kitchen island, wearing a sweatshirt topped by a quilted vest, and carefully built an egg sandwich on a square of tinfoil. His thermal coffee cup stood nearby, ready to go.

"Hey, hon. How are you doing? Harry called. He said the office is closed, so I

74

didn't wake you."

"I heard. He just sent a text." Suzanne poured herself a mug of coffee and sat on a stool across from him.

"Lucky you. Some of us zombies need to march on."

She felt bad for him. He'd missed a lot of sleep last night, too. "Sorry, honey, but I just remembered. We left my car in the village. Can you give me a lift? I'll jump in the shower and be ready in two minutes."

She knew it would take a bit longer than that. She was sure he did, too. But he nodded. "Okay, I'll wait. Not a problem."

He sighed and picked up the newspaper, then bit into the sandwich he'd been packing to take along.

Suzanne dashed back to the bedroom, quickly made the bed, and grabbed a towel for her shower. She was aching to tell her friends what had happened, but decided to text from the truck, on the way into town.

She hoped that Dana and Lucy could meet up this morning. Suzanne had a feeling that once everyone learned that she had discovered Liza Devereaux's dead body last night, they'd find a few minutes in their busy schedules to hear the gritty details.

A short time later, Suzanne sat center stage on the front porch of Maggie's shop, answering questions about her horrid adventure. Last night's cold snap had passed and the day was sunny and mild for the first week in October. It seemed a shame to waste the fair weather by sitting inside.

Maggie had spoken to Charles, and already knew about Suzanne's gruesome discovery. But not much more. Suzanne didn't doubt it. Charles was notoriously discreet about his investigations.

Lucy had come to town for her usual morning jaunt with her dogs, Tink, her golden retriever, and Wally, her chocolate Lab. The dogs sat at her feet, working on their chew toys while she worked on her knitting. Lucy's dogs were usually so calm and well behaved, you'd hardly know they were around. Except when Phoebe's cat, Van Gogh, escaped from the apartment above the shop. Suzanne hadn't seen the cat lately, but he did have a way of appearing at the most unexpected moments. Dana had a convenient break between clients and had quickly run up from her office. Though not so quick that she'd forgotten her knitting bag either.

"She was just lying there," Suzanne explained, "with this incredibly surprised expression on her face. Her eyes wide open. Just staring up at me." Suzanne felt a lump in her throat but pushed on. "I felt for her pulse and listened for her heartbeat. But I knew she was gone."

"How awful." Maggie pressed her hand to her mouth.

"I kept talking to her, hoping she'd wake up and answer. I've been present when someone's passed away. Like my dear Grandma Bella. But that was expected. This was just out of the blue. I finally got a grip and called nine-one-one."

Suzanne sipped a cup of coffee Maggie had fixed for her. Relating the events left her shaken. But it was comforting to be surrounded by her friends and look out at Maggie's garden and feel surrounded by the flowers, too. Had this all been here last night? Why hadn't she noticed?

Phoebe was unpacking skeins of yarn from a paper carton balanced on her lap. She looked up and met Suzanne's gaze. "There are some things you can never un-see, know what I mean?"

Suzanne definitely did. "I felt as if she wanted to say something, but couldn't get the words out."

"Do the police know how she died?" Lucy asked.

"They didn't know for sure yet. It must have been a heart attack, or maybe a stroke.

Or something burst in her brain? I felt so bad. What if the argument we had did that to her? What if it caused her to just burst a blood vessel or have a cardiac arrest? Maybe she had some awful condition and had never told anyone."

"Oh, Suzanne. Don't even say that. You can't blame yourself. Believe me." Maggie gazed at her with sympathy.

"Kevin and Charles said the same thing. It's just how I feel. I can't help it."

No matter what people said — her husband and friends, even Charles Mossbacher — Suzanne couldn't get past the dark, self-blaming thoughts.

"Charles was there?" Lucy looked surprised. She glanced at Maggie. "Is he investigating Liza's death?"

"Seems so." Maggie shrugged. "We spoke this morning and he told me that he's on this case. Though I doubt there's much to investigate."

"It's just that I left things on such an ugly note with her," Suzanne said. "If I'd only known yesterday what I know now, I would have acted a lot differently, believe me."

Maggie shook her head and sighed. She was checking the labels on the skeins and recording the new items on her laptop. "I'm sure you would have. But we can't see around the corners in this life. For better or worse."

Dana hadn't said much so far. She glanced at Suzanne over the edge of her glasses. "So you told Charles that you felt guilty about making her upset?"

"Yes, I did. I was sort of rambling. In shock a bit, I guess. But he told me that he'd never heard of anyone accused of murder simply because they'd argued with the person who died."

"Didn't that make you feel better?" she asked.

Suzanne shrugged. "A little."

"Oh bother . . . I wasn't going to say anything and Charles will strangle me if he finds out." Maggie sighed and shook her head. "But I can't hear you going on about this heart attack thing. Please don't fret, Suzanne. You didn't have a thing to do with Liza's death."

"Did he tell you the cause?" Lucy leaned toward her, and her golden retriever, Tink, sat up with one ear cocked to the side, as if she was interested in the answer, too.

"He did tell me. They're not certain yet. But it wasn't what you think. That's all I can say." Maggie looked back at her record keeping with an intent expression. Suzanne could tell she was bracing herself for every-

79

one's reaction.

"Come on, Mag. You can't leave us hanging." Phoebe whined as if she'd been stuck with a knitting needle.

Maggie sighed but didn't look up. "Yes, I can. I've already said too much."

"If the police are *almost* certain, it will be in the news soon. Probably by tonight," Lucy predicted. "Surely we can all avoid Charles until then?"

"You know we can keep a secret, Maggie. Think of poor Suzanne. You'd really take a load off her mind by telling us the whole story," Phoebe coaxed.

"All right. I give up. But you never heard it from me. The medical examiner said last night it was pretty clear that she'd died of anaphylactic shock — an extreme allergic reaction."

Phoebe looked surprised. "My boyfriend is allergic to tree nuts. He always carries an EpiPen, just in case. His lungs can close down in less than a minute. It's really scary."

Dana nodded. "My stepson, Tyler, has that problem, too. If you don't get help, your breathing passages swell up and close. With no air going into your lungs, the person can die from lack of oxygen. Or maybe a heart attack," Dana explained. "But either way, it still had nothing to do with you, Suzanne."

Suzanne felt so relieved at the news, she thought she might cry again. "Thank you for telling me that, Maggie. It really is a load off my mind. You have no idea."

Maggie smiled, looking as if her good deed had been worth breaking her word. "I couldn't watch you beat yourself up about it anymore, honestly. The police won't know the details until the autopsy is completed. But as Dana said, you may have regrets about leaving things on a sour note. But your argument, however passionate, had nothing to do with Liza's death. You can rest easy about that at least."

"I was tying myself up in knots, thinking I'd caused it. Even remotely." Suzanne couldn't help recalling Liza's shocked expression, her staring, surprised eyes. "It must have been a frightening way to go. I wouldn't have wished that on anybody."

"You don't need to explain to us. We get it," Lucy replied in a comforting tone.

"We know you'd never harm a fly," Phoebe added. "Except for shouting 'Get away from me, you fly!' really loud. And waving your arms around like a wind turbine."

Suzanne gave Phoebe a look as her young friend acted out the insect-chasing technique. "Don't argue with success. That

81

works, doesn't it?"

Phoebe kept her eyes on her task. "Only because the fly laughs itself to death."

"Good one, Phoebe," Lucy said.

"I have my moments." Phoebe shrugged, patting the skeins into a neat pile.

"You're sharpening your game, girl. I'll give you that," Suzanne said.

Dana had a copy of the *Plum Harbor Times* open on the table, and had been thumbing through the pages while they chatted. "Nothing in here about Liza. I guess the news hit too late to be included in today's edition."

"Channel five was there," Suzanne said, mentioning a local TV station. "I saw the van as we were leaving. We slipped past just in time. I would have hated to be on TV about this."

Maggie looked up from the computer. "A reporter asked Charles a few questions. Since she seemed to have died of natural causes I doubt there's much of a news story there."

"Let's look online. I bet Plum Harbor Patch has something." Lucy picked up Maggie's laptop, which sat on a wicker end table. She quickly struck the keyboard to bring up the local news site that covered events faster than the newspaper or sometimes even the TV news.

"Here we are. 'Liza Devereaux, found dead last night on the premises of Prestige Properties, Main Street, Plum Harbor, where she worked in real estate sales. Police were called to the building when the body was discovered and are investigating the cause of death. Devereaux family is planning a memorial service and will make information about the arrangements known soon.' "

Lucy looked up from the computer screen. "I guess the family is waiting for the police to release her body. Whenever there's an autopsy it takes time."

"Nothing we didn't know. But enough for me," Suzanne murmured.

She felt relieved to hear it would be a day or two before the memorial gathering. A bit more time to process the event. She had a feeling Harry would be among the first to hear the details from Liza's family and had no doubt he'd send the information to his staff.

"I feel awful for her mother," Maggie said quietly. "It's positively unnatural to outlive a child. Such an unthinkable loss."

"There aren't any words to describe it," Dana said.

"I only met Ruth Devereaux once," Maggie said. "Liza brought her here to talk about the knitting demonstration. She's a lovely woman. I feel I should pay my respects. I'll attend the service. Send flowers, or something."

"Liza knew everyone in town. I have a feeling the service will be standing room only," Suzanne said.

Dana took off her reading glasses and slipped them in a case. She looked as if she was getting ready to go. "At least Liza's sister lives in town and her mother has someone close, to take care of her right now."

Maggie rose from her chair and helped Phoebe place the new yarn skeins back in the box. "That should be some comfort. They have each other."

Suzanne and her friends sat quietly, at an unusual loss for words. She heard her phone buzz with a text and checked the screen.

"Thanks for listening again, gang, but I have to run. An SOS from Alexis. She forgot her lacrosse jersey and she has a game today. And I just realized, I can even go and cheer her on, since I have the afternoon off."

Suzanne loved to watch her kids play sports, or perform in concerts or plays, but she was always sandwiching in the events between business appointments and was rarely there from start to finish. Today, she'd even be able to get a good seat and not stumble over all the other parents in the grandstands.

"It's a perfect day to watch a lacrosse game. It will be great to be outside in the fresh air." Lucy had packed up her knitting and looked ready to leave, too.

"Definitely beats my first plan — hang around in my pj's and watch the shopping channel all day. Maybe have some frozen waffles for lunch?" Suzanne's confession made her friends laugh.

Maggie stepped forward and gave her a hug. "Try to put that dreadful episode out of your head. If you want to talk some more, just call me. Any time."

Everyone else repeated the offer and Suzanne left with a warm, comforted feeling. She cruised down Main Street, planning a quick stop at home to pick up the jersey and a healthy snack that would give her girl an energy boost for the game. But she couldn't help slowing down as she passed her office. The yellow police tape was still in place, and a blue and white cruiser was parked in front.

Why were the police still poking around in there? According to Maggie, they knew how Liza had died. The only question was what had brought on the allergic attack, and how did she accidentally eat it? Or breathe it in, or whatever.

It might not have been food, Suzanne realized. She'd heard of people being insanely allergic to all sorts of things — bee stings, latex gloves, even some hand creams and face lotions with nut-based ingredients could set off sensitivities.

All she knew was that their argument had nothing to do with Liza's death. Suzanne would never have guessed, but the mere thought that she was somehow — even distantly — to blame for Liza's demise was her very worst nightmare.

The Plum Harbor Sea Hawks were victorious, pushing their record to six straight wins for the season. Watching the game had been the perfect distraction, just as her friends had promised. Suzanne had been riveted by the action on the field, jumping up and down in her seat so many times, she felt as if she'd made it through a double Zumba class.

She'd definitely burned enough calories to enjoy the taco dinner her daughter had requested. Suzanne often skipped the shell and some of the trimmings to save calories. But tonight she piled her taco high —

practically a work of art, she decided as she prepared to take a bite.

The rest of the family was already a taco or two ahead of her. Fresh from a shower, Alexis sat in her comfy clothes — a cotton hoody and sweatpants, her long hair still wet and tied in a sloppy bun. Suzanne's twelve-year-old boys, Ryan and Jamie, sat side by side, as intent on the meal as if they were competing in an eating contest.

Kevin was at the opposite end of the table, adding some shredded cheese to his dish.

"I have to go to games more often. I got a workout just from watching. Alexis was awesome," she told the family. "I wish I had a video of you scoring, honey. She spun around and jumped in the air before she made the shot. I think those ballet lessons finally paid off."

"Thanks, Mom. It was just a goal. No big deal." Alexis was acting her cool teenage self, but Suzanne could tell she was proud.

Before Suzanne could reply, her phone rang. She sat very still, though her first impulse was to reach into her pocket and answer it.

She and Kevin had a family rule — no electronic devices at the dinner table. Which included keeping the TV off during mealtimes. She had read that kids were less likely

87

to get involved with drugs and other risky behavior if the family had dinner together most nights, and talked and shared. Without screen distractions.

Suzanne didn't want to set a bad example, though she was itching to know who had called and why.

"Just my phone. I'll see who called later," she said above the ring tone.

"You know the rule, Mom," Jamie chided in a parentlike voice.

She glanced at him, but had to smile. The kid was a total wise apple. But she knew it was genetic; he couldn't help it.

"I know the rule and I'm keeping it. See?" she put both hands in the air just as the ringing stopped.

There was a moment of silence as they all continued eating. Then Kevin's phone rang. He glanced at her across the table.

"I guess someone is trying to reach us. Could be important. I'd better get it."

He stood up and walked over to the kitchen counter where his phone was charging. Suzanne felt a frisson of nerves. She hoped it wasn't a family emergency. Was it her sister, calling about her mom, or dad, down in Connecticut? They weren't that old but they weren't that young anymore either, and both had a myriad of health complaints lately.

Kevin stood with his back turned toward the table and spoke in a quiet voice. She couldn't make out a word of the call. Which made her even more anxious.

"Sure . . . I understand. We're just finishing dinner. Be there in half an hour. Or sooner," she heard him say.

"Who's Dad talking to?" Ryan asked.

"I don't know, honey. Maybe somebody from work." The answer seemed logical. Kevin sometimes had calls from clients who had suddenly sprung a leak, or flipped a circuit breaker. Or had some other little complaint he had to solve.

She met his glance as he walked back to the table. His expression was grim, making her worry all over again.

"What's up, honey? Did something go screwy at one of your jobs?"

"That was Charles. He needs to ask you a few more questions. He wants you to go down to . . . to his office."

Suzanne's mouth grew dry. Kevin had been about to say "police station" and had caught himself just in time. So the kids wouldn't start asking a million questions.

Quick thinking. She doubted that Charles even had an office.

89

"Tonight?"

Kevin nodded. "That's right. It's okay," he added quickly. "No big deal. I'll go with you."

"Um . . . okay." Suzanne tried her best to sound calm. "I guess we're all done here. Kids, can you just put your dishes in the sink? I'll put the leftovers away and we can go."

She and Kevin exchanged another glance. They hadn't told the children, not even Alexis, where she'd really been last night, and it still didn't seem the right moment to tell them she'd found a dead body.

Alexis picked up a few dirty dishes and followed Suzanne to the sink. "So I guess I'm in charge of the gruesome twosome again. You'd better tell them to behave. I have a ton of homework."

"Daddy will talk to them," Suzanne promised. She looked over at Kevin. "Tell those boys if they act out, no video games for a week."

"Two weeks. And no pizza either," Alexis chimed in as Kevin headed out of the kitchen to lay down the law to his sons.

Suzanne loaded a few dishes into the dishwasher, but quickly shut it and left the rest in the sink. Her hands were shaking. She wasn't sure why, but she didn't want her daughter to see.

Alexis gazed into the refrigerator, looking for something else to eat. She ate more than Kevin these days, bless her, and was built like a string bean. A lean, mean string bean.

"Are you going to talk to Charles Mossbacher, Maggie's boyfriend? Isn't he a police detective?"

Suzanne was glad her daughter couldn't see her face. She rinsed her hands and wiped them on a paper towel.

"Yes, I am. Something happened last night. I wasn't stuck in town with car trouble. We told you that because . . . well, it was sort of upsetting and we didn't want you and the boys to get scared."

Alexis had chosen a large Macintosh apple. She turned to Suzanne, looking puzzled. "You can tell me, Mom. I'm not a baby."

"I know that." Suzanne nodded. "I'm telling you this because you're old enough to understand. But don't tell the boys. Dad and I will explain this to them soon."

"Okay." Alexis looked even more curious now.

"Do you remember that woman I work with, Liza Devereaux?"

"Sure. The one you always say you hate?"

Suzanne sighed. Her ill-considered words

were going to haunt her, weren't they?

"I didn't hate her. Not really. Hate is a very strong word. We should never say that about anybody," she added, knowing full well she was facing the typical "do as I say, not as I do" parenting conundrum. "The thing is, I went back to the office last night after the knitting meeting. And she was dead. I found her, in her office."

"OMG . . . you're kidding? Did you scream and stuff? Was her body all cold and stiff? Like they show in the movies?"

Suzanne knew that a full reel of horror flicks was now running through her daughter's head . . . starring her mother. She thought it best to downplay her reaction.

"I may have screamed a little. Not that much," Suzanne replied.

Alexis squinched up her face. "How did you know she was dead? Did you have to touch her?"

"Of course I touched her. I wasn't sure if she was . . . I mean, I had to check her pulse. To make sure."

Her daughter didn't answer, just stared, the apple hanging limply from one hand. "Wow . . . That is so creepy."

"The police came and asked a lot of questions and now they need to ask more." She shrugged, trying to act as if this was no big deal. As much for her daughter's sake as her own. "It won't take long."

She wasn't sure of that either but hoped just saying it would make it true.

"Okay. I'll watch the little monsters. No worries. Catch you later." Alexis, who wasn't prone to spontaneous shows of affection since she had been about five, hopped over and planted a quick kiss on her mother's cheek.

Suzanne was so shocked, she lifted her hand to touch the spot.

"See you later, honey." The sweet gesture made her feel a little better. Though the request from Charles was definitely a surprise.

But there's no reason to worry, she reminded herself. Hadn't Charles said last night that he might need to ask a few more questions? Well, this is a few more questions.

She had just about talked herself into a semicalm state when Kevin came back into the kitchen. He was already wearing his jacket and picked up his car keys.

He turned to her, with a surprisingly serious expression. "I don't know, Suzanne. Do you think we should call a lawyer?"

CHAPTER 4

"A lawyer? What do I need a lawyer for?" The question seemed totally out of left field.

Kevin shrugged his big shoulders. "I don't know. Charles sounded so official. Why does he need to talk to you at the police station? Why can't he ask you questions over the phone?"

Suzanne wondered about that, too. But again, she tried to minimize the implications. "For one thing, when he did call, I didn't answer the phone."

She had listened to Charles's message. It had been brief, giving no hint of his reasons or intentions.

"It could be worse. What if he'd come to the door, like they do in the movies? It would have scared the kids silly and then we'd really be answering questions. I did let Alexis know what happened, but asked her not to tell the boys," she added.

"I guess that's the best thing. For now.

We'd better leave. He must be waiting for us."

Kevin stared straight ahead and headed for the side door. She could tell by the set of his jaw he was worried, but trying not to show it. Outside, they climbed in his truck. He quickly started the engine and drove toward the village. It was a dark night. Suzanne stared out at the road where bare branches swayed and dipped overhead.

"I'm not going to get bent out of shape about this. And I really don't think I need a lawyer sitting there for no reason. Charging a zillion dollars a minute," she added.

But her mind jumped to Dana, the only person she knew who could find a lawyer on such short notice. Dana's husband Jack was an attorney in town and, before that, had been a detective for the county. He had a lot of connections in law enforcement.

Should they call Dana, just in case?

"I thought you said the police found out Liza died from an allergic reaction. Why do they need to ask anyone more questions?" Suzanne knew Kevin was just thinking out loud. He sounded annoyed and even angry — an emotion she'd discovered men often expressed to mask their worry and fear.

"Your guess is as good as mine. I bet the police are still talking to a lot of people from my office. Not just me," Suzanne insisted.

"Could be," Kevin said quietly. "Maybe we're getting upset over nothing. Let's just see how it goes."

About two hours later, Suzanne had to face the fact that it was not going the way she had expected. In fact, it was not going well at all.

She wished with all her heart that her husband had been allowed to stay with her, but soon after they arrived at the station and gave their names to the officer at the front desk, Charles had come out to meet them.

Kevin was directed to a waiting area and Charles led Suzanne into the deep maze of the Essex County police station, which the public didn't often see.

They walked down a sterile-looking hallway with a linoleum floor, the walls painted a color Suzanne called "hospital green." They passed a few gray, metal doors with stenciled numbers and a small window on top. Then they came to one that was open.

"Let's step in here and we'll talk," Charles said. He politely stood aside to allow Suzanne to enter first. She saw another man seated at a narrow table, with chairs set up on either side.

The man looked up at her, with dark eyes, close set. He had a narrow face and a shiny, bald head. An impressive black mustache covered his upper lip. She recognized him from the night before, one of the police officers who had been scurrying around the realty office. She had guessed he was another detective, Charles's partner, and now she was sure.

"Suzanne, this is Frank Oliver, my partner. Frank and I have some questions for you."

She sat down in a molded plastic chair and squared her shoulders, a technique she'd learned in a business course about negotiating. Poor posture sends a bad signal. You need to take up as much space as possible to intimidate your adversary. Like certain reptiles in the rain forest that blow themselves up three times their size when facing down a predator.

"Hello, Frank." She smiled at him, but didn't overdo it. He met her gaze. "Hello, Mrs. Cavanaugh. Thank you for coming in to talk to us."

"Not a problem. I want to help."

"Good. The more truthful you are with us, the easier this will go."

His words were alarming. Suzanne glanced at Charles. But if Charles thought his partner's words were inappropriate, his

97

expression didn't show it.

"I thought I told Charles everything I know last night. But if you have more questions, that's fine. I'll answer them."

You have nothing to hide. Or worry about. Disliking someone — even trash talking them — is not a crime, she reminded herself.

Charles cleared his throat. He had been carrying a dark green folder and it now sat in front of him on the table. He looked up at her, without opening it.

"You told me last night that you and Liza didn't get along. That you'd had an argument in the office on Thursday afternoon."

Suzanne nodded. "That's right."

Detective Oliver spoke next. "Can you tell us what that argument was about?"

Suzanne was fairly certain that they knew the details of the argument by now. They must have spoken to everyone in the office, and had heard about the incident again and again. With many embellishments, she had no doubt.

But she had to keep her cool and answer their question as calmly as she could. Suzanne took a breath and related the story — how she had been running an open house at an exclusive listing and how Liza had stolen her clients and squeezed an offer out of them.

"I was very surprised when I found out what she'd done. Though it wasn't the first time," Suzanne added. "Any real estate professional will tell you that was totally unprofessional behavior. Naturally, I was upset. Anybody would have been."

Suzanne stopped herself from saying more. She could see it would be unwise to sound angry. She needed to spin this as more of an ethical disagreement.

"It was the principle of the thing," she said finally.

She sat back and looked across at Charles, hoping for some sign of support. But his expression was as unreadable as a stone lion's.

Detective Oliver caught her attention. "So you were upset. How upset? Would you say that you were angry?"

Suzanne thought a moment, wondering how honest she should be. She suppressed a sigh. No sense lying about it. There were too many people who would contradict her.

"Yes, I was angry. She'd stolen my clients. And my sale. As I just said, this was totally unprofessional behavior. I had to speak up for myself. Wouldn't you?"

She glanced at Charles, hoping he'd be the one to answer this time. But again, he sat silently, his mouth set in a tight line, his jaw jutting out a bit. She had a feeling that he wanted to reply, but the two detectives had a game plan and Oliver had the ball.

The realization that they had probably strategized on the best way to question her was alarming.

"One of your coworkers, Lyle Croddy, described your reaction as more than upset, or even surprised and angry. He said . . ." Frank Oliver opened the folder on the table in front of him and read from the top page: " 'She was over the top. Like a crazy woman. Screaming expletives. She jumped up and tried to attack Liza. She even pulled Liza's hair.' "

Detective Oliver looked up at her. "Is that true?"

Lyle, Lyle. Crocodile! Of course you would exaggerate and get me in even more hot water.

"Yes, I raised my voice, though I was definitely not screaming. And I may have even leaned toward her, across the table. But I never pulled her hair," she stated flatly. "That's not true at all."

Only because Lyle held you back and you couldn't reach it, a small voice clarified.

Before Detective Oliver could reply, she hurriedly added, "I certainly don't think Lyle Croddy is the best source of information. His beat is commercial listings, which are slim picking in this town, and he's always been very jealous of me."

Finally Charles spoke. "Please calm down, Suzanne. We're just trying to get a picture of the events at the office on Thursday. The day Liza Devereaux died."

Suzanne didn't want to cry in front of the two men, but she suddenly felt as if she might. "I understand. But I told you all about the argument last night, Charles. And you said that even if I had made her upset, you'd never heard of anybody accused of murder or even manslaughter, just because they'd had an argument with the person who died. . . . And besides," she added, turning now to Detective Oliver, "I heard today that she died from a severe allergic reaction. We certainly didn't like each other, but as far as I know, Liza wasn't allergic to me. So I couldn't have caused that, either."

She sat back and crossed her arms over her chest, staring at Oliver with her best, "How do you like them bananas, pal?" look.

Charles's gaze narrowed, his expression darkened. "How do you know that?"

Suzanne took a breath and shook her head. "Heard it around town, I guess. News like that gets out quickly."

She could tell he didn't believe her. And

she was instantly sorry that she'd lied. *But only to protect Maggie and keep your promise to her,* she reminded herself.

When neither of the men replied, she said, "She had a food allergy or something like that, right?"

Detective Oliver leaned toward her. "You seem to know a lot about it, Mrs. Cavanaugh. Why don't you tell us?"

Suzanne sat back, feeling stung. What was going on here? Why were they treating her like this? Talking to her as if . . . as if she'd been involved in Liza's death? That couldn't be right. She felt her heart race. She looked from one man to the other.

"Why are you saying these things to me? I went back into the office last night to talk to her. To apologize for losing my temper at the meeting. But when I found her . . . Well, she was lying on the floor. Dead. That's what happened. That's all I know."

Charles looked at his partner. Suzanne had a feeling her appeal had moved him. Maybe they would let her go home now?

Detective Oliver avoided Charles's gaze. He had opened the folder and was paging through the contents. "Let's move on. We'll get back to the argument again, later."

Later? How long did they plan to keep her there?

Suzanne nearly jumped up in her chair, about to protest. But looking at the demeanor of the men, she caught herself and settled back in her seat. Oliver, at least, was ready to categorize her as a nut job. She didn't need to provide any more evidence of that.

Charles's voice broke through her thoughts. His tone was almost friendly. She met his glance, but she was still on her guard. "Where were you yesterday morning, Suzanne? What was your schedule like?"

She sat back and gazed at the ceiling, badly in need of a paint job. "Let's see . . . dropped my daughter at the high school around eight and drove up to Newburyport. There was an open house on a condo for salespeople only. Waterfront, in a warehouse. Very nice property."

"Go on," Detective Oliver prodded her.

"That ended around ten. I drove out to Peabody next, to have my teeth cleaned. The dentist office was backed up and I wasn't done until noon. Maybe later."

Oliver had been taking notes. He glanced at Charles and then looked back at Suzanne. "What route did you take from Newburyport to Peabody?"

Suzanne thought it was an odd question. How did this have anything to do with Liza's death? "I was right near the entrance to the highway, so I jumped on, and jumped off in Peabody. What route would I have taken?"

"You're sure that you didn't travel down on 1A?" Oliver asked.

"Who would do that from Newburyport? It's like driving in a big circle. And so slow, going through all of the villages again."

"You're sure that you didn't pass through Plum Harbor on your way to the dentist? Take your time answering," Charles advised.

"I don't have to take my time. I know how I got from A to B, okay?" Suzanne was getting annoyed at these cat and mouse games.

"Was anyone in the car with you?" Oliver asked.

"I was driving alone the whole day. As usual," she added. "What is this about? Do you want to give me a clue?"

Detective Oliver took out a photograph and pushed it across the table toward her. "Do you recognize this car?"

Suzanne glanced at the picture. A white Mercedes SUV, with a long, jagged, black scratch running from the front bumper to the back. "I can tell you the model. And that Liza drives one just like it. Drove one, I mean," she added quietly. "And I heard that her car was vandalized yesterday, so it must be hers. Right?"

"Yes, that's her car," Detective Oliver replied. "We're wondering if the same person who did that caused her death."

Suzanne felt her mouth grow dry.

"I didn't do it. I was nowhere near her car on Thursday morning."

The two detectives stared at her, neither of them answering.

"Do you have a way of proving that, Suzanne?" Oliver asked.

"If there was a toll booth, or security cameras on the highway between Newburyport and Peabody, we could verify your story that way," Charles suggested.

"But there aren't any," Detective Oliver added, squelching that hope.

She could tell Charles was trying to be helpful. Even though the information he'd offered had not helped at all. But it did remind her of something that might.

She clapped her hands together. "Wait a minute . . . I stopped at a drive-thru on the highway. I got some streusel bites and a coffee. I'm sure I saved the receipt, since meals during work hours are deductible for me. And I talked to Mr. Streusel," she added, referring to the plastic dough man that hid the drive-thru microphone. "They probably have cameras in those things, don't you think?"

Charles was trying hard not to smile. Suzanne could tell.

Detective Oliver had his head down again, making more notes. "Possibly. We'd like to see your receipt at some point. I'll look into this to verify your story."

Suzanne sat back, feeling vindicated. She'd felt so guilty after being seduced by Mr. Streusel. Yet again . . . But thank goodness for that sugar craving. Her old pal was a solid alibi for the car thing.

"All right. Let's go on. Here's another photograph we want you to look at. Can you tell me what you see?"

Suzanne glanced at the next picture and recognized it immediately. "Liza's desk? The way it looked last night?"

"That's right. Do you see what's on it? Next to the lamp?"

"A bottle of diet shake. I saw it there last night. She practically lives on that stuff. . . . *Did* live on it, I mean."

There was a lesson, Suzanne thought. The woman tortured herself to stay so lithe of limb. What good had all that deprivation done? Gather ye rosebuds . . . and yes, streusel bites . . . while ye may.

"We actually drank the same brand," Suzanne added. One thing they had in common. One tiny, little thing. "Though she definitely got better results."

Charles looked as if he wanted to chuckle again, but was holding it back. The humor had not registered on Frank Oliver.

He showed her another photo, the inside of the office refrigerator where a myriad of take-out containers and convenience foods sat on the shelves, each marked with different names and initials. On the bottom shelf, Suzanne saw her pack of diet drinks — Dreamy Creamy Chocolate — with four containers left in the six pack. "Can you show us which bottles are yours?"

Suzanne pointed to a photo. "That pack on the bottom. I mark them with my initials." She looked up at Detective Oliver. "That's the system we have in the office. Though food does disappear."

"Initials. Right." Detective Oliver took out two more photos and turned them around so she could see them clearly.

The diet drink bottle again, eight-by-ten glossies. Suitable for framing, Suzanne thought. The shots looked as if they'd been taken in a laboratory, the background in both stark and clinical looking.

In one picture the focus seemed to be the white sticker on the front of the bottle, with initials *L.D.* scrawled in blue pen. The other showed the side of the bottle, where a "use by" date and some other numbers had been stamped.

Suzanne looked down at the photos, then up at the detectives.

"This is the bottle we found on her desk, which was empty," Detective Oliver explained. "The autopsy and lab tests show that Liza Devereaux died of an allergic reaction to a substance that was added to that bottle."

Suzanne wasn't sure that she'd heard correctly. "Added to the bottle? You mean someone put something in the drink that they knew she was allergic to?"

Charles nodded. "That's right. The drink was tampered with, tainted. Someone set out to deliberately elicit an allergic reaction, which they probably knew would be life threatening."

Suzanne took a breath and sat back, putting distance between herself and the photographs. "That's awful. . . . I mean, if that's what really happened. That means someone set out to . . . to kill her?"

"That's right." Detective Oliver's reply was clipped and quiet. He pushed the photos closer to her and pointed to the photo on the right that showed the side of the bottle enlarged. "The funny thing is, Suzanne, when we checked the serial numbers on the side of this bottle they matched up with your pack."

Suzanne felt a jolt. She pressed her hand to her chest. "My bottles? Are you sure? Maybe we bought them at the same store and all the bottles in that batch have those numbers."

Charles shook his head. "Part of the code matched, since the product was produced and shipped from the same location. But the last few digits are different. The numbers on that bottle match your six-pack."

Suzanne shook her head, refusing to accept what the detectives were implying. "All right. If you say so. But . . . I didn't put anything in a diet drink and pass it off on her. Is that what you're trying to say here? I didn't even know she had allergies. I didn't know that much about her. Honestly."

She turned her head back and forth, looking at each of the men who sat across from her. She could hardly believe this was happening. She could tell her voice was rising, but she couldn't control her reaction.

"Are you sure?" Detective Oliver persisted. "You never heard her say she was allergic to *anything*? You never heard anyone in the office talk about that?"

Suzanne shook her head. "Never. She was a very private person. Even with people she was friendly with. Which didn't include me."

Detective Oliver nodded. "I think we've established that, Suzanne. You two were like oil and water, weren't you? The day that she died, she was stealing a huge commission from you. And it wasn't the first time," he reminded her, reading from notes he'd made earlier. "Lyle Croddy said you were 'Wild with rage. And tried to attack her.' You must have been very, very angry." He paused and glanced at Charles.

Charles had his notepad open, the one he carried around in his pocket. He flipped it back a few pages and looked up at her. "You know, Suzanne, when I first spoke to you at the crime scene, you seemed very distraught. You told me that 'I never got along with Liza but I never meant to hurt her.'" Suzanne could tell he was reading her exact words off the pad now. He must have made notes after he left her. "'I never imagined she'd end up like this,' meaning her death, I'd assume." He looked up at her again. "Isn't that what you said? Or words to that effect?"

Suzanne's heart was pumping so loud she heard ringing in her ears. "I did say that. But later, when you asked me, I told you

110

what I meant. I was worried that the argument at the meeting had made her sick somehow. Given her high blood pressure or something."

"You said that later. But maybe that's not really what you meant at all when you first saw Detective Mossbacher," Detective Oliver cut in. "You were very angry at her. You tried to assault her. So maybe you just wanted to teach her a lesson. Make her feel a little sick, a little scared. You had no idea it would go that far. Is that how it happened, Suzanne?"

For one weird moment, there was just the sound of Detective Oliver's voice, drilling into her head. The pale green walls in the room were dissolving, melting in on her. Suzanne squeezed her eyes shut, thinking she might faint. Or puke. Or make a run for the door.

She gripped the arms of the chair, her sweaty palms sliding on the cold metal. She was suddenly struck by a horrifying realization — these men actually believed she'd killed Liza Devereaux. They were trying to say that she'd slipped some weird substance in a diet shake, something she knew Liza was allergic to — and planted it in the fridge with Liza's initials on it, then waited for her to drink it.

And die.

"Suzanne? Can you answer us?" Charles's voice sounded a bit softer. Almost concerned, she thought in some dim, distant part of her brain.

But Charles Mossbacher was not going to help her. He was the enemy now. Much to her surprise. Wasn't that painfully clear?

Suzanne opened her eyes and took a deep breath. "I know my rights. I want a lawyer. I'm not answering another question until I have an attorney in here."

Detective Oliver glanced at Charles. He looked annoyed. Charles didn't meet his partner's gaze, just stared down at the table a moment. Suzanne had a feeling he felt relieved. As if he'd been waiting for her to say those words but wasn't able to suggest it.

Maybe I'm just projecting, she thought, still wanting to think of Charles as an ally, when clearly the lines were very blurred. To say the least.

Detective Oliver's eyes widened in surprise. "We're just trying to understand what happened, Suzanne."

"Ha! That's a laugh. How dumb do you think I am?"

"I think you're pretty sharp. Believe me." Detective Oliver nodded, his words edged with double meaning.

Suzanne glared at him. "I just told you, Detective. I'm not going to answer another question without a lawyer."

Before his partner could reply, Charles nodded. "You can call an attorney. That's your prerogative."

"Okay by me," Detective Oliver muttered. "I don't punch out until six AM. Is that how you want to play it?"

A sassy reply nearly left her lips. Instead, she shrugged. She pointed an index finger at her lips and did a pantomime of a zipping gesture. Then met Detective Oliver's gaze with an angry smile.

Despite Detective Oliver's warning, Suzanne did not remain in the small room answering questions until dawn. Though it did take nearly two hours for Helen Forbes to arrive and be briefed on Suzanne's situation.

The criminal attorney, who was about Maggie's age, Suzanne guessed, quickly cut through the bluster and bluff of the two detectives. Jack Haeger, Dana's husband, had reached out to make the connection. Suzanne knew right away she was fortunate to have Helen rush to her aid. Not to mention that she liked Helen's style — the black, oversized eyeglass frames, which contrasted sharply with bright red lipstick and a shock of white hair.

After Helen had settled in at the table next to Suzanne, Detective Oliver began talking again about the diet shake, explaining there were only two sets of fingerprints on the bottle. "Liza Devereaux's and that of one other person. We believe the other set is yours, Suzanne. Of course, we can't confirm that until we examine your prints. You can let us take them voluntarily. Or we can compel you." His harsh tone alarmed her. But Suzanne reminded herself she was protected now.

"Why wouldn't they be Suzanne's? You've already told us the bottle came from her package." Helen ran her hand through her short, thick hair, then tossed her glasses on the table. "That doesn't prove squat, gentlemen, and you know it. Nothing you've said so far will even squeak past the DA. No less stand up in court. Did forensics work hard on that shocking bit of evidence?"

A DA? A courtroom? Suzanne stole a glance at her attorney. Was it really that serious?

Charles showed no reaction to Helen's words. His partner however, looked as if she'd insulted him personally. Maybe she had, Suzanne reflected. Touché, Helen. One for our side.

"So, you agree that Suzanne Cavanaugh's fingerprints are on this bottle. Is that what you're saying?"

"I did not. I'm simply pointing out that it's possible and, if so, would be no proof that she was the one who planted the bottle for the victim. The person who did that was probably wearing gloves. As criminals often do." She glanced at Suzanne and then at her watch. "And no, my client is not going to give you her fingerprints, either. Unless you have a court order. Is there something else you want to ask? If not, you have nothing here to hold her on. . . ."

"Not so fast, Ms. Forbes. We're not finished," Detective Oliver said curtly. He turned to Suzanne, paging through the folder again. She thought he looked rushed, set off his game, which was a good thing from her perspective.

"Well, what's the question? I think you've detained this woman long enough. Without any legal grounds, I might add."

Detective Oliver held up his hand, without making eye contact with Suzanne's attorney. "Just a moment. I'm getting to it."

Helen Forbes let out a noisy breath, but didn't interrupt him.

"Did you and Liza Devereaux ever talk about Botox?"

Suzanne could not have been more surprised by the question if the detective had asked her if they'd talked about their first boyfriends.

"Botox?" Suzanne shook her head. "I just told you. We weren't friends, in any sense of the word. We didn't get all girly and talk about stuff like that. We didn't talk at all, really."

"Are you sure? Did you ever hear her talking about it with anyone else in the office?" Charles asked.

Suzanne thought about it a moment. She did remember something that related to this odd line of inquisition. But before she could answer, Helen leaned forward, holding up a hand to Suzanne like a school-crossing guard signaling to a child it was not safe yet to leave the sidewalk.

"What's the punch line, Detective? Where is this going?"

Detective Oliver sat back. Suzanne could tell he didn't want to show his hand.

"If you don't explain, she's not going to answer." Helen shrugged and glanced at Suzanne. "I guess it's not that important."

Charles and his partner exchanged a glance. Then Charles said, "The medical

116

examiner determined that Liza Devereaux died of anaphylactic shock, after ingesting Botox."

"Are you kidding? You mean, someone put that in her diet shake?" Suzanne didn't mean to speak without Helen's approval, but the news was so bizarre.

Detective Oliver nodded. "That's right. Normally, the substance is not poisonous and wouldn't cause much harm if ingested. Even a good amount of it."

"Botox is derived from botulism, which is highly toxic, even in small amounts. But the brand name solution that's injected into the skin by cosmetic surgeons is purified. So it's not harmful, even if it gets into a patient's eyes or mouth by accident," Charles explained.

"Except in rare cases, like Liza Devereaux's. She was highly allergic," Detective Oliver broke in. "According to interviews with your coworkers, this was common knowledge. Do you still insist you didn't know?"

Suzanne leaned her head back. She was exhausted. She could barely keep her eyes open. How would she ever get up for work tomorrow morning?

She glanced at Helen, not sure what to

do. Helen nodded. "I think you can answer that one."

Suzanne did get up and staggered into the shower then dressed quietly while Kevin snored into his pillow. It was Saturday morning, her kids were sleeping in, and the house was blessedly quiet. Suzanne appreciated the silence as she crept down to the kitchen and started the coffeemaker.

Their family dog, Barkly, nosed her hand. He was a gentle soul for such a big hound, part Bernese mountain dog, part Labrador, and Suzanne had always thought part polar bear. She let him out and sipped the strong coffee, standing at the counter.

But she had to get to work. The office was open for business. *And I have to show up and act as if nothing unusual is going on in my life — if you don't count sitting in a police station and being interrogated all night.*

A text message made her phone buzz where it sat on the countertop. It was from Dana.

Hope Helen Forbes was able to get you out quickly. Coming into town this morning? I have a yoga class but if you can meet at the Schooner, I'll rally the troops. I told them you were at the police station last night and they all want to see you.

Suzanne sent a text back quickly.

The office is open today and I have to show face. But can definitely stop at the Schooner on the way. That will give me a reason to live.

Helen was amazing. But can't believe how the police treated me! Even Charles.

She didn't often use emojis, but put a sad face after his name.

It wasn't pretty. And I can definitely use a waffle.

A short time later, Suzanne sat shoulder to shoulder with her friends at their favorite local eatery, the Schooner Diner. As usual on a Saturday morning, the place was packed, but they had some pull since Maggie was good friends with the owner, Edie Steiber.

Edie was always trotting across the street to Maggie's shop, for first aid with her knitting mishaps or to buy yarn for her projects, which were mostly gifts for her many grandchildren and even great-grandchildren. The Steibers were a prolific clan.

Most of the time at the diner, Edie sat up front behind the counter, a bouffant Buddha in a flowery dress, watching over her domain, and her cash register. Like a gatekeeper at a hip nightclub, no matter how long the line, Edie would wave in her favorites, like Suzanne and her friends, ahead of others. This practice made some customers irate and complain that they wouldn't come back. But Edie didn't care. She had more than enough customers for two restaurants, Maggie always said. Suzanne often thought Edie's blasé attitude made the retro diner seem more exclusive than it actually was. And that made more people want to eat there, too.

They all knew the menu by heart and ordered quickly. While waiting for their food to come, Suzanne told her friends about the call from Charles and being questioned by him and his partner, Detective Oliver.

"Finally, I realized it was getting too crazy and I really needed a lawyer. So I called Dana, and Helen Forbes came right away. She was terrific. Wonder Woman and Perry Mason wrapped into one."

"Helen is terrific. She helped me a few years ago, when Amanda Gorman died and the police kept badgering me." Maggie's expression was grim and Suzanne could see the memory still stung. "It's no joke when they have you in one of those little rooms and start hammering away. You're likely to say anything."

"Tell me about it," Suzanne agreed.

The waitress arrived and served their

dishes, setting a fluffy, golden waffle in front of Suzanne first.

Dana, the healthiest eater in the group, had ordered avocado toast, a trendy addition to Edie's traditional menu.

Lucy always ordered the same thing, scrambled eggs with cheddar cheese and whole wheat toast. Unexciting, but it did look tasty. "Were they really accusing you of causing her death? But how? She died of an allergic reaction."

"Yes, they were. Or about to, before Helen put the brakes on. Liza was highly allergic to Botox and they think someone put the solution in a diet shake and planted it in the office fridge with her initials on it."

"Charles told me, but I didn't really believe it. It's too bizarre for words." Maggie shook her head and took a bite of a toasted bagel.

"When they first asked me, I couldn't remember about the allergy. Then the police reminded me of that silly Botox party I went to. Janine, our receptionist, was trying to earn a little extra money, so she hosted this party. She did demonstrations and sold do-it-yourself kits of Botox. She held it right in the office, so it was pretty hard to avoid attending. Just about everyone was there. Even Harry and Lyle. Their wives were curious. Except for Liza. She said she'd tried it once and had a bad reaction."

"And that's how you were supposed to know that she was allergic?" Dana asked.

"That's right. But as Helen pointed out, everyone in the office knew, too. And they all went to the party and bought the stupid stuff. Which didn't work that great anyway."

Lucy caught her eye as she sipped her mug of coffee. "I remember now. The eyebrow incident?"

Her friends laughed quietly. Maggie rose to her defense. "This is not a good time for teasing. Suzanne is upset."

Suzanne sighed, but she also had to smile and even laugh at the joke, too. "All right, I can take it. You'll never let me live that down, will you?" she asked Lucy.

Lucy quirked one eyebrow up and even tilted her head a bit, for emphasis. "I'm sorry. . . . I didn't mean to make you feel bad . . . Sherlock."

Suzanne had looked like Sherlock Holmes. She couldn't deny that. All she'd needed was a curvy pipe and one of those peeked hats with the earflaps. "At least it wore off quickly, once I sought medical help. I did learn my lesson. Who knows? Maybe I'm allergic to it too and that's why it made me look so funny."

"I think you stuck the needle in the wrong spot," Dana said quietly. "Luckily, it didn't do any lasting damage."

"Except to my credit card. I didn't dare tell Kevin I bought it. I didn't even take it home."

"What did you do with it?"

Suzanne shrugged and took a bite of her breakfast. "I couldn't return the kit so I just threw it out."

Dana squeezed a bit of lemon and a pinch of salt on top of her avocado toast. "What did Helen say when the police were trying to connect all these crazy, random dots?"

"She was awesome. She tore their theories to shreds." Suzanne sat back and did her best to mimic the commanding voice and manner of her attorney. " 'What is that supposed to prove? Suzanne was not the only person at the party who bought this product. Everyone in her office was there. Except the victim. And anyone can buy this stuff online, twenty-four/seven.' And then she said some other things that more or less forced them to let me go."

Suzanne felt a chill recalling those moments. She was honestly scared. "Thank goodness I had Helen with me. She is one cool customer. Nothing they said rattled her. When I was alone with them, they twisted around every answer."

Suzanne looked across the table at Maggie. "Not Charles. He didn't say that much. The other guy, Detective Oliver, did most of the talking."

Maggie nodded. Suzanne could tell she felt self-conscious talking about her boyfriend's role in Suzanne's trouble. Suzanne wondered if Maggie and Charles had spoken much about her — whether he thought she was innocent or really capable of such an act. But of course, Maggie would never say.

"So Helen got you out of there, finally?" Maggie asked.

"Yes, she did. Poor Kevin. He waited for hours. Again. Sitting on a hard plastic chair." Suzanne sighed and ate another bite of the waffle, which was still warm and cooked just the way she liked it, crunchy on the outside and fluffy within.

"What else did they say? How did they leave it with you?"

Lucy leaned closer, eager to hear her answer.

"Helen backed them down. But it's not like I'm off the hook. Detective Oliver told me not to leave town."

Lucy sighed and shook her head. "What is that supposed to mean? Like you're going to run off to Tahiti or something?"

"That doesn't sound too bad right now. I might check my frequent flyer miles." Suzanne tried for a light tone, but she knew her friends could tell that she was worried.

"Whatever twisted, far-fetched scenarios they come up with, you didn't do it. They'll finally have to move on and find the person who did," Maggie insisted.

"Sounds as if there are plenty of possibilities at Prestige Properties. So many people in your office had access to the Botox and knew about her allergy. And you told us Thursday night that other people you work with had grievances with her, too," Lucy pointed out.

"Yes, but Suzanne had the worst relationship with Liza. I think that's why she was singled out," Dana said. "It was very convenient that you both used the same diet drink. Anyone who wanted to implicate you could have taken the bottle out of your package, knowing it was covered with your fingerprints, and used it to kill her."

Dana's summary made perfect sense, but also took Suzanne's breath away. Then Lucy said, "Sounds like the police haven't even finished investigating. There might be more."

Suzanne wanted to reply but a bite of her breakfast stuck in her throat. She sipped some water, then said, "Gee, guys . . . you make it sound as if someone is trying to make me look guilty. As if they've purposely framed me."

"I think you are being framed, Suzanne," Dana replied quietly.

Lucy nodded and touched her hand. "Sorry, but . . . I don't think there's much question about it."

CHAPTER 5

"Really?" Suzanne asked the question, but knew in her heart it was true. "Who'd want to do that? Why pick on me?"

"Your contentious relationship with Liza is well known. That must have put you at the top of the list," Maggie said in an even tone. "I don't mean to hurt your feelings, but that imbroglio at the meeting Thursday set the stage perfectly."

"The . . . what did you call it?" Confident of her own vocabulary, Suzanne knew Maggie had her beat.

"The brawl. The shouting match. The battle royal," Lucy filled in.

"How I regret that wretched day! If I could only go back and do it over again." Suzanne sighed. "And isn't it just like Liza to get back at me? Even from the other side? Maybe this is it. She's finally won."

"Come on now, Suzanne." Lucy slung an arm around her shoulder, her voice comforting and commanding at the same time. "You can't think that way. It doesn't do any good at all. If the police can't see that all these clues are a complete hoax, we have to find out who did this."

"And we will," Dana promised.

Maggie sat silent, Suzanne noticed. Ever since her relationship with Charles had begun, she'd been torn about sticking her nose into police business and had even promised him a few times that she wouldn't — always breaking those promises later.

Lately, they'd been talking about moving in together, though no plans had been set. With Charles on this case, Suzanne could hardly blame her for hanging back. This one was close to home. Suzanne would never want to cause friction between Maggie and Charles. Not even over this.

"You don't have to say anything, Maggie. I'm giving you a pass," Suzanne said quickly. "I'd hate to be the cause of any problems between you and Charles."

Maggie poured a drop of milk in her coffee and slowly stirred. "It's the same old thing with us. I keep promising to mind my own business, but it never sticks for long. This time is different. If someone is really trying to stick you with the blame for Liza's death, how can I sit idly by? I'll help, if I can, Suzanne. You know I will. I'll work it out with Charles when the time comes. Don't you worry."

Suzanne hoped if the time came, it was as easy as Maggie made it sound.

"Honestly, since he does know you socially, I think he should recuse himself from this case," Maggie added. "I've been meaning to speak to him about that. We just haven't gotten the chance."

Because he's been busy every night, investigating the murder he thinks I committed . . . and interrogating me at the police station. Suzanne wanted to say that, but held her tongue.

Lucy had pulled a copy of the *Plum Harbor Times* from her knapsack. It was opened to a back page and she set it on the table. "Liza's obituary is in the paper today. There's going to be a memorial service tomorrow."

"I knew it had to happen. But I've been dreading it," Suzanne said honestly. "Even more, after my night at the police station. Word gets around so quickly," she said, lowering her voice a notch.

She glanced over her shoulder, wondering if people in town already knew the police had singled her out, and were those people talking about her?

"Her obit says she died of heart failure,

129

brought on by anaphylactic shock. Which is certainly true. But there's nothing in the news section that embellishes on that. I guess the media will find out soon that the police are investigating," Lucy said. "If they don't know already."

"I wouldn't worry about anyone knowing you were questioned. Other people will be called in, too," Dana assured her.

"You need to go to that service tomorrow with your head held high. You've nothing to be ashamed of, Suzanne. You're totally and completely innocent." Maggie's tone was firm and bolstering. "Remember what you told us about Annie Oakley? How you used to pretend when you were a little girl? I think it's time to saddle up and channel your inner Annie O. You've faced worse than this. You'll get through it."

Suzanne had to smile at the reminder. One night while stitching merrily away, they had started talking about their childhood imaginary friends and heroes. At the age of five or so, Annie Oakley had been Suzanne's secret playmate and even her alter ego.

"You're right. I have to keep reminding myself, I've done nothing wrong. It will be hard, but I have to stick with my routine. Go into the office today and go to that service tomorrow with the rest of the staff.

Even if they are all gossiping their heads off about me."

"If it's any help, I'll be there, too," Maggie promised. "I want to pay my respects to Ruth. And to Liza and her sister."

"I only knew Liza by reputation, but I'll go for your sake, Suzanne," Lucy said.

"Me too," Dana leaned forward and caught her eye. "We'll be there for you. We can all sit together. It will give us a chance to scope out the players, don't you think?" she asked the others.

"That's what I was thinking, too." Lucy spread out the newspaper and looked down at the page with Liza's obituary. "Should I read this out loud? It's not that long, but interesting."

"I'd like to hear it," Maggie said.

Suzanne glanced down at the page and read the headline. LIZA ANN DEVEREAUX, PROMINENT BUSINESSWOMAN AND PHILANTHROPIST. Philanthropist? Was that really true?

Liza's head shot, the one she used for business cards and advertising listings, was enlarged to a prominent size on the page. She was wearing a big, friendly smile, along with a satin blouse with a shawl collar and her pearls, of course. Below that, a long article was printed.

"Let's see . . . I won't read it word for word," Lucy began. "Sounds like she had a privileged upbringing. She was raised outside Boston, in Cambridge. Her father was a college professor and taught at MIT. The family also had houses in Kennebunkport and Florida. Prep school education, too. The Ackerly School in western Mass."

"I've heard of that place," Dana said. "Difficult to get accepted there. Students are very bright and motivated."

"She was all that and more," Suzanne murmured.

"She also had an MBA in finance and worked for a big investment firm in Boston right out of college. Did you know that, Suzanne?" Lucy sounded surprised at Liza's many pedigrees.

"With all that high-powered experience, I wonder why she ended up out here? No offense, Suzanne," Dana added quickly. "But sounds like she was more qualified for a job in a bank, or as a financial advisor somewhere. Why real estate in Plum Harbor?"

"She gave up her job in the city when her husband bought a restaurant out here. I think they wanted to start a family, but that didn't work out. Maybe for the best, all things considered now. That's the story I heard," Suzanne recalled. "Now that you

132

mention it, she was a big fish in a small pond. The way she acted at work makes more sense now."

"It is interesting to hear about a person's background and the experiences that shaped their personality." Maggie leaned over, curiously peering at the article. "I think I know a bit about the philanthropy side. But what does it say there?"

"Let's see . . . She volunteered at the high school, in the Business Club and mentoring students, especially young women, who were interested in careers in finance and sales."

"I should do that," Suzanne broke in. "When I have some spare time."

"Let's put that one on your to-do list. You have some other priorities now," Maggie suggested in an appeasing tone.

"She was also on the board of an organization that helps homeless families and moves them out of the shelter system. She was a big fund-raiser for that cause."

Suzanne felt suddenly deflated and embarrassed. "For goodness sakes, the woman was practically a saint. You would have never known it, being around her day to day." She glanced around, wondering if even her own friends would believe her. "I didn't know half of this stuff. I mean, she acted like a snob, to the manor born, and all that. So of course I could tell she came from money. But all this charity and community service?" Suzanne shook her head. "She sure kept a low profile on that. Maybe she didn't want anyone at the office to think she was a pushover."

"Maybe," Maggie agreed. "Or maybe she was just . . . modest?"

Suzanne had not considered that possibility, immediately assuming Liza had some defensive motivation for her secrecy about these matters.

"Either way, she did some good in the world, that's clear." Lucy looked up from the paper. "That's saying a lot for a person. I think so, anyway."

"I agree," Maggie replied.

"The paper says she's survived by her sister, Kira, her mother, Ruth, and husband, Nicolas Sutton." Lucy looked up. "I wonder why it doesn't say former or ex-husband? Maybe that's a typo. Didn't you say she was divorced?"

"I thought she was," Suzanne said. "I did hear it's been going on a long time and he really dragged it out. Trying to get alimony. She was the big bread winner."

"That shows how far women have come. We were barely able to join the workforce

134

not too long ago," Maggie pointed out. "Still, I hate to see anyone take advantage in a divorce. Dissolving a marriage is hard enough."

"Sounds as if they were never officially divorced," Dana said. "Which means he could inherit all of her estate. Never mind fighting for a slice in court."

"Good point, Dana." Suzanne could tell the wheels in Lucy's blond little head were turning. "A solid motivation to do away with your stubborn, almost ex-spouse. I'm going to look into that guy on the Internet."

"It is interesting to know more about Liza. It seems there was a lot to her life that she kept hidden. At least from the people she worked with," Dana pointed out. "Maybe, down the road a bit, something in her past will help us figure out who's trying to frame Suzanne."

"That could be. I'll hold on to this." Lucy closed the newspaper and slipped it back in her knapsack.

Suzanne noticed Edie squeezing and wriggling her way to their table. She stood beside Maggie, nearly breathless. "Did you girls see the TV? That Liza Devereaux was murdered. It just came over the news." She glanced toward the counter where an overflow of customers sat on stools. A large, flat screen TV hung over the cake stands and a pyramid of mini cereal boxes.

Suzanne met Edie's surprised expression and then glanced at her friends.

"I think we did hear that someplace, Edie," Maggie said vaguely. "It's a terrible shame, but I'm sure the police will figure out who did it quick enough."

"I saw her around town a lot. She never came in here," Edie added. Suzanne got the feeling Edie felt insulted by Liza's slight. "I hear there's a memorial service for her tomorrow."

"We were just discussing that," Maggie said. "Are you going?"

Edie shrugged. "I don't think so. But I bet half the town will be there."

"From what I hear, I don't doubt it," Maggie replied.

Edie was called away by a waitress and bid them a quick good-bye. Once she was gone, Lucy said, "Well, the news is out. If Edie knows the police are calling it murder, I give it five minutes to travel down Main Street."

"I'll give it three, but I get your point," Maggie countered. "So, we'll go to at the memorial service tomorrow? It's at one o'clock, at the church on the village green. Maybe we should ride over together?"

"Good idea. I can pick everyone up." Suzanne was relieved to have her posse with her, right from the start. Especially since the whole town would soon know that Liza was murdered.

She glanced at Maggie. "Do you think Charles and his partner will be there?"

"Possibly. They may want to see who attends. Just like we do." She paused.

"And they might be following me around now." Suzanne didn't mean to sound so glum and rattled, but she couldn't help it. "Gee, Mag . . . I thought Charles liked me."

Maggie looked surprised. "Of course he likes you. But he has to do his job."

"Can't you put in a good word for me or something?" Suzanne knew the question sounded whiny and childish. But she really meant it.

Maggie seemed half amused and half thrown off balance by the appeal. "Oh, Suzanne . . . you know it doesn't work like that. Please don't worry. Let's have a little faith in the police department. I know they got off to a bad start, but I'm sure they'll soon see you had nothing to do with Liza's death. The attempt to point the investigation in your direction seems very clumsy to me."

"Okay. But I sure hope you're right.

Clumsy or not, I'm still on the hook." Suzanne tried to smile. It was hard. She didn't know what else to say.

Maggie smiled back. Suzanne could tell that her good friend didn't know what else to say, either.

Breakfast with her friends had been both emotionally and physically fortifying. Suzanne felt ready to face her coworkers at Prestige Properties.

Nobody knows you were at the station last night and you don't have to tell anyone if you don't want to, she reminded herself. Just show your face, act busy, and when you've had enough, pretend to have an appointment.

It seemed like a good plan and Suzanne felt calmer. Though her confidence began to melt as soon as she walked through the door and the receptionist, Janine Osborn, didn't even say hello before she started talking about Liza.

"It's awful about Liza, isn't it? Here one day, gone the next. What a shock. Now the police are saying she was murdered?"

"Yes, awful. A real shock," Suzanne echoed. The upgrade to murder had been breaking news five minutes ago on TV, but had obviously traveled like a flash fire down

Main Street.

"The memorial is tomorrow. Are you going?" Janine glanced down at her desk and slipped a sheaf of time sheets over the celebrity magazine she'd been reading.

"Of course I'm going. I'm sure everyone in the office is." Suzanne didn't mean to bristle but the question caught her by surprise.

"Right." Janine nodded. "I just thought . . . well, since you two didn't get along."

"We didn't. But I certainly want to pay my respects. I didn't dislike her that much." Suzanne's tone was curt.

"Of course not," Janine replied. She put her hands up in mock defense. Suzanne noticed her fresh manicure. Tall and thin with dark hair and eyes to match, Janine was young and attractive. And always on the lookout for a boyfriend. She never seemed to meet Mr. Right, though from what Suzanne could see, the young woman didn't have very good judgment about men and was always attracted to the toubled type, guys with enough baggage to fill a carousel at Logan Airport. Still, Suzanne didn't envy her. Being single in a small town like Plum Harbor had to be tough.

"Didn't mean anything by it, honestly,"

Janine said.

"I'm sure you didn't," Suzanne replied in a calmer tone. "I'm sorry if I snapped. I didn't get much sleep."

"We're all a little out of sorts around here today. Join the club." Janine gave the sort of eye roll Suzanne usually got from Alexis. "Wait until you see Harry. He's a mess, poor guy."

In her sigh Suzanne heard a certain telling note of devotion, one she'd heard before. Janine had a little crush on Harry. Maybe not so little, actually. Suzanne wondered if, with Liza gone, Janine had plans to comfort the "poor guy"?

The phone lit up and Janine answered in an efficient voice. "Prestige Properties. How may I help you?"

Suzanne felt relieved and headed to her cubicle. But she was alarmed to find it messed up, with gritty powder on her desk and chair. It looked as if the drawers of her desk had been pulled out and the papers riffled through. She opened a cupboard to find the contents rearranged.

The detectives had asked for her fingerprints last night, but maybe just to make their case files official. She knew what the stuff looked like and it seemed they had already dusted the room thoroughly for her prints.

She hung up her jacket, dusted the desktop and her chair with a tissue, and set down her leather bag. She'd just settled in when she heard a light tap on the metal molding of the cubicle and then, a throat-clearing sound. It was funny how, when there were no doors, people had different styles of getting your attention.

She turned to find Harry. He looked bleak, his dark eyes wide and sad, his mouth sagging at the corners. Suzanne knew that most women, especially in her office, would say that Harry Prentiss was good looking. Maybe he was, though he wasn't her cup of tea. But he was successful and wealthy, which did affect the eyesight of a certain type of person.

Tall and fit, he still had most of his hair. His features were rather ordinary, with a thin nose and sharp chin. He did have very nice eyes, which could bestow a certain glow of warmth and approval. Other than that, he dressed well and looked like a man who didn't work that hard but enjoyed a very comfortable life. He sailed and played golf, then drank aged whiskey and vintage wine, and ate well, too.

Today, as she expected, he looked lost.

His eyes were red rimmed from crying, or drinking too much. Or maybe both. It was hard to lose someone you loved. A cut that went deep. Despite her opinion of Liza, and even ignoring his marriage, she did feel sorry for him.

"The whole place is a mess. Not just your spot, if that's any consolation," he said, taking a step in.

"Not much." She took another wad of tissues and dusted off her computer screen. "Geez, if I wanted to clean today, I would have stayed home and pulled out the vacuum."

She saw Harry's mouth twitch, almost forming a smile. "A top salesperson like you? I thought you'd have a cleaning service by now."

Suzanne had tried weekly cleaners. But the house got messed up within minutes once the family marched in, and it made her even crazier, because she'd actually paid for it to be neat.

"What can I say? Housekeeping keeps me humble." She dabbed the desktop again but tissues were not going to do it. She needed some paper towels and spray from the kitchen. She tossed the last wad in the wastepaper basket, dusted her hands, and turned to him.

"I'm sorry, Harry. . . . I'm sorry for your loss. I know that you . . ." How to say this in the most delicate way? Suzanne suddenly regretted starting the condolence, but she felt Harry's sorrow had to be acknowledged. It was a fine needle to thread, that was for sure. "You valued Liza very much, as part of this staff," she added. "And you valued your . . . personal relationship. I'm sure this must be very hard for you."

Harry seemed touched by her words, however awkward they'd spilled out. "Thank you, Suzanne. It's no secret that you two didn't get along, but I know she respected you."

"I respected her," Suzanne said quickly. Which she realized was true. "I feel bad about the way I acted on Thursday at the staff meeting. You don't know how much I wish I could start that entire day over," she said honestly. "I was so ashamed of myself. The things I said. That's why I came back in that night. I wanted to apologize to her."

To apologize . . . and try to save my job. Though she didn't think he needed to know all that.

"Don't beat yourself up. What's done is done. We all have bad days, and even lose our temper. At least you wanted to make it right. You were just . . . too late."

Harry's sympathetic words surprised her. She'd braced herself for a harsher reply. But it seemed that the wake of Liza's death had left him with a kinder and gentler perspective. Which was fine with Suzanne. But it was not like him and she wondered how long it would last. He cleared his throat and blinked. Pushing back a sudden bout of tears? He took out a handkerchief and quickly got hold of himself.

He met her gaze again. "You know what they say. 'No one is guaranteed tomorrow.' Liza died well before her time. What a fluke. And they still don't know what set off that allergic attack. Not that I've heard."

"Oh yeah, they do. Turn on the news, pal," she was about to say. Harry obviously hadn't heard yet that the police knew how Liza had died and were calling her death a homicide. Suzanne was about to break the news, then caught herself. Once she started down that road, it would be hard to keep her interview with the detectives a secret.

"It was a tragedy. No doubt. But I know the police are on it. They'll figure it out soon. With the autopsy and all. The investigators certainly tore this place apart."

She wondered when she would get her office computer tower back, but thought it wasn't a good time to ask.

"I'd gladly see the whole building knocked down to rubble, if that would bring her back," Harry said quietly.

She never realized he had a poetic side. Maybe only Liza brought that out in him.

He gazed at the floor, lost in his thoughts, then suddenly looked up. "When this is all over, we'll talk, Suzanne. There's a big gap to fill with Liza gone. I'd like you to take over her clients. What do you think?"

Harry was bestowing an unexpected gift and Suzanne knew he expected surprise and gratitude. But she didn't know what to say. Ordinarily, she would have whipped out a pom-pom and done a leap for joy. She was always the Can-do! Girl when it came to taking on more work. And making more money. But inheriting Liza's clients? With the police sniffing and snapping at her heels? The proposition seemed ghoulish and just the thing Detective Oliver would love to hear — and twist all around to smear her even more.

"You know, Harry . . . I'm so flattered that you thought of me. Can I think about it a bit? I've got such a heavy load now, and things are just wild at home. I'm not sure I can do the kind of job I'd want to do for you. One that would do Liza's reputation justice."

Harry looked surprised. "I understand. It's probably too soon to bring up business. This is a sad time for all of us. But think about it. I only ask because I know how motivated and skilled you are, Suzanne. A real role model for the others, believe me."

Lead dog in the sled, now that Liza's gone, he meant to say. Suzanne heard the whip crack and replied with a silent "Woof!" At the same time, she felt undeserving and weighed down by his praise.

"Thanks, Harry. I try my best."

"I'm sure." He glanced at his watch, a slim, gold Rolex. "I've got to get going. We're managing the reception tomorrow after the memorial service. The Devereauxs are in shock. They weren't able to handle it, and we wanted to help."

"That's very generous of you. I'm sure they appreciate it."

Harry waved his hand. "It's nothing. The least we can do. I'll see you tomorrow, Suzanne."

At least he hadn't insulted her by asking if she was going to the service. Suzanne appreciated that. "See you," she said.

The conversation with Harry had been draining and distracting. She was glad for the simple task of cleaning up her cubicle before she settled down to do real work.

Though her productivity today was questionable, with her office computer gone and her thoughts so scattered.

She suddenly wondered about Harry's lack of knowledge about Liza's death. Was that just a cover-up of some kind? Maybe he did know but didn't want to talk about it. Was he trying to find out how much she knew?

Suzanne gave up on trying to clean her cubicle with tissues and headed for the kitchen. She searched under the sink for spray and a sponge or some paper towels, but supplies were scant. Everyone needed to do the same thing here today, she realized, and Beth Birney, their office manager, was careful with expenses and fell into a tizzy if she found two sponges or two rolls of towels in use at the same time. Flustered, but never really sharp in her rebukes, Suzanne amended. Beth took such things so to heart, you wanted to cooperate just to be nice to her.

Suzanne found a petrified sponge in the back of the cupboard and ran it under hot water. As she stood at the sink, the rest of the sales team, Anita Fleming and Lyle Croddy, walked in.

In her midfifties, with long, brown, silver-streaked hair, Anita had a perennial bohemian look that had recently come back into style. She favored swinging skirts or leggings, and high boots with blowsy tops and layers of costume jewelry. Her jingling bracelets always warned of her approach, like bells on a cat's collar.

Anita's laid-back personality matched her vintage outfits. She worked part-time, covering apartment rentals and low-end properties, and Suzanne had never noticed any friction between Anita and Liza, mostly because Anita seemed to know her place in the food chain and was marching to a different drummer entirely.

But maybe under all of that peace, love, and understanding, Anita was really seething? Suzanne knew that her husband had lost his engineering job last year and hadn't found a good paying position yet, working now as a barista in a Starbucks at the mall. Watching Liza pull down commissions on million-dollar properties left and right had to sting Anita a bit. No one was that laid-back.

"Here we are, the last three on the island. Who will be the . . . *survivor*?" Lyle met her gaze and wiggled his eyebrows in a meaningful way.

Did he mean they were going to get "picked off" one by one, as in a dumb reality TV show? Leave it to Lyle to come out with that tasteless quip. Did he know Liza's death was not due to natural causes? It seemed so.

Suzanne glanced at him, nearly blinded by a typically mismatched outfit — a blue striped shirt with a patterned tie, covered by a lumpy green sweater vest. A fringe of white and orange hair stuck out in all directions — a few, select strands carefully combed across a bald spot and fixed with hair gel.

Anita poked him with her elbow. "Have some respect. Poor Liza isn't even laid to rest."

Lyle shrugged. "A little gallows humor. Didn't mean to offend."

Suzanne met his gaze, remembering now how he'd sold her out to the police, wildly exaggerating her behavior at the infamous meeting. Was it Lyle? Was he the one who had set her up to take the blame for Liza's death?

He acted nice enough face to face, but she always got the feeling that deep down, he didn't like her very much. He was normally on the cranky side, but always seemed extra bitter about her victories. He'd been that way with Liza, too, come to think of it. Often dropping hints that made Suzanne think that, just because he was a man, he believed he should have seniority on the team. But it didn't work like that. "You have to sell stuff, Lyle. Duh . . . ," she had often wanted to tell him.

He'd also felt the sting of Liza's client-stealing ways, she recalled. And had tried to horn in on Liza's residential listings and Suzanne's, even though he was supposed to stick to commercial sales and leases.

The grass was always greener in the real estate biz. And so were the commissions, Suzanne reflected. Maybe Lyle and Liza had some private vendetta that she had no idea about?

Lyle, Lyle, Crocodile . . . ? Something to consider, later, when she was alone.

"No worries, Lyle. No offense taken," she replied smoothly. "Anybody know when the network will be back up?"

"I asked Harry, but he couldn't say. He's in a daze today." Anita shrugged and cast Suzanne a meaningful look. "If I knew the system was down, I would have worked from home."

"Me too." Lyle had turned to the counter to make a cup of coffee. He pulled open several cupboards before he found a coffee pod and a clean mug. "This place is a mess. Didn't the service come this week?"

"If they did, they need to come back. I'm trying to clean my space with a Dustbuster. It really needs a Shop-vac," Anita said.

Suzanne was relieved to hear her cubicle had not been singled out for investigation. If anyone in their group, or even a stranger, had harmed Liza, surely the police would find some evidence of that?

Evidence that didn't point to her.

Suzanne squeezed the sponge and pulled off a wad of paper towel from a dwindling roll next to the sink. "Beth should ask the cleaners to come back. Maybe the police wouldn't let them in while they were working here."

"Just like on TV. The crime scene can't be contaminated." Lyle spoke with the authority of a man who watched a lot of police procedurals. "I think they suspected foul play from the start. Even though they kept telling us all this detective work was routine. Did you see the news today? The police are sure now that she was murdered."

"I heard that, too. On the radio, driving over this morning." Anita had found a plastic cake holder on the table and checked under the lid. She pulled out an oatmeal cookie, sniffed it, and took a bite. Beth's doing, Suzanne guessed. She probably made

151

the cookies thinking they might cheer every-one up.

Anita glanced at Suzanne. Her flea market earrings — large golden circles etched with an Indian design — bobbed up and down. "Gosh, it's weird to think that she was really murdered, right here in the office. Gives you the creeps, doesn't it?"

Suzanne met her gaze and nodded, feeling like a bobblehead doll on a car windshield. "Yes . . . yes, it does."

In an effort to hold her tongue, she squeezed the sponge so hard water dripped on her shoe. For once, she was not going to play the office know-it-all. If Lyle and Anita had just found out Liza was murdered, maybe they didn't know that so far, she was the prime suspect?

And she wasn't about to tell them, either.

"Talk about the creeps, Suzanne found her body, for Christmas' sakes." Lyle waved his coffee mug in her direction. "You're the one who found her, didn't you?"

Suzanne nodded again. "I saw her car outside and came in to talk to her, to apologize about the fight we had in the staff meeting. And . . . there she was."

She was unsure how much detail to give. Lyle and Anita stared at her, Anita quietly munching the cookie.

"Wow, that's heavy," Anita said.

"Yeah, it was," Suzanne agreed.

"I wonder what she was doing here that late at night." Anita brushed some crumbs off her blouse. "She was a real workaholic, wasn't she? Just goes to show, life is short. You can't postpone your happiness. You have to be in the now, and just enjoy it."

Suzanne wasn't sure how to respond to this dose of coffee room philosophy. She glanced at Lyle. He looked amused. "I'd like to enjoy some of Liza's commissions. I wonder how Harry is going to deal out her client list. I'd like a few of those plums."

Anita shrugged. "I guess we'll just have to wait and see. It's really up to Harry."

"Right, Harry will decide," Suzanne said. Which was almost true. She didn't want to admit that Harry had just offered her the whole basket of plums. She didn't want to sound as if she was bragging, and she hadn't accepted the offer either. She also wondered now if Harry might change his mind, as time went on and his thoughts were clearer. And why give her coworkers even the slightest reason to suspect she might benefit from Liza's passing?

Lyle lifted his chin and rattled the coins in his pocket, a nervous tic he had. "There's a lot of ball game left, I'll tell you that much."

"I think you're right," Anita replied. "And there's a lot the police aren't telling us. I don't know about the rest of you, but I'm not likely to hang around here after hours anymore."

"I wouldn't worry about that. Someone was out to get Liza. The police probably know who it was already. They can't keep something like this under wraps for long." Lyle's coffee had dripped through. He picked up the mug and slurped up a bit. "Believe me, it all comes out in the wash."

Suzanne wasn't sure what that was supposed to mean. He always peppered his conversations with hackneyed expressions, announcing them in a meaningful tone: Takes one to know one. Empty barrels make the most noise. Don't kill the messenger. And, don't throw the baby out with the bath water. One of his favorites.

"I'd better get back to my office. I have to make some calls." Suzanne turned and left her coworkers, knowing they would immediately start talking about her.

Nothing she could do about that. She sighed and headed back to her private, padded space. *If they think they have something to gab about now, wait until "the other shoe*

154

drops," she chided herself.

She did hope the police had found more evidence by now, clues that made them see she was being framed by the real killer. But who could that be? She still had no idea and wondered how she could figure it out.

Lost in her thoughts, she nearly walked right into Beth Birney, who was heading up the hallway toward the kitchen. Despite the near collision, Beth smiled, looking happy to see Suzanne. It took a lot to rub Beth the wrong way. Except wasting paper towels or using the printer for personal copies. Or, when someone dared to crank up the thermostat on a bitter cold winter day. "I have a sweater in my office if you'd like to borrow it," Beth was likely to say with a pleasant smile.

If Harry was the star of the production, Beth was the stage manager, who made the lights go on and the curtain rise every night, right on time. She was the glue that held the place together, Suzanne had often thought. Unfailingly loyal to Harry, who would probably go broke without Beth's watchful eye.

Her mild personality and Mother Hen looks fit the role well and she genuinely enjoyed her job, keeping the company humming along, like a well-oiled machine.

"Oh, Beth . . . excuse me! I don't know where my head is today." The sponge had left a damp mark on Beth's blazer, which looked new. A stylish change from Beth's ubiquitous cardigans. Suzanne felt embarrassed. "Your jacket. I'm so sorry."

Beth patted the spot with her hand. "It's just water. It will dry in no time. We're all upset today about poor Liza," she added in a quieter voice. She shook her head, her eyes going foggy a moment behind her glasses. Suzanne thought she might cry. "Such a shock. Right here in the office. I didn't know her well. But she was so young. Too young to lose her life in such a senseless way. She was always nice to me," she added in a wistful tone.

Suzanne certainly couldn't echo that last sentiment. Was it intended as a backhanded rebuke? Suzanne doubted that. Beth didn't mean anything personal. She wasn't that way.

"I didn't know her well either. And she was young," Suzanne said finally.

Beth looked down at the sponge and the spray Suzanne carried. "I know the police left the place a mess. Sorry about that. We'll get the cleaning company in tomorrow. The computer towers should be back early next week. The network will be up again soon after that. I'll get the technicians in here ASAP."

"Sounds like you have it covered. As usual."

Beth nodded and smiled at the compliment. She hugged some folders to her chest. The wet spot on Beth's jacket was drying quickly. Suzanne felt relieved.

Beth had upped her game in the appearance department lately. She had recently confided that she was trying online dating. Suzanne hoped it worked out. Beth was such a lovely person and had so much to give. She'd been divorced for many years and her children were grown, living in New York. Poor woman, she was lonely. But at least she was willing to be proactive, starting with a mini makeover, a new hairstyle and designer eyeglasses. Some new clothes, too. She'd never be a supermodel, but a lot of men would be happy with such a gentle, thoughtful woman, Suzanne thought.

"Computer problems are easy to fix," Beth promised. "It will take longer for everything else to settle back to normal. How are you doing, Suzanne? It must have been a terrible shock, finding her."

"Oh . . . I'm okay. Trying to process it all. Just like everyone else." Suzanne shrugged and forced a small smile.

"It's good to see everyone back. I know it wasn't easy to come in today. There's no pressure to stay if you feel upset. Or uncomfortable."

"I have an appointment soon, to show a little cottage in the Marshes. I guess I'll head home after that."

"Such a trouper." Beth smiled and patted Suzanne's shoulder. "One more thing, dear. I have something for you." She opened the folder and Suzanne saw a stack of envelopes. Beth flipped through with fleet fingertips and pulled one from the pile. "With the computers down, I couldn't do direct deposits this week. I don't want you to leave without that."

"Thanks, Beth." Suzanne glanced down at her paycheck. It was good of Beth to make the extra effort and get the checks out on time, all things considered.

"We don't want anyone to be stressed by this unfortunate situation any more than is absolutely necessary."

Stressed? Beth didn't know the half of it.

"You just do what you can today, Suzanne. Don't push yourself," Beth advised in a serious tone. "We can only do our best, right?" Beth nodded good-bye and continued down the hall, the firm's friendly little paycheck fairy.

Suzanne slipped into her cubicle and started to clean again. She wasn't sorry she'd come to the office today. It had been a good thing to show up. She had no reason to hide, as her friends had reminded her.

But she'd definitely felt a strange vibe around here. More than just the shadow of Liza's death, casting a cold gray light.

Suzanne couldn't quite say what it was, but it was there, lurking beneath the surface, dancing in the shadows, slipping up behind her, with icy fingers that traced her spine.

"Honestly, Charles. Do you really think Suzanne — *our Suzanne* — is capable of murder?" Maggie had not intended to get into the subject at all. Not even a tiny bit. Charles had Saturday night off and she'd planned a romantic evening at home, including his favorite dinner, grilled lamb chops with fresh rosemary and plenty of garlic, oven roasted potatoes, and string beans. He was not a hard man to please. Not in the culinary sense.

They were having a completely lovely, relaxing evening. Sipping wine in front of the fire and talking more about Charles possibly moving in with her soon.

Charles loved her home, often saying that everywhere he turned, there was something interesting or pretty to look at. He felt very comfortable there and she hoped he'd soon be sharing the space with her. Though she knew that living with someone after all these years would be a shock. But she was more than willing to make a go of it. She wasn't sure how they had wandered into the quicksand subject of Suzanne, but when he'd asked about her day, she couldn't help mentioning breakfast with her friends at the Schooner, and their main topic of conversation.

"Between you and me — I'd never peg her as the type. But one thing I've learned in this job — never assume. You never really know about a person, what goes on deep inside."

She knew he was just talking in general. But his reply still got under her skin. "Come on, Charles. That answer is so . . . pat. You sound like a character in a film noir, for goodness sakes. Where's the suit with the big shoulders?"

Her question made him laugh, encouraging her. He would look good in that era of men's wear. She'd have to tell him that later. For now, she stuck to Suzanne.

"You know Suzanne as well as I do. She's a good person, kind and generous, and loving to a fault. Sure, she's emotional and has a temper at times. But she's an open book. Not that she's even capable of such a thing, but if so, she'd never be able to hide it. She'd be bursting at the seams with the secret."

Charles shrugged and sipped his wine, a smooth Pinot Noir he'd contributed to their dinner. "Everything you say about her is true. I'm not debating any of it. But it would be completely irresponsible — not to mention, sloppy police work — if we didn't follow through on this lead. There's just too much evidence pointing in her direction."

"Of course you need to do that. To eliminate her," Maggie added quickly. "You'll come to a dead end with Suzanne very soon. You'll see that someone has planted all this evidence. I'm surprised you haven't already."

"I expected that at first, too."

His reply was alarming, and Maggie tried to hide her reaction. "Why do you say that?"

Charles tilted his head, the way he often did when he had something serious and maybe even confidential to say. "Unfortunately for your friend, the more we dig, the more we find."

Maggie was unhappy to hear that, but rallied quickly. "Someone has framed her, Charles. I think that's obvious. And in a very clumsy, amateur way. If there's a more polished way to do that sort of thing, I don't know. But I'd think it would be clear to a seasoned professional, such as yourself, that she's been set up. And she was a very easy, obvious target, considering her contentious relationship with Liza Devereaux."

Charles sat with his shoulders back, his mouth a straight, hard line. He waited a moment or two before speaking. "Are you done now?"

"Yes, I think so." Maggie nodded. She knew that she'd gotten too excited and maybe, gone too far. But how far is too far when the reputation, and possibly the very fate, of one of your very best friends is at stake? Charles wanted to say something, she sensed, but before he could, she felt compelled to continue.

"What did you mean when you said 'the more we dig, the more we find'? Have you found more evidence that implicates her?"

"You know I can't tell you that."

Maggie sighed. "I do know that. I just forgot for a minute, sorry."

"Forgot? Or thought you'd catch me off guard?" He was teasing her a bit, but also serious.

She shrugged. "A little of each," she admitted. She leaned toward him. "I've been thinking. Maybe you should take yourself off this case. You know Suzanne so well, and she's one of my best friends. Doesn't that muddy the waters?"

It certainly muddied the waters between them, she wanted to add. But she was afraid where that line of conversation might go.

"I'd only do that if I was unable to be impartial and objective. But I believe that I am."

"What about doing it for my sake? It's hard for me to see you investigate one of my very best friends in the world as possibly guilty of murder. Isn't that a conflict of interest for you?"

She watched Charles mull it over, spinning the sips of wine left in his goblet. She wondered what he'd say. She was used to these long pauses. He always considered his replies carefully, especially important questions, like this one. A trait she loved about him. Though tonight, it seemed darn right frustrating.

"I really don't think of it that way," he said finally. "I don't believe it's a conflict for me. I don't believe I'd cut her any slack even if she was your blood kin, Maggie. But I suppose, the connection might look questionable to an outsider. Especially if I let her off the hook when there's enough evidence to make an arrest."

"An arrest? What in the world are you talking about? This is Suzanne. Zany, funny, big-hearted Suzanne. It's very upsetting for me to hear you even talk that way."

Charles pulled back into his corner of the couch, turning to face her. "It's upsetting for me to hear that you expect me to take a back seat and look the other way, because she's your pal. Let me ask you something. If I were to take myself off this case, would you do the same?"

"What do you mean by that?" Maggie stared back at him, honestly confused by the request.

"I think you know what I mean." He sat back, crossing his arms over his chest.

She did know. But she didn't know how to answer. Not without fudging the truth a bit. "I have to be honest; if she's in trouble, I'll try to help her. Any way I can. That's just who I am. I think you know that by now."

"Fair enough. I think you know who I am by now, too."

Maggie felt upset. She didn't like where this conversation had led. It did not feel like a good place at all. But she knew it would not help to let the argument go further. He seemed to feel his honor was at stake. She knew she'd never persuade him to her point of view when that was the issue.

"I think you misunderstand me. I know you're totally ethical in your work, Charles. More than ethical. Let's skip it for now. I'm sure this investigation will lead somewhere else, to the *real* killer. Did you know that Liza and her husband were probably not officially divorced? Even though they've been separated at least two years? Suzanne says the husband has a gambling problem and now he's in line to inherit her estate."

Charles met her gaze, his expression even more displeased. She realized that he knew the lowdown on Liza's marital status and all about Nick Sutton's gambling, but didn't realize that she did, too.

"I wish you and your friends would stay out of these situations. I hope you're not going to the memorial service tomorrow."

Maggie didn't answer right away. She met his gaze a moment, then looked back at the fire.

"You are, aren't you?" he said.

She picked up her wine and turned to him. "I knew Liza. She was a customer at the shop and took classes with me all the time. I've even met her mother, Ruth. I want to pay my respects. I don't think there's anything wrong with that. And Suzanne has to be there, since Liza was a coworker."

"And your other friends, are they going, too?"

"We want to give Suzanne some support, all things considered."

Since the police — my own significant other, in particular — is hounding her and making her miserable, Maggie thought.

"Suzanne is a big girl. She doesn't need her friends to hold her hand," Charles said curtly. Then, in a softer tone, "I wish you wouldn't go. You barely knew the woman. You say you want to pay your respects. But to me . . . Well, it seems more like sheer snooping."

Maggie bristled. He didn't have the right to say that or judge her that way. "That's a harsh thing to say. I told you honestly why I'm going. And I don't need your permission to be there, either."

They sat in silence. A fire in the hearth that had started out full and bright had burned down to embers. The logs Maggie had set with such care and anticipation were crumbling into gray ash. No one rose to stir it back up to its former glory, though that would have been an easy task, Maggie thought.

"You don't need my permission. I know

166

that." Charles set his wineglass on the side table, taking care to use the coaster. He was always very neat. He sat back, his hands on his big knees, and suddenly stood up. "Well, guess I'll get going. Early day tomorrow."

Maggie came to her feet, too, surprised at his announcement. He usually — practically always — spent the night, and if he was off on Sunday, they had a leisurely morning reading the newspaper, with the Baroque Hour on the radio, and then spent the day together, too. Taking a long walk or a relaxing drive out to Rockport.

They both planned to attend the memorial service tomorrow, but Maggie thought they might find an orchard after that and pick some apples. She'd make a pie with Sunday dinner. She'd seen so little of him lately, she'd looked forward to this weekend together.

But she quickly guarded herself from showing her reaction and admitting her disappointment. He was obviously angry, but she wasn't going to unpack that now and make a big thing out of it.

"I have a lot to do tomorrow, too. It has been a long week."

"A very long one. Always is when we have a murder case going on," he added in a quieter tone. "Thanks for dinner. It was terrific. As usual."

"No trouble." Maggie had followed him to the foyer. He took his jacket and hat off the coat tree, then planted a quick kiss on her lips. It was something, she thought. Maybe he wasn't that mad? Though there was no lingering embrace as she'd come to expect.

He stepped back and tugged on his hat brim. "I'll call you."

Maggie didn't feel reassured. Was he really going to call her? Or had he tossed off the phrase the way men do when they mean just the opposite?

"Good night, Charles." She looked up at him, feeling sad and empty. And frustrated about the way the evening had ended up.

She felt even worse as he stepped outside and she watched him walk to his car.

What had just happened here? Maggie was confused. It felt as if some small but very important cog, deep in the machinery of their relationship, had gotten stuck. Worse yet, snapped and broken.

But so quietly, one would hardly notice.

It would have been better if we'd had a screaming fight, Maggie thought. *At least then, everything would be out in the open.*

But now, she wasn't sure where things stood. Except that it was Saturday night, barely eleven o'clock, and Charles was not at work, but he wasn't with her either.

That didn't seem right at all.

CHAPTER 6

Suzanne was so nervous about attending the memorial service, she changed her outfit three times, finally settling on her "go to" navy blue suit, with brand new black heels that pinched a bit, but did make the most of her figure. She wanted to look respectful but not overdo it in "widow's weeds." Everyone would know that wasn't genuine.

She usually wore pearls with the outfit — large earrings and an opera length strand — and reached for the set automatically. The glistening string hung in midair, but she couldn't put it on. She put the necklace back in its case, the reminder of Liza much too strong.

Since Suzanne's SUV comfortably sat five, she was usually the chauffeur for outings with her friends. Today she was especially happy to play that role. While everyone chatted, she kept her eyes on the road, not saying much. No one remarked on her quiet mood.

As they approached the church, Maggie said, "How did it go at the office yesterday? I bet it was a very somber atmosphere."

Suzanne nearly laughed at the understatement. "Let's put it this way — the Devereauxs didn't need to hold a wake; we had one at Prestige Properties. Harry wasn't exactly carrying around a box of tissues, but he should have been."

"He's taking it hard? Interesting." Dana sat in the front passenger seat. She glanced over her shoulder at Maggie and Lucy in back. Phoebe had never met Liza and events like a memorial service made her uneasy. She was content to take care of the shop and keep it open regular hours.

"Sounds as if he was carrying a torch, as we said back in the day," Maggie replied.

"No news there. Truth be told, we were all bummed out and the office was upside down from the police pawing through everything. That didn't help morale much either," Suzanne added. "All my records had definitely been tossed and the police took the tower from everyone's office computer. I guess they're going through the files."

"Probably looking at phone records, too," Lucy remarked.

"I'm sure." Suzanne had already thought of that.

Dana glanced at her. "You sound nervous. You shouldn't be. Once the investigators sift through everything with a fine-tooth comb, they're bound to find clues that point away from you. I bet the person who's trying to frame you has messed up somewhere. There's no such thing as a perfect crime."

Her words made sense and gave Suzanne a bit of hope. But she also knew there were a lot of "ifs." "Let's hope the culprit messed up a lot. Sometimes the police get tunnel vision. They just want the pieces to fit so they can get on to the next crime."

"Any ideas at all who it could be?" Lucy asked. "Seems to me it has to be someone who knows both you and Liza. And who has access to the office. Someone who knows what goes on there. Probably a co-worker."

"And who had motivation to harm Liza. Let's not forget that," Maggie chimed in.

"And motivation to screw up my life, too," Suzanne pointed out.

"Not necessarily." Dana had been looking out the window but quickly turned. "You were a good target for the blame. But that doesn't mean the killer has anything against you."

Suzanne laughed, her gaze fixed on the road. "I see the logic in what you're saying. But being framed for a murder sure feels personal."

"Hang in there." Maggie's voice was full of sympathy. "Maybe we'll get some insights at this gathering. Everyone from your office should be there. Sometimes you just have an intuition about these things."

Suzanne didn't want to depend on the intuition of one of her friends to save her. But it appeared she didn't have much else to pin her hopes on right now.

The church parking lot was almost full, but Suzanne spotted a space not far from the entrance. She slipped out of the driver's seat and quickly scanned the parking lot. "I don't see Charles or Detective Oliver. I expected them to be here, making a guest list."

"Charles told me he was coming," Maggie said. "Maybe they're not here yet."

"Maybe because they're so sure it's me?" Suzanne asked.

"Don't be like that." Dana took her arm. "You know what she meant."

Suzanne sighed and allowed herself to be led into the church. It was hard to attend this event, but the company of good friends did cushion the sharp edges.

The church was classic New England, with a tall, peaked spire and large wooden doors. Whitewashed clapboard outside and creaky floorboards within.

Soft organ music played as she and her friends entered the narrow sanctuary. Hazy autumn afternoon light filtered in through long, arched windows. Suzanne thought they were on time, even a little early, but the pews on either side were practically filled, so many had come to honor Liza's passing.

Suzanne and her friends found seats toward the back, but still had a clear view. Several large flower arrangements were displayed on the altar. Suzanne had heard that Liza's body had not been released yet by the police, and when it was, she would be cremated. The family had wanted the service carried out promptly, for a sense of closure.

A minister walked to the center of the altar and welcomed everyone, particularly the Devereaux family, who sat in the front pew on the pulpit side.

Suzanne spotted an older woman, with upswept silver hair and a clear-eyed, striking profile. A black shawl rested on her shoulders. Ruth Devereaux, Liza's mother, she guessed. Next to her, she saw a younger woman with long, dark hair, also wearing black. Suzanne could only see her from the back, but assumed it was Liza's sister, Kira.

There were a few others nearby who looked like they might be family or close friends. Still, Ruth and Liza's sister seemed solitary, and very much alone, Suzanne thought.

She noticed her office mates, scattered among the crowd. Anita had come with her husband and they sat with Beth a few rows ahead. Lyle and his wife sat on the opposite side of the church, and Janine sat closer to the front, not too far from Harry and his wife, Claire.

The minister spoke glowingly about Liza's life and achievements. Nothing that was a surprise to Suzanne after hearing the obituary. He also noted her intelligence, charm, and "sparkling sense of humor."

Suzanne had to acknowledge the first two traits but had never seen the latter. But maybe Liza could be funny and clever when she wanted to. *She just didn't feel relaxed enough around me to show it,* a small voice noted.

Life was mysterious. That's all you could say. One minute you're screaming your head off at someone, trying to pull their hair out, and the next . . . you find them stone cold dead.

Suzanne could hardly believe she'd never see Liza again. She'd never bicker with her, or be looking over her shoulder to make sure her rival was not gaining the advantage in some shrewd way.

Liza had been a sharp salesperson, maybe the best Suzanne had ever seen. She had to grant her that. Suzanne knew she ought to feel relieved that she didn't have to compete with Liza anymore. But she didn't feel that way at all.

She felt . . . lonely. Deserted. As if she'd lost a partner of some kind. Wasn't that strange?

Liza had not been her friend. Anything but. But she had been an impressive adversary, one who had pushed Suzanne to do her best, and then some. Now it felt as if she was Serena Williams, all set to receive a smoking first serve, and left staring across the net at an empty court. Her most worthy opponent had vanished.

The minister announced the hymn "Amazing Grace" would be performed. While a local soprano offered a respectable rendition of the ageless song, heavy thoughts of mortality circled Suzanne, like dark winged birds.

She was hardly aware that the music had ended, when she heard the minister return to the pulpit. "And now, Kira Davenport will read a poem in honor of her sister."

As Suzanne expected, the woman seated beside Liza's mother rose. Before she had even turned around and started walking toward the pulpit, Suzanne felt her pulse quicken.

When Kira had taken her place behind the microphone and looked out at the gathering, Suzanne's heart skipped a beat.

It was Liza. Her exact double.

Kira Davenport squared her shoulders and unfolded a single white page. Even her gestures and postures seemed the exact same as Liza's. When she spoke, thanking everyone for attending to honor her sister, it was as if Liza's voice was being channeled from some distant dimension.

Why didn't anyone tell me? An identical twin. A complete doppelgänger. Suzanne realized her mouth was gaping open and quickly shut it.

Maggie sat to her left and leaned closer. "Did you know?" she whispered.

Suzanne shook her head and whispered back, "At least, hearing you ask, I know I'm not *hallucinating.*"

"It is . . . eerie," Maggie admitted, then

turned and faced forward again.

"My sister loved poetry," Kira told the audience. "She even wrote poems from time to time and gave poems as gifts in our family."

She wrote poems as gifts for her family? Really? The woman was truly a saint. How wrong could I have been?

"This is one of her favorites, by Emily Dickinson. It's in the program, if you'd like to follow. I know it would have pleased her to hear me share it with you today."

As Kira began to read the poem, Suzanne noticed that it was printed out in the program for the service, and she followed along.

I'm Nobody! Who are you?
Are you — Nobody — too?
Then there's a pair of us!
Don't tell! they'd advertise — you know!

How dreary — to be — Somebody!
How public — like a Frog —
To tell one's name — the livelong June —
To an admiring Bog!

Suzanne felt confused. That was Liza's favorite poem? Had she felt invisible, like a "nobody"? To the contrary, Suzanne

178

thought of her more as the head frog, croaking on the biggest bog at Prestige Properties. She'd been a private person. Aloof, one might say. But never a wallflower. She'd been out there, networking, socializing, doing what good salespeople do in a small community like Plum Harbor. Had that all been an act? Suzanne would have never guessed.

And why "a pair"? Who was the other nobody — Harry? Suzanne could see it that way. They did have a secret, didn't they? She'd have to ask her friends what they thought. Perhaps there was some cryptic meaning here that would help them understand who had killed Liza. Or, maybe it was just a poem that she had enjoyed. Sometimes, you can't read too much into these things, Suzanne reminded herself.

She sighed and sat back as Kira, Liza's body double, left the pulpit. A latecomer made his way up the center aisle, a bit noisy and distracting as he hobbled along on a cane, with one arm in a sling. He took a seat in one of the pews a few rows up and across the aisle and Suzanne soon recognized him.

Liza's estranged but not quite divorced husband, Nick Sutton. Tall and dark, he was very well dressed in a navy blue, pin-stripe suit that looked custom made. Stark white shirt cuffs secured with gold cuff links extended from the suit jacket sleeves just the right amount.

She could only see his face in profile but he was as handsome as she remembered — in a shady, slick way. He'd come to an office Christmas party before the breakup with Liza and she recalled now how Janine and some other women there had been smitten. That had been a few years back. But his good looks were not marred much by time or a black eye, among other injuries.

She wondered if he'd been in a car accident, or maybe taken a bad fall. He still had good hair, dark and thick, touched with silver at the temples. Maybe at a hair salon? Lucy would have called it the "gravitas sideburn" look. But he wore it well. Suzanne could understand how Liza had been attracted, though from what she'd heard, it was hard to fathom why they'd stayed together so long.

The service ended soon after Kira's recital. Most who had attended filed into the church hall for the reception. Suzanne stood with her friends, wondering if they should go in as well.

"The service is one thing. But we don't really know her, or the family. It might be awkward," Lucy said.

Maggie nodded. "I know what you mean. But I came to offer a word of sympathy to Liza's mother. I think I'll do that and then go."

"My coworkers are heading in. I guess I should go in, too. At least to offer condolences," Suzanne decided.

Lucy and Dana agreed to tag along. "We'll just mingle and eavesdrop a bit," Lucy said quietly. "You never know what you might overhear at these things."

Suzanne knew she was only joking, but secretly wished that Lucy did overhear some valuable tidbit.

Talking in the car, it had seemed very obvious that Liza's murderer would be here. But in the midst of the crowd, Suzanne realized how naive it was to think that either she or any of her friends could easily pick that person out.

Unless they wore a stick-on badge, like the ladies from the church who manned the refreshment tables. "Hello! My name is Betty. I killed Liza Devereaux!"

It was a typical church affair, with big coffee urns, small sandwiches, and cookie platters set out on folding tables. The offerings were good quality, Suzanne noticed. From a high-end catering shop in town. Harry's contribution, she guessed. She hadn't eaten lunch yet and would have been tempted, except for the cement mixer churning in her nervous stomach.

Maybe being the prime suspect in a murder investigation would help her shed a few pounds? It wasn't a diet she'd recommend, but she was trying to look at the upside.

Suzanne helped herself to a cup of coffee, then scanned the room for her office mates. Anita stood near the door with Beth and Janine. Lyle was already waiting to talk to the family, angling for a quick exit, she guessed.

Harry and his wife, Claire, walked in and Harry stopped for a brief word with his employees.

"Lovely service," she heard him say to them. "Just lovely."

He kept tugging at his collar, as if his tie was too tight. Suzanne thought he looked nervous. But maybe that was because she rarely saw him dressed so formally?

Claire gazed around with a placid expression, her eyes wide behind her large, tortoiseshell-framed glasses. She wore one of her many, very expensive, nondescript suits. It hung on her thin body without any style or flair.

Not the type for makeup either. Though her straight, fair hair and blue eyes screamed, "Make me over! Pl-eeeze," to Suzanne each time they met.

Those eyes would pop with a little mascara and smoky shadow, Suzanne always thought. And her hair just needed a better cut and some product. Today it was tied back in Claire's usual style, a haphazard ponytail.

Harry's wife was an academic, everyone knew, with a master's in education and a PhD in child psychology from Ivy League universities. She was devoted to her school and theories about teaching gifted children. She'd even been the subject of a documentary that had played on WGBH, the public broadcasting station. Suzanne had taped it, but never watched.

At the end of the day, she needed something light and amusing, with plenty of romance. Or a thriller that kept her on the edge of her seat, knocking back the popcorn and digging her manicure into Kevin's arm.

Claire leaned toward her husband, then pointed across the room to where Ruth sat in a large chair. Kira stood beside her, talking to the minister. An older woman, who looked like she might be a relative or a member of the church, approached with a little girl whom she held by the hand, leading the little one's careful steps.

The child was adorable, not more than two years old, Suzanne guessed, wearing a fancy dress, tights, and patent leather Mary Janes.

"There's Mommy. We found her, Emma. Mommy is right here." The older woman's tone was comforting and singsong. "And Nana is here, too. See?"

Ruth turned and waved a vein-covered hand, offering the child a thin, shaky smile. Kira lifted the little girl and balanced her on a slim hip. She kissed her daughter's cheek and smoothed her hair back with her hand.

"Liza's niece. Cute little thing." Suzanne turned to find Anita standing beside her, balancing a cup of tea in one hand and a finger sandwich in the other.

"She is cute. I barely knew Liza had a sister, no less a niece," Suzanne replied honestly.

"She didn't talk about her family much. The twin thing is hard for some people to handle. I've heard Kira is the artistic type. Not big on nine-to-five, cubicle life. She paints flowers on silk fabric, or something like that. Liza was paying all the bills in that big house on Hickory Hill."

Aside from painting on silk, it seemed Kira was also a single mother, no husband or partner in sight.

"Liza was a good egg to support them." Suzanne had to give her that.

"She was. But she kept it under her hat. Maybe just scared to show her softer side?" Anita nibbled the sandwich, just cucumber and watercress, but it looked good.

Suzanne had not known Liza even had a softer side until yesterday, when Lucy read the obit. She had no theories to offer about why Liza may have wanted to hide her tender underbelly. Maybe to keep up a strong front at the office, so no one — especially me? — would take advantage of her?

Maybe just to protect her privacy? To be a nobody, like the poem?

Suzanne saw Maggie approach the family and thought she'd join her friend. It would be easier to talk to the bereaved with Maggie at her side. "I'd like to speak to Liza's family," she said to Anita. "I can't stay very long."

"Sure. See you at the office," Anita replied.

There was a line of visitors waiting for a word with Ruth and Kira. Suzanne took a place at the back of the cue, beside Maggie, while Harry and Claire stood at the front. She couldn't help but overhear the conversation.

". . . And if there's anything you need, anything at all, please call on me." Harry held one of Ruth's thin hands in both of his own. "I can't tell you how much we'll miss her," he added, his voice shaking a bit.

"I didn't know her well. But I did know she was a very special person. We're so very sorry for your loss," Claire added.

She either has no clue about Harry's attachment to Liza, or she's a very good actress, Suzanne thought. It was probably the former. Claire seemed very much in her own world.

Claire met Ruth's gaze, then looked up at Kira, who still held Emma in her arms. "At least you have this beautiful girl to brighten your days. What's her name?" Claire asked.

Kira smiled and turned her daughter to face Claire. "This is Emma." Suzanne heard a note of pride in her voice. "Say hello, Emmie." The toddler glanced at Claire, then buried her face in Kira's shoulder. "She can say a few words, but she gets shy."

"She must be tired. So many strangers and totally out of her routine. She's a very good girl." Claire reached out and gently touched Emma's soft curls. "A beautiful girl," she added quietly.

Emma seemed fussy. She shook off Claire's touch and pulled her head away.

She frowned, as if she might cry. Kira bounced the toddler in her arms. "There, there. It's okay. . . ."

Claire pulled back. She looked disappointed. Maybe even a bit hurt by the rejection, Suzanne thought, as if she took it personally. She was touted to be an expert with children Emma's age and should have been the Baby Whisperer. Maybe she was just embarrassed.

"Sorry, she's a little cranky today. She's usually very even tempered," Kira said, looking back at her child.

"It's my fault. Entirely. Though she might benefit from a little more socialization," Claire added. "Is she in preschool yet? You should start her right away. Come visit my school, Prentiss Academy. It would be perfect for her." Claire had taken a card from her purse and held it out to Kira. "Call me when you're ready. I'd be happy to waive the tuition. I know Liza would have wanted the best for her niece."

Kira glanced at the card and back at Claire. "Thank you. There's so much going on right now. I will think about it. Liza did want the best for her. She was very devoted to Emma," Kira said, gazing down at the child again. "As much as any aunt could be."

Harry stood by but did not interrupt the conversation. Suzanne wondered what was going through his head as he stood with Kira, who was an exact double of the woman he had loved and lost.

Claire turned to him. "Say hello to Emma, Harry. Isn't she darling?"

Harry looked uncomfortable and put on the spot. He leaned over awkwardly and waggled his index finger. "Hello, Emma. How are you?" he asked in a formal tone.

Emma stared at him, wide eyed. Suzanne thought she might burst into tears. But a smile appeared as she reached out and grabbed his tie.

Harry pulled back, chuckling, but looked self-conscious, too, as he gently loosened her hold. Claire was amused. "She likes you, Harry. She didn't react to me that way."

Harry smoothed his tie under his jacket again. "All the girls like me, dear," he joked. "I can't help it." Finally he said, "I think we'd better move on, Claire. So many people are waiting."

"Yes, of course." Claire nodded, with a solemn expression. She briefly touched Kira's arm in a comforting gesture. "Please stay in touch. The coming weeks and even months will be hard for you. We really do understand. And we're here for you — all of you."

Harry said good-bye, too, then took Claire's arm and steered her toward the refreshment table.

Maggie had found an opening to speak with Ruth, and Suzanne slipped up next to her. "I just wanted to let you know how very sorry I am for your loss," Maggie said sincerely. "I didn't know Liza that well, but I so enjoyed her visits to the shop. She was always a bright spot in my day."

Ruth nodded graciously. Her thin face was crisscrossed by the signs of age. But Suzanne could see, in her bright blue eyes and delicate features, that she had once been a very beautiful woman. And her daughters had taken after her that way.

"A bright spot. Yes, truly. She was the light of my life. Now that light has gone out forever," she said sadly. "It's hard to believe."

"I'm sure," Maggie murmured. She turned to Suzanne. "This is Suzanne Cavanaugh. She worked with Liza at the realty office."

"We're all very shocked and so sorry," Suzanne said. She realized it didn't sound like much, but it was impossible to put such a loss into words, or express the sympathy you really felt.

189

"Thank you. She did love her work. That's something to remember." Ruth looked up at her. "Your name sounds familiar."

"Really? I know we've never met," Suzanne said quickly. If Liza had ever mentioned her to Ruth, Suzanne was sure it had not been in a flattering light. Or maybe the police kept the family apprised of their investigation and Ruth knew Suzanne had been questioned?

Maggie seemed to have come to the same conclusion. She smoothly changed the subject. "I'd love to visit you sometime at Brookside Village, Ruth. If that would be all right. We could do some knitting."

"I'd like that." Ruth nodded. "I used to knit with Liza all the time. I'll miss that."

Maggie seemed sorry to hear that admission. "I imagine that you will. But I'll be in touch. No pressure. Whenever you're ready."

"Thank you for coming today." Ruth turned to include Suzanne. "So many people here. From all over. It's a bit overwhelming. So many names and faces, I can hardly keep track. But Liza was respected and even loved wherever she went. It's a comfort for us to see that."

"She was," Suzanne agreed. *More than I'd ever guessed or would allow myself to acknowledge before today.*

Maggie and Suzanne said good-bye to Ruth and moved along the line. Kira was talking with a large circle that she seemed to know well.

"Kira seems involved. Let's not intrude," Maggie said quietly.

"I agree. I guess we can go. Do you see Dana and Lucy?" Suzanne glanced around the room and noticed Nick Sutton approaching Ruth, making his way slowly with a swinging gait, caused by his cane. Even with his injuries, he was even better looking and well turned out than she'd remembered.

She was not the only one who noticed him. Suzanne watched Beth and Janine huddled nearby, whispering to each other with bright eyes. If the occasion hadn't been so solemn, Suzanne suspected some girlish giggles would have wafted her way as well.

Good looking or not, it quickly became apparent Sutton was the skunk at the garden party.

Silence fell over the room as Ruth shouted at him. "You? You have the audacity to come here? How dare you show your face! Get out! Right now! I'll call the police. . . ." She was very upset, and struggled to rise up from her wheelchair.

Her daughter and a few others rushed to Ruth's aid, making her sit back down as she

191

wheezed out the last few words. "Get him out of here. I can't even look at him. . . ."

Sutton stared back at her a moment. Suzanne wondered what he might do or say. The minister approached and said a few quiet words Suzanne couldn't hear.

Sutton's mouth twisted in a frustrated expression. "I'm leaving. Don't worry." He headed for the exit, hobbling on his cane. "It's no use with you high and mighty Devereauxs," he called back over his shoulder. "You always want the last word. It won't work this time. I'll guarantee you that."

Finally, he was gone. The room had grown silent, but conversation quickly started up again.

"Who was that man?" Maggie looked at Suzanne with a startled expression.

"Liza's estranged husband, Nick Sutton," Suzanne replied. "Not on good terms with family, it seems."

"Obviously," Maggie echoed.

Dana and Lucy had walked over to join them. They were wearing their coats and ready to go. "You said that their divorce was contentious. But it seems there's more than the typical amount of bad feelings there," Lucy said quietly as she led the group toward the door.

"Much more. Ruth was beside herself. He

must have treated Liza very badly. Or done something to the family to earn such disdain," Dana said.

Suzanne fished around her big purse for her car keys. "The police always look at the spouse in situations like this, don't they?"

"That's what I've always heard." Maggie was carrying her sweater coat over one arm, a handmade masterpiece of stitchery in which she took great pride. She opened it up and slipped it on.

"I hope Charles and his partner take a good, long look at this guy. There's some bad blood there. No question." Suzanne felt a twinge of hope. No one she'd met at the gathering had seemed the least bit suspicious, except for Nick Sutton.

"Maybe we should give him a look, too," Lucy suggested.

"You won't get an argument from me." Suzanne followed her friends out of the dimly lit church into the late day sun, feeling warmed and relieved. She had not realized how much she'd dreaded this event. Thank goodness it was over.

She felt her phone vibrating wildly in her pocket. She'd shut off the ringer in church and had forgotten to turn the sound on again. She pulled it out as her friends continued walking. "Hubby" had appeared on the screen.

"Kevin's calling. I'd better take it." She pressed the phone to her ear and greeted him. "Hi, hon. What's up?"

Kevin was fine with the kids, but when things went over the top, she was the final arbiter. Alexis must be whining about wanting to hang out with friends before she'd finished studying. Or maybe one — or both?–of the boys had stretched Kevin's patience too far?

"The police are here, Suzanne. They have a warrant and just started searching our house."

The news stopped her in her tracks. "The police? Searching our house?"

She screamed. She couldn't help it. Her friends turned and ran back, quickly surrounding her. She felt Lucy on one side and Dana on the other, catching her under the arms as her knees buckled.

"What is it, Suzanne? What happened?" Lucy asked.

"The police are searching my house. They have a warrant. . . ."

Suzanne was terrified. She heard Kevin's voice, calling out to her. She quickly put the phone back to her ear.

But before she could reply, she saw Charles and Detective Oliver, in their dark blue sedan, driving toward her. Her stomach dropped, as if she was on an amusement park ride, and everything started spinning.

"Charles and Frank Oliver . . . look." She pointed at the car. "They have a wrecking crew tearing my house apart, and now they've come to get me."

Lucy put her arm around Suzanne's shoulder. "Calm down . . . It's all right."

Suzanne met her gaze. "It's not all right. It's not all right at all."

"Suzanne? Are you still there?" Kevin's voice shouted from her phone. She still hadn't answered him.

"I'm here. But so are the police. I'm sure they've come to take me to the station again. Oh, Kev . . . I'm so scared." She started crying and couldn't say more.

"I'll be right there. I'll call the lawyer. Don't say a word this time until she gets there. Promise me, Suzanne."

"Don't worry. I learned my lesson," she managed as Kevin said good-bye and ended the call.

Maggie patted her arm and handed her a pack of tissues. Suzanne wiped her eyes as her friends looked on with wordless sympathy. She felt like a sitting duck. Or a fish in a barrel. Or whatever expression Lyle Croddy would have come up with to illustrate how she just had to stand there and wait for the police to drag her away.

She'd been so naive and forthcoming the first time the police interviewed her, thinking it was best to be completely honest. *Where did that get me? In more hot water.*

Her friends stood around her in a protective circle as she finished her snivels. "My eye makeup is a mess, right? I look like a raccoon with a hangover."

"Not at all," Dana insisted.

"Liar," Suzanne said, with a shaky smile. She sighed. "I hope they give me a minute to freshen up before the mug shot."

"Stop that! There will be no mug shot. Let's not even go there," Maggie insisted.

Visitors from the memorial gathering were drifting out of the church, heading to their cars, totally unaware of the dilemma she was caught in. Suzanne searched the lot again, looking for the detectives.

"Where are they? I don't see them anymore."

Had they possibly left, deciding not to bother her until they searched her house? But the dim hope was quickly squashed.

"Here they come." Dana glanced over her shoulder. "They're walking this way. I don't see the car. They must have parked it somewhere else."

Suzanne turned and saw the two men walking her way. She looked back to her friends and winced. "Why did I wear these heels? My feet are killing me and I can't even make a run for it."

She was only half joking and the humor fell flat.

Lucy squeezed her shoulder and Maggie took her hand. She felt Dana's gentle, soothing touch on her back.

The support was a comfort, though she knew there was no way they could hold on to her. In a heartbeat, the police would whisk her away.

Charles, who was steps away now, met her gaze, and she felt her stomach churn with anxiety.

"Just remember, you are completely and totally innocent." Maggie's tone was quiet, but stern.

"You've done absolutely nothing wrong," Dana reminded her.

"Thanks, guys. . . . Why don't I feel like that right now?" Suzanne heard her voice quiver.

"Suzanne," Charles said. "New information has come up in the investigation of Liza Devereaux's death. We have more questions for you."

Did she hear a note of reluctance in his

voice, or was that just wishful thinking? He did look tired. She guessed he'd been working long hours. Trying to build a case against her?

Before Suzanne could answer, Detective Oliver said, "You need to come with us to the station, Mrs. Cavanaugh. Right now."

His tone is cold, almost gleeful, she thought.

She nodded quickly. "I understand."

She glanced at her friends, her dear, dear friends who would have stepped between her and these men if she'd asked them to. She reached in her pocket and handed her keys to Lucy.

"Here, take my car. I'll pick it up later."

Before Lucy could take the keys, Detective Oliver stuck out his hand. "I'll take those. We have a warrant to search your car, too."

"Don't worry, we'll be fine." Maggie said quietly. "You'll be fine, too. Let us know how it goes."

Charles had stepped aside, Suzanne noticed, letting Detective Oliver take over. Perhaps he was embarrassed to drag her off to the police station with Maggie watching. Suzanne saw Maggie glance at him, a silent plea, Suzanne thought. But Charles didn't respond. Didn't even meet her gaze. He glanced at Suzanne and then at his partner.

"Let's go, Mrs. Cavanaugh." Detective Oliver met her gaze and she started walking before he could take her arm or escort her in an even more embarrassing way. She set off at a brisk pace, walking between the two detectives as they led her to their car. Thank goodness they hadn't put handcuffs on her. She was sure she could never bear that humiliation. She felt people in the parking lot watching, but she forced herself to keep her gaze forward, acting as if she was leaving the service with two rather grim male companions.

As Charles helped her into the backseat, Detective Oliver spoke to a uniformed officer who had pulled up nearby in a blue and white police car. He handed the officer the keys to Suzanne's SUV and explained where it was parked.

Charles sat in the passenger seat. "Please put your seat belt on," he said quietly.

Suzanne did as she was told. She wanted to talk to him, to ask him questions in their familiar way. But something about his demeanor kept her silent.

Across the parking lot, she saw her friends standing by the church, watching. Powerless to help her, though she knew how much they wanted to.

She stared back at them, remembering

Maggie's words.

Of course I didn't do it. Of course I'm totally innocent. But that fact doesn't seem to matter. Not so far.

She felt so lonely and frightened.

What was going to happen now?

CHAPTER 7

"Hey, I'm not sorry. Okay? And I'm not going to say I am."

Suzanne glanced at her son, Ryan, who sat beside her in the front seat as she drove toward home. His defiant declaration was practically an echo of words she'd said last night to the detectives, who had questioned her relentlessly.

He stared straight ahead, holding an ice pack against his nose. A spot above his left eye had puffed up and turned a deep shade of reddish purple. He definitely needed more ice when they got home, but he'd still have one heck of a shiner. A medal of honor for a boy that age, she guessed.

Wait until Kevin sees him. He won't be happy about this. Not one bit.

Her first impulse was to scold, but she decided to take a softer approach. Her family had been through a lot the last few days, all on her account. She felt bad about that, as if Ryan's acting out was really her fault.

"It's not like you to fight. I'm surprised. Who started it? Can you at least tell me that?"

"He did. Andy Stahl. I already told you and I told Krugman, too," he added.

"*Vice Principal* Krugman," she reminded him. "Let's show respect to adults, please."

Even if you don't always hear your mother speaking respectfully. Ugh . . . she had to get a handle on that. She'd definitely learned her lesson.

"Vice Principal Krugman," he corrected in a pained tone. "Andy started it. I don't go around just slugging kids for no reason, Mom."

"I know you don't. That's why I'm surprised."

Suzanne had a good idea why and how this clash had come about. She was almost certain.

"Did this boy, this Andy . . . did he say something about me? Is that what made you mad?"

Ryan glanced at her and then out the window again. He didn't reply.

"Come on, honey. You can tell me. I had a feeling kids might talk at school today." She did have a feeling, after she saw the local news last night that included a video of her slinking out of the police station with her coat pulled over her head.

Not to mention, the surprise and confusion the children had experienced, watching the forensic team march in to search the house. Kevin had quickly whisked the kids over to his mother's, but when they were able to return last night, the wake of the search was disturbing. Suzanne had stayed up into the small hours, putting her home back together again. As much as she was able.

She'd been so tired this morning, Kevin had brought the boys to school and she had no chance to warn them. He obviously had not, even though they had watched the news coverage together.

The report had been horrifying, but she'd been unable to take her eyes away. Like watching a slow motion train wreck.

Suzanne Cavanaugh has been named as a person of interest in the murder investigation of Liza Devereaux.

Of course, there had been more. But her heart had nearly stopped when she'd heard those words, and she had barely listened to the rest.

She pulled the car into the driveway, relieved there were no media vans parked on the street, or reporters waiting on the porch to interview her. To be on the safe side, she opened the garage door with the remote, pulled the SUV inside, and closed the door quickly behind them. With the driveway empty, maybe the media would think she wasn't home.

She and her son got out of the car and headed into the house. "I should have warned you," she said. "You know about that woman in my office who died, right?"

"Liza something? You found the body the other night, and called the police." They stood together in the mudroom and he pulled off his jacket.

"Her name was Liza, that's right. She died in the office and I found her." She swallowed hard, trying to sound calm. "The thing is, the police are trying to find out who killed her and . . ."

They think your Mom did it?

No . . . that was not a good thing to tell your child.

"They need my help." *That was not a lie,* she comforted herself. It was definitely true, from her perspective. She was helping by trying to convince them she was innocent and they had to look harder for the real killer.

"That's why they need to keep asking me questions," she explained.

204

"Andy said you killed her. He said his parents saw it on TV."

"That's not true. That's not true at all, honey. All they said on TV was that the police asked me questions. That's all . . . honestly." Suzanne thought she might burst into tears but blinked them back furiously.

"I know, Mom. That's why I punched him."

"Oh, Ryan . . ." Suzanne leaned over and hugged her son, pressing his head to her chest. "You wanted to defend me. I understand. I'm touched, honey. Honestly. That means a lot to me." She ruffled his hair, then stood back and looked down at him. "Next time, please just ignore those wise guys? Your mom didn't do anything wrong."

Except to say really bad things about someone, which has gotten me in all this hot water, she silently added. *And which I've always told you not to do.*

"This might go on for a while," she warned him. "Until the police find the person who did it. You can't come home from school with a bloody nose every day."

She and Kevin definitely needed to have a long talk with the kids tonight. She wasn't the only one affected. The family needed a game plan.

Ryan stared back at her. She wondered if

205

anything she'd said had gotten through. "I believe you. But if you didn't do anything, why are you wearing that weird outfit?"

Her outfit was strange — a black hoody and matching spandex yoga pants, a baseball cap, and large glasses. Perhaps drawing more attention than it deflected? But it seemed a good idea early this morning, when the vice principal had called, before she'd even had a cup of coffee. She'd peered out the window, car keys in hand, to find at least five reporters on the lawn and a minivan with a transmitter on top.

It had taken driving skills worthy of an action film hero to escape the paparazzi. When the call had come from school to collect her son, combat mode seemed the only choice. She'd hunkered down behind the steering wheel with a baseball hat covering her head and big sunglasses obscuring her face.

She'd opened the garage door with the remote, and backed out as fast as she dared, praying the daredevil photographers would jump out of her path in time. She didn't want to maim anyone on top of all her other legal troubles.

A few had pursued, but she'd shaken them off and finally arrived at the middle school with no one tailing.

All in all, it had been quite a morning.

After a long and unhappy night.

"The outfit is not my usual style. I need to keep a low profile."

"I know. Just yanking your chain." He laughed and picked up his backpack. "I don't know about ignoring kids who diss you, Mom. Getting the day off from school isn't so bad."

"Very funny. You'll do your schoolwork before any video games, my friend." She took off the glasses, which had been a silly touch, since it was cloudy outside.

He could find the day's assignments online. The school was very efficient that way. The police had taken her laptop but had left the other computers. She was thankful for that much.

Suzanne hadn't even removed her baseball cap when she heard the doorbell buzz as if someone was just leaning on it. More reporters. What had she done to deserve this?

"Should I get the door?"

Suzanne shook her head. "Just ignore it. They'll go away soon."

"Can I have some lunch?"

She knew he ate early at school, but this was ridiculous. Her boys were at an age when they could eat twelve meals a day. "It's not even ten o'clock. Make a snack and start your schoolwork."

She heard her son groan, but he dutifully followed her from the mudroom toward the kitchen.

She stopped in the hallway and listened. Someone was on the deck, knocking on the glass slider. She pressed herself against the wall, as if they were on a secret mission, and placed a finger on her lips.

"Hold up," she whispered. "Sounds like they came around the back. I should have locked the gate."

The knocking grew louder and she heard someone shout her name. More than one person, it sounded like.

"Sounds like they know you, Mom."

"Just a trick. Didn't you ever see reporters call out to celebrities? Do they say, 'Ms. Jolie!' or 'Ms. Kardashian!'? No, they say, 'Angelina!' or 'Kim! Kim!' "

He rolled his eyes but didn't reply. The voices grew even louder.

"Suzanne? It's us. . . . We just want to know if you're all right."

Through the haze of her media paranoia, she recognized Maggie's familiar voice. She peered around the doorway and, instead of a pack of rabid reporters on the deck, saw only her friends, their faces pressed against the glass of the French door slider.

They spotted her and jumped up and down, waving wildly.

Ryan had been excited at the prospect of reporters trying to break into the house. But now said, "Just your crazy friends. Better let them in before they bust the door down."

"Yeah, I'd better." Suzanne had never felt happier in her life to see them.

She pulled open the door, and they entered, single file. Maggie led the group and hugs were exchanged all around.

"Sorry to scare you but we tried the front door," Maggie said. "And we left a million messages on your cell phone and the landline. I guess you shut the sound off the message machine?"

"Had to. And the police took my cell phone . . . and my laptop," she reported.

"Bummer!" Phoebe sounded genuinely shocked at the thought of being stripped of all technology.

"We figured that." Lucy reached out and patted her shoulder.

"I thought you were reporters. They've been hounding me all morning. I think that video clip of my perp walk went viral."

"It was not a *perp* walk," Lucy cut in. "You were leaving the station. Not even charged with a parking ticket."

"Thanks, pal. But do you really think anyone knows the difference when you're filmed running with your coat over your head and the police call you 'a person of interest'? Hey, I'm a celebrity now. Fleeing the paparazzi. Everyone gets their fifteen minutes, right?"

She tried to strike a light note, as if none of this upset her. When in fact it had shaken her to the core.

"You're definitely dressed for the part." Dana's sweeping glance took in Suzanne's sleek black outfit.

"Wait." Suzanne picked up the dark glasses and her hat. "The accessories make the look, right?"

"As always." Maggie sighed but definitely looked amused. "We just wanted to know that you're all right. We don't have to stay. You must be exhausted."

After being released from the police station late last night, Suzanne had sent her friends a group text to let them know she was out and basically all right.

She knew they were dying to hear the details of her latest ordeal, but never would have asked them to upset their Monday morning schedules like this for her. It appeared that Maggie had even closed the shop. Now that they were here, she couldn't let them leave that easily.

"Exhausted, yes. But I can definitely use some company. I had to run over to the school as soon as I got up this morning. Long story, but *somebody*" — she pointed upstairs as she lowered her voice — "got a black eye, defending his mom's honor." Her son had gone up to his room, but she guessed he was listening.

"Oh my, that sounds painful. Is he okay?" Maggie asked.

"He'll be fine. I think he's proud of it," Suzanne replied. "Still, I don't like hearing he got into a fight at school because of my problems. And all the gossip about me."

"Which will pass soon, we hope," Lucy said.

Suzanne didn't see even a flickering light at the end of this dark tunnel, but didn't want to be contrary.

"Hope being the operative word." She forced a smile. "I didn't even have my coffee yet. Anyone interested in a cup? And maybe some scrambled eggs?"

Lucy looked interested. "Sounds good to me. I skipped breakfast, too."

"I'd love some tea," Dana said.

"We brought some treats from the bakery. To lift your spirits." Maggie produced a white bakery bag from her tote, the fragrance of fresh bread and coffee cake wafting in Suzanne's direction, an instant elixir.

"And we brought our knitting, of course." Phoebe pulled out her latest project, multicolor-striped booties for the baby wear donation.

Her friends quickly shed their jackets and joined her in the kitchen. A short time later, they sat at the big kitchen island, enjoying the late breakfast Suzanne had whipped up with their help — scrambled eggs with cheddar cheese, tomato bits, and avocado. With plates of buttered toast and bakery confections on the side. Even Dana could not resist.

Suzanne slipped in to her usual role of hostess and chef with ease, though worries that these gatherings — and her entire way of life — were now threatened, crept across her consciousness like small black spiders.

Dana met her glance and smiled, but with a somber light in her eyes. Suzanne guessed what Dana was thinking — that she'd slipped in to denial about her situation. Well . . . maybe a bit. It was easier with her friends here, than when she was alone.

"Okay, we're all fed and fueled. Tell us what happened. Why did the police drag you down to the station again?" Lucy prodded.

"We heard the police say they found new

evidence. What was it?" Maggie asked.

Suzanne sat back and licked a cake crumb off her fingertip. Scrambled eggs were easy. This part was hard.

"Files from Liza's office computer turned up on the desktop of my office computer. Private files. Her earnings and leads, her special client list, and her "hot" file, notes about leads on new listings. We all save notes like that — keeping track of gossip you pick up around town. Like learning that an old person is going into a nursing home, or a retired couple is downsizing. Or someone is being transferred. Or divorced. You want to be the first to make contact and swoop in," she explained. "It's hardly the sort of information you give to other salespeople."

"The police found her files, of that type, on your computer? How could that have happened?" Maggie was the least tech savvy in the group, though Suzanne didn't pretend to be any sort of computer geek.

"We have an office network and you can share files between computers, if you want. But she didn't share them with me; I can promise you that." Suzanne took another slug of coffee, though she knew she'd had more than enough for the day.

"So someone got on her computer and

sent the files to yours. To make it look as if you'd hacked into her private, valuable information?" Lucy asked.

"That's right. When the police accused me of doing that, I had to laugh. I need one of my kids just to print out a contract, no less hack into someone else's computer. What am I, a 'dark web' spook? The entire idea is preposterous."

Suzanne was trying to laugh off this latest accusation, but it was getting harder every day.

"What did the police say?" Lucy had her knitting out. She'd started on the baby jacket and it was coming along quickly, Suzanne noticed.

"As usual, they just kept asking the question different ways. As my attorney pointed out, even if I was capable of such a thing, it still doesn't prove I killed Liza. And, why would I steal the files and leave them on my office computer? Where someone else could easily see them? That part is plain dumb. I'd definitely be smarter than that."

Suzanne heard her voice getting louder and forced herself to simmer down.

"Totally smarter. And smarter than using a bottle of your own diet drink. Or vandalizing her car the same day you planned to kill her. It's so obvious someone did all that stuff to mess you up." Phoebe was knitting quickly, the tiny boots taking shape.

"When were the files transferred? Did they tell you?" Dana asked. "The computer would have recorded that information."

"The police didn't tell anyone at first, but Helen made them. The files were moved on Wednesday, the day before the murder. Unfortunately, I was in the office that day, but I never noticed," Suzanne admitted. "Somebody stuck the files in different folders on my desktop — Quick Chicken Recipes. And Cute Shoes."

"You keep a folder of cute shoes?" Lucy munched on a piece of toast crust.

Suzanne shrugged. "So? What do you save? Cute dog toys?"

Lucy laughed. Suzanne could see she'd caught her. "Point taken."

"It's just more circumstantial evidence." Dana snipped a strand of yarn as she finished off a row. She was also making a baby jacket in a rich, turquoise blue.

"But all this circumstantial evidence is piling up," Maggie cut in. "Like one of those days when the weatherman predicts a flurry and a few hours later you look outside and there's a foot or two of snow. It's worrisome. Did the police come at you with anything else?"

Suzanne bit her lip and nodded. "This one is even worse. They must have been searching since Liza's autopsy. Some empty vials from a Botox kit turned up in the town dump. From the same type of kit I bought at Janine's party."

"Well, the killer tossed them out and didn't think the police would look that hard," Maggie said calmly.

"The police knew what they were looking for and must have put a lot of man power on finding those vials," Dana said. "Are they trying to link you with fingerprints?"

"Better than that. The trash came from a house that's one of my listings. A cute little saltbox, in Lucy's neighborhood. An older couple, the Gertwigs, have it listed for a low price. I got a lot of action on an ad and I'd been in and out of there a hundred times last week. The vials were in a bag that definitely came from their house. It had some junk mail in it and a few other bits with their names on it."

"That was clever. It's almost as incriminating as if it came from your house," Lucy said.

Phoebe was clearly upset by the direction the conversation had taken. She'd tangled up her yarn and she never did that, Suzanne noticed. "Yeah, well . . . maybe even worse.

It makes it look as if Suzanne was trying to hide the vials. But the police were smarter. I hate when that happens."

Suzanne sighed, appreciating her concern. "Me too. I really hate that."

"It's got to be someone in your office. Someone who knows your movements." Maggie looked upset, too, the little crease in her brow that only showed when she got worried or angry getting deeper the more they talked.

"I agree, but let's not narrow the field too quickly," Lucy said. "It's definitely someone who's close to the office, but maybe not right inside. For example, the listing for the Gertwig house is in the window of Prestige Properties with Suzanne's name on it. It doesn't take an insider to know Suzanne would be there frequently."

Suzanne agreed, but was starting to feel overwhelmed. Her friends were trying hard and were usually so clever at untangling these puzzles. But could they figure this one out in time to help her?

Maggie had just started a baby sweater. It looked like a basic garter stitch and Suzanne guessed she'd whip right through it. "Did they ask you about anything else?"

"Don't they have to let her know everything that they know?" Phoebe seemed affronted by the suggestion that the police might hold back.

Dana shook her head. "They don't. Not unless Suzanne is charged and a trial is imminent. Then they need to turn over all the evidence they have against her. At this stage, they can hold back a lot of what they may have discovered."

Suzanne didn't like hearing that. "Oh . . . brother . . . I can't go through any more of these all night questioning sessions. It's too exhausting. Even with Helen there, after a while I start babbling. I don't know what I'm likely to say just to get them off my back."

"They're trying to wear you down. You can't let them." Maggie reached over and squeezed her hand. Suzanne felt Maggie was remembering her own experience of being a suspect when a rival knitting-shop owner was murdered. It had happened years ago, but the trauma of that experience had left its mark; Suzanne had no doubt.

Phoebe turned to Suzanne with an intense expression. "Think, Suzanne. Who could have done this? Who could have fooled around with the computer files and planted the drink? Who knew that Liza had that allergy and that you were at the Botox party? Who dislikes her even more than you did?"

"Dislikes her . . . or just has some reason to want her out of the way?" Lucy clarified. "Who stands to gain once she's out of the picture?"

"I've been asking myself that for days now. I just can't figure it out." Suzanne's brash, funny mask melted. She looked around at her friends, feeling helpless.

"Let's pretend we're the police," Maggie said suddenly. "They must be sorting this out in a careful, logical way."

"Right, with one of those big whiteboards with photos and arrows drawn in marker all over the place." Lucy was getting into the idea.

"I don't have a whiteboard, but here's a pad." Suzanne found a pad on the kitchen counter and pulled off her shopping list to reveal a blank page.

Lucy snatched it up and fished a pen out of her handbag. "I'll be in charge of writing stuff." Suddenly all business, her gaze swept around. "Let's round up the suspects in your office. What are their names again?"

"Anita and Lyle are in sales. Beth is the office manager, and Janine is the reception-ist. And there's Harry, of course. Our boss," Suzanne added.

Lucy had recorded the names, writing them in bold, block letters across the top of the pad. Down the margin, she wrote the words: "Means," "Motive," "Opportunity." Then drew lines to make a grid of boxes.

"Nice, Lucy. This is like Clue, my favorite board game," Phoebe said.

"Colonel Mustard did it in the drawing room, with the candlestick," Dana quipped.

"If only," Suzanne sighed.

"Logic, ladies. Focus, please?" Maggie implored them. "Suzanne, you need to lead here. How can we fill in this grid? You know the players best."

Suzanne pondered the blank squares. "I'm sorry . . . but they all knew about the diet drinks we both used and about the Botox party and Liza's allergy. I'm not sure who knows how to move files around the office network, but I don't think it's that complicated."

"What about the car vandalism? You told us someone had keyed her car really badly, earlier that day?" Maggie had taken a break from her knitting to study Lucy's chart.

"I wasn't in the office but I heard later on that Liza had gone out to her car around eleven o'clock, to leave for an appointment, and found a huge, ugly scratch from one end to the other. And I think a headlight was broken, too." Suzanne sipped her coffee, thinking. "Janine, the receptionist, told

220

me when I got in. She said Liza was very upset, but she didn't call the police to report it. She didn't want Beth to report it either, even though she had offered."

"So the police think the vandalism is related to her murder?" Dana asked.

"They would have really loved it if they could have blamed me for it somehow. But I was cruising down the highway, popping down streusel bites. I even kept the receipt. Personally, I think we should just put the car thing aside. We have plenty on our plate already."

Dana glanced at the pad and then back at her knitting. "This is a good start. But Lucy's right. We have to be open to the possibility that it could have been someone who isn't an employee. But just close enough to know how to manipulate the situation."

"How to frame me, you mean," Suzanne clarified.

"I didn't want to put it that way, but yes — how to frame you."

"In that case, it could have been anybody. People are coming in and out of the office all day. Clients, food deliveries, the office cleaners . . ." Suzanne could have named even more traffic, but stopped herself. "The office is always cleaned on Thursday night, but last week, for some reason, the cleaners

221

didn't come. And I couldn't help thinking that if they had been there, Liza would have had help and she could have survived."

"Interesting." Maggie glanced at Suzanne over the edge of her reading glasses. "Why did they miss the visit?"

"I don't know."

"Why don't we find out?" Lucy already had her phone out. "What's the name of the service?"

"Spotless Cleaning Service." Suzanne felt encouraged by Lucy's can-do spirit. Lucy quickly looked up the number and dialed, with her phone on speaker.

A woman answered on the first ring. "Spotless Cleaning. How can I help you?"

"I'm calling from Prestige Properties in Plum Harbor. The service didn't come last week. It was very inconvenient and no one here recalls canceling." Suzanne was impressed by Lucy's assertive and snappy business voice. She'd never seen that side of her before.

"I'm sorry to hear that. I'd be happy to take your name and number and look into it."

Suzanne was alarmed at the reply, but Lucy took it in stride. "That's okay. . . . I can hold. We'd like to get to the bottom of this today, if we can."

222

"All right. If you prefer. Let me see what I can find out. Please hold."

The call clicked over to elevator jazz. A saxophone solo intended to sound soulful came out of the phone speaker as pure screech. Everyone winced and put their hands over their ears.

"Lower it, Lucy. Please," Maggie begged.

"Maybe the phone Muzak made all the cleaners call in sick," Phoebe mumbled.

"Maybe they quit in protest," Suzanne offered.

The voice on the phone returned. "Hello? Are you still there?"

"Yes, I'm here," Lucy replied quickly.

"I spoke to the person who books the appointments. She's sure that someone from your office canceled. A message was left on our machine Wednesday night."

"Really? That's funny. Because I handle that sort of thing on this end, and I know *I* didn't call." Suzanne suppressed a laugh. Lucy was really getting into this, wasn't she? "Can you just tell me one more tiny thing? Did a man call? Or was it a woman?"

The receptionist replied with a pained sigh, clearly irritated and losing her patience. "Hold again. I'll ask."

Lucy muted the phone before the music could come on.

"Good one, Lucy. Fast thinking," Dana said.

Lucy shrugged with a modest grin. "It just came to me. There are men in this mix, too."

"Absolutely," Maggie agreed. "We have to cover all bases, though they do say that poison is a woman's preferred murder method."

The woman at the cleaning service came back on the line. "The appointment manager doesn't remember and the message tape has been erased."

"Bummer!" Suzanne blurted out. Then covered her mouth with her hand.

"Excuse me?" the woman replied.

"Sorry, someone just walked into my office. Thanks so much. You've been very helpful."

"No trouble. We appreciate your business. Have a good day."

"You have a good day, too," Lucy said, and clicked off the call. "Well, we found out something. Someone was smart enough to cancel the cleaners."

"And that someone knows the cleaners come on Thursday night," Dana noted. "Once again, points to an inside job."

"Yes, it does. But if Liza's killer is smart enough to frame Suzanne this way, they could be smart enough to be outside the circle," Lucy countered. "But somehow have privy to all the important info."

Suzanne's head was spinning. She felt dispirited again. "Sure, that could be it. But now it opens the door to the entire world."

"There are more possibilities. But not that many more," Dana reminded her. "Someone close, but maybe not a coworker."

Maggie was concentrating on her stitching. She didn't look up but Suzanne could tell she was following the conversation closely. "What about Nick Sutton? I don't know how he rates as far as means and opportunity. But he probably has enough motive."

Suzanne had thought of him, too. "Plenty of motive. And never trust a man who wears French cuffs. That's a given."

Maggie smiled as she continued stitching. "I'm not sure about the cuffs, but didn't you hear that their divorce was contentious?"

"Contentious barely covers it. I heard it was a clash of the Titans. A battle to the death."

"Maybe literally?" Dana asked quietly. "I think we're pretty sure the divorce decree was never finalized. If so, he's entitled to part of her estate. Or even all of it."

"She called him her 'ex.' But maybe that

was just wishful thinking." Suzanne considered the possibility. "He was in the office last week, on Tuesday. I was on my way out to meet a client, but I saw him at the reception desk, sweet talking Janine. No great challenge there. She turns to mush at the sight of any attractive guy. He wanted to see Liza, but she was out. He didn't believe that and barged past Janine to check Liza's office for himself. He was definitely hot under the collar about something."

Lucy looked like a dog who had just heard a sharp whistle. "Really? What happened after that? Was he alone in her office at all?"

"I saw Janine run after him. She couldn't get him to leave, so she called Beth. I guess he was alone for a few minutes at the back of the office. And Liza's cubicle is near the kitchen."

"What happened after that?" Lucy asked.

"Beth came running and Lyle came to help her. I guess they got him out, eventually. I don't know. I had to leave. I was already late for my appointment."

It didn't seem important then, but Suzanne wished now she'd stuck around longer to see what had happened next. "They were married a long time. He must have known that Liza and I didn't get along. I'm sure she complained about me plenty at

226

the dinner table."

A fact that made Suzanne ashamed now and even a little sad, to think she was such a bane to someone else's existence. But it was true.

"I was thinking that, too," Dana said. "And he probably knew about the allergy. The fact that there was a Botox party and you attended was a lucky bonus. He could still have framed you by leaving some vials that he used in the trash at one of your listings."

Maggie picked up her knitting again. She examined the stitches on a row and turned her work over. "Whether or not the divorce was final, there were certainly bad feelings left with the family. Ruth couldn't even stand to look at him," Maggie reminded them. "I do wonder what that was all about."

Suzanne had wondered about that, too. "I guess I should ask around at the office. Maybe someone knows the history. If I ever go back to the office, that is." She tried not to sound too glum but she couldn't help it.

Dana looked up and met her gaze. "What do you mean by that? Harry didn't fire you . . . did he?"

Suzanne shook her head. "Not yet. He has a little style about these things. He'll draw it out and make it seem like he's doing it for my own good." She laughed at her analysis, though her assessment was true. "He did say he thought it was best if I took a few days off. Worked from home, if I felt 'up to it.' He's sure it's a huge misunderstanding but he has to think of the company's image. All this negative press about Liza's death and the investigation is hurting business, and 'there's enough gossip about Prestige Properties already,' he told me. I know that's probably true," she reluctantly agreed. "Having the police suspect one employee of murdering another really smears the place."

Lucy bit her lip. Suzanne could tell she wanted to say something but was holding back. "Go on, Lucy. What is it? I can take it."

Lucy glanced at the others, then pulled the *Plum Harbor Times* from her knapsack. "I guess it's best if you hear it from us. The headline in the newspaper today . . . BETTER HOMES AND HOMICIDES?"

Suzanne stared at the page, another picture with her coat over her head, going into the police station. She didn't know if she was going to laugh or cry. "For once, that front page editor came up with a decent pun." She looked back at her friends. "Maybe Harry saw the headline this morning and decided I was bad for business."

Her friends exchanged glances, but didn't argue with her. "He acted all sympathetic about what I'm going through, and said he knows it's a huge misunderstanding." She paused, then imitated Harry's deep, smooth voice. " 'You'll be back soon, Sue. But I want something left for you to come back to, right? Ha-ha.' He tried to make a joke out of it. That annoyed me. And I really hate when people call me Sue."

A small point, but one that got under her skin.

"Anyone who really knows you would never call you *that,*" Lucy murmured, as she folded the paper and put it out of sight.

"However he put it, that must have hurt," Dana said. "This is the time when you need more support. Not less."

"Gosh, he's acting like you have a contagious disease or something," Phoebe said.

"Yeah, it's called prime suspect-itis. I wish I could just take a pill and make it go away."

"I'm sure," Lucy was sympathetic, too. "But it's interesting, too. I mean, if you're not in the office, it's harder for you to figure out who really did this. Maybe he's keeping you away on purpose."

Lucy was clearly pointing a finger at Harry, but Suzanne didn't see it. "I know we can't rule anyone out yet. Especially my coworkers. But Harry worshipped the ground Liza walked on. I think he still harbored hopes they'd get back together someday."

"I was watching him at the memorial," Dana said. "I don't doubt what you say is true. But even the deepest passion can turn to the complete opposite. Maybe he tried to repair their romance and she rejected him again?"

"And if he couldn't have her, no one else ever would?" Lucy finished sketching out the scene.

Dana nodded. "Something like that. It wouldn't be the first time a forlorn lover ended the life of the object of his affections."

Maggie shrugged. "Happens in the opera all the time."

"Not a fan. But I'll take your word." Suzanne sat with that theory a moment. "I won't argue with you, Dana. You're the expert in the obsession department. But aside from romance, she was his star earner. The goose that kept laying golden eggs. Harry's heart definitely watches the bottom line. Why would he give up such a good thing? It still doesn't make sense to me. But his hot and cold attitude toward me doesn't make sense either. One minute, he's offering me Liza's listings, and the next, banning me from the office."

Phoebe picked up the chart. "Sounds like a split personality. He did have means and opportunity, but the jury is still out in the motive category." She checked off two boxes in Harry's column, and put a question mark in the last.

"I'm not sure how I feel about your boss, Suzanne." Maggie had come to the end of another row and seemed satisfied to put her work aside. "But we definitely need to add Nick Sutton to the chart. And I need to visit Ruth Devereaux and find out why the mere sight of the man sends her into paroxysms."

CHAPTER 8

"I'm surprised she agreed to see us. She probably doesn't remember that we're friends with Suzanne." Lucy sat beside Maggie in the Subaru on Tuesday afternoon, as Maggie drove toward Peabody and Brookside Village, where Ruth Devereaux lived.

"I wondered about that, too. Even if she doesn't watch the local news — and that's a long shot — the police must be filling her in on their progress. But she didn't mention Suzanne, and I didn't either. At the memorial service, I asked if I could visit and she seemed pleased by the idea. When I called last night, she didn't mind hearing a friend would come along, so . . . Oh, here we are. It's closer than I thought."

Maggie saw a sign, BROOKSIDE VILLAGE — AN ASSISTED LIVING COMMUNITY, and turned into the entrance. She slowed the car as they approached a security booth.

The guard asked whom they were visiting, a gate was raised, and they drove on.

"This isn't a bad place," she said, glancing around.

"Not at all. Though all the 'brooks' look carefully planned and constructed."

Maggie smiled. "That's a given. I did expect something more stark and austere. Even with the name Brookside."

The architecture was acceptable; two- and three-story apartment buildings surrounded by pleasant landscaping, fountains, and gazebos. Bridges connected some of the structures. So that the occupants could still get around in the winter without braving the cold weather, she guessed. The roads had picturesque names, like Willow Walk and Canterbury Court.

"It's not so bad. I mean, when one is ready," she added quickly.

Lucy glanced at her. "Don't worry, I know you're not ready for assisted anything. You can barely tolerate an assistant in the shop."

"Assistant manager, now," she replied, reminding Lucy of Phoebe's promotion. "But thanks for the compliment. I know I'm getting older but I still do everything I've always done. Just a little slower," she admitted with a laugh.

Maggie hated talking about her age and

getting older, being of the mind that if she didn't pay much attention to it, the years wouldn't catch up with her. Even though she saw the signs very clearly among her contemporaries. Lately, she had to admit the years were passing faster and faster; though her life was as active and full as ever, she often felt a little scared of what was to come.

Now, just when she'd expected to make a big, important move in her relationship with Charles, their romance had run out of steam.

As if reading her mind, Lucy said, "I didn't want to say anything in front of Suzanne, but how are things with Charles? I know he doesn't want you involved in any police business — no less, a case he's working on."

Maggie saw a sign for Ruth's courtyard and turned into the parking lot. "We had words. I'm sure he thinks she's innocent. But he just can't admit it. Not even to me. He got all officious, spouting things about police policy and procedure. And his professional ethics."

Maggie stopped. She felt upset just recalling it.

Lucy looked concerned. "You had an argument?"

"I guess you'd call it that. Not a shouting match or anything like that. That's not our style." She sighed and brought the car to a stop. "Let's just say things have cooled off considerably. We were talking about Charles moving in. And right now, we're barely talking."

Maggie couldn't hide her disappointment. Not in front of Lucy. "He is working long hours and I usually don't get to see him when he's on a big case. I asked if he'd take himself off this one. But he won't. So why should I sit back when Suzanne needs our help? Especially now that she's been singled out as a person of interest."

Lucy met her gaze. "You're a very loyal friend. But I'm sure Suzanne wouldn't want you to lose Charles over this."

"I know. But it's hardly her fault. He's being so stubborn. It's just common sense. Suzanne is *not* a murderer. We all know that. I know Charles can't just punch her ticket and give her a free pass. But I'm not sure the police have given any thought at all to the notion that someone has framed her."

"And done a good job," Lucy pointed out.

"Too good. That's why it's up to us now to find out who's done this to our Suzanne. And killed Liza."

Ruth lived in a ground floor apartment.

Maggie rang the buzzer and they heard a voice call out, "Come in. It's open."

Maggie swung open the door and stepped inside, followed by Lucy. She paused a moment, her eyes adjusting to the light.

It was a spacious apartment, larger than Maggie expected, with one room flowing into the next. Still, elegant pieces of furniture and artwork looked a bit out of place, and spoke of a grander home. Maggie recalled Suzanne talking about a big house on Hickory Hill and she guessed these were a few of the furnishings Ruth could not part with.

Across a light-filled living room, she saw glass doors that framed a view of a man-made pond and bubbling fountain. Ruth sat in her wheelchair, a knitting project in her lap. Maggie greeted her, and Ruth watched as the two visitors walked toward her.

"What a lovely place. Liza told me that you haven't been living here very long," Maggie remarked.

"I've tried to make it comfortable. I left the big house right after Liza moved to Maine. It was too much for me. Then I had the stroke and the girls came back to help, with little Emma in tow. The house had never sold, so they moved in. We all could have lived there and never bumped into

236

each other for days." She shrugged. "But since I'm in the chair now, we decided I'm better off here. I didn't want to burden them."

"Thank you for having us," Lucy said.

"It's nice to have some company. Take off your things, sit down. My aide made some tea." She waved at a cart that held a china teapot, cups, and a plate of plain butter cookies, the type that came in a large, round tin and older people seemed so fond of. "She'll be back in a while."

Maggie took a seat on the couch and Lucy next to her. "This is my friend, Lucy Binger. She was at the memorial. There were so many people there, you probably don't remember her."

Ruth had picked up her knitting. She examined Lucy over half-rim glasses that were balanced at the tip of her nose.

"I'm sorry. I don't recall. Too many introductions. Were you a friend of my daughter?"

Maggie could see that Lucy felt put on the spot. "Liza was so well known around town. We all wanted to pay our respects."

Ruth seemed satisfied with the explanation. "There was an impressive turnout. It was a wonderful tribute to her."

"Yes, it was," Maggie agreed. "My knitting group has been inspired by all the good work she did for charity. We set a goal of one hundred knitted baby items by the holidays. I thought we'd make the donation in her name."

"That would be a lovely honor to her."

Lucy glanced at Maggie, but didn't say anything. Maggie hadn't cleared the idea with the group yet, but doubted anyone would object. Even Suzanne. In fact, she thought it might help Suzanne feel better. And she hadn't said it just to butter Ruth up. She really did think it would be a fitting tribute.

Lucy nodded and held up her project. "Baby jacket number one. It's almost done."

Ruth nodded. Maggie could see she was impressed. "Do you have any children of your own, Lucy?"

Maggie saw color rise in Lucy's cheeks. Too many people had been asking her that lately. "No, I don't."

"Don't wait too long. Kira got in just under the wire, I'd say. But Liza missed out. Maybe that's why she put so much time into her charity work, knitting for other people's children."

That thought had crossed Maggie's mind, too.

"Liza would have liked to see your knitting circle involved. She got me working on the donations, too. I don't think anyone knew what a charitable soul she really was. Until she died, that is."

"She was very modest." Maggie wasn't saying this just to get on Ruth's good side. She knew it was true. Maggie had taken out her knitting and started to work.

"Modest in the goals she set for herself, too," Ruth said. "She could have been anything she set her mind to. She had brains and ambition and never shied away from hard work. Loved numbers. She had a knack for mathematics, even as a child. She started off with a big job in Boston, right out of college. Investments or something like that. How she ended up in a dinky real estate office in this backwater burg, I'll never understand. Nick Sutton dragged her out here. He ruined her life. That was just the start."

"So you blame him for that? For pulling Liza off track?" Maggie wondered if she'd answer.

Ruth's mouth tightened, her eyes narrowed. "That's certainly part of it. He's a weak, self-centered man. Always blaming the world for his failings — a total narcissist. I never wanted my daughter to marry him. He was like a vampire, draining her energy. Liza wanted a family. But I was relieved that they never had children. It made the divorce easier."

Maggie wasn't sure how much she should say, but decided to take a chance. "Really? I heard the divorce was very complicated and even contentious."

Ruth glanced at her, but didn't question her sources. "He dragged it out. Liza was the breadwinner in that household, even though he has that restaurant. It never made a dime. He's a terrible businessman. Liza knew first-hand. She did his bookkeeping for years. He gambled away any profit and then some. So he demanded alimony." She shook her head in disbelief. "A grown man. That's pathetic, don't you think?" She didn't wait for Maggie's answer. "He has a gambling problem. And he's in with the wrong class of people. A very low element. He always expected Liza to bail him out, even after they were separated."

"But she drew the line," Maggie added.

"Too little too late, if you ask me. But finally, she'd had enough." Ruth turned to her knitting and took a deep breath. The conversation was upsetting her but she seemed relieved to share her opinion of her former son-in-law "He didn't like that. It made him very angry."

"Really? What did he do? Did he threaten her?" Maggie asked.

"She didn't tell me much. She didn't want me to worry. But I wouldn't doubt it. The man is a natural-born bully and desperate for money. It's very clear. My daughter wasn't even laid to rest when we got a letter from his lawyer, demanding her estate."

Maggie tried to hide her surprise. And her pleasure at hearing their suspicions confirmed. So that was why Ruth kicked him out of the memorial gathering. One question was answered.

"How could he claim a right to her estate? Weren't they divorced?" Lucy hadn't said much so far, but Maggie knew she was particularly curious about confirming this point. Lucy's research had hit a snag. The records were public but not available online, and there had been no time to visit the county clerk's office.

"I honestly don't know. My attorney is looking into it. Liza always spoke as if the divorce was signed and sealed. But he claims it was not."

"That must be very distressing. On top of your great loss."

"I try not to think about it. Kira is taking care of all of Liza's affairs. She says not to worry. She told me that Liza's estate is protected. My daughter was too smart to let a man like him get the best of her."

Maggie didn't doubt that, though she wasn't sure what Ruth meant by "protected." She didn't want to seem too nosy. She certainly seemed snoopy enough already, she thought. She did have one more prying question and wondered if Ruth would answer.

"You say Nick Sutton was desperate for money. Desperate enough to have harmed Liza?" She waited, wondering if she'd gone too far.

Ruth raised her chin but sat silent for a long moment. Maggie wasn't sure she would answer. Finally, she said, "The police think it was someone in her office — Suzanne Cavanaugh. Liza spoke about her."

Ruth had obviously forgotten that she'd met Suzanne at the memorial service. Maggie was not about to remind her.

"She sounds like a ruthless woman, willing to do anything to get ahead, or beat my daughter out of a sale. That's how Liza described her to me."

Maggie's heart sank. Ruth must have told the police the same thing. "They were office rivals. Very competitive with each other. But we know Suzanne well. We'd never describe her as ruthless."

"She's just the opposite, honestly," Lucy said.

Ruth did not look convinced "So, she's your friend?"

Maggie nodded. "A good friend. She did not harm Liza. We're sure of it. No matter what the police say. I hope you can believe me."

Ruth sighed. "Frankly, I was expecting the police to tell me Sutton did it. Expecting and hoping, too. What does it matter what I believe? It's what the police decide."

"Not necessarily." Lucy put her knitting down. "Somebody is trying to make it look like Suzanne killed your daughter. But the police haven't investigated that possibility. Not that we can see."

"We hoped you could help us," Maggie admitted.

Ruth looked surprised. "To clear your friend's name? Why would I do that?"

"Because she's innocent." Maggie couldn't help the sharp note in her voice. "Would you rather an innocent person went to jail for this crime and the person who really killed your daughter went free?"

Ruth bowed her head. When she looked up again, Maggie was sorry to see the older woman's eyes glazed over with tears. But under the tears, a steely resolve, too. "I want

243

to see whoever did this put behind bars and have them throw away the key. Though there's nothing that can ever make up for losing her."

"I understand," Maggie said quietly. She would feel the same way, heaven forbid, if she'd been in Ruth's place. "It wasn't Suzanne. She's a good person. A loving mother and friend. She has three growing children. She's just not capable of such a thing. I would stake my life on it."

Lucy leaned forward, clutching her knitting on her lap. "Can you think of anyone, besides Sutton, who had a grievance with Liza? Someone who would have benefitted from her death?"

Ruth dabbed her eyes with a tissue. "No one besides that dreadful man comes to mind. Liza always put on a brave face, though I'm sure she had her ups and downs. She didn't want to worry me. Especially after the stroke."

"Anyone could see she was independent," Maggie agreed. "But mothers have an instinct about these things. You never felt she was hiding something? Something worrisome going on in her life?"

Ruth put her cup aside. "She was upset last week, when her car was damaged. She told me about it over the phone. A little more upset than I'd expect, to be honest. Someone ran a key along the driver's side and scratched the finish. It was a simple repair. But she seemed very . . . rattled."

Suzanne had mentioned that. Maggie thought it was probably random vandalism, unconnected with the murder, but now she wondered.

"Did she have any idea who did it?" Lucy asked.

"Nasty teenagers, she told me. But I think she did know who was responsible. And why. I just got a feeling from the way she talked about it. A mother's instinct, I suppose." She cast a meaningful glance Maggie's way.

"Who do you think it was?" Maggie had some theories but wanted to hear what Ruth thought.

"I'm not sure. Competition in the office came to mind. Frankly, I thought your friend was probably the vandal."

Maggie cringed. Poor Suzanne. Liza had given her the same bad press that Suzanne had given Liza.

"It wasn't Suzanne. She was covering appointments far from the village at the time it was damaged. She has proof." Lucy had put her knitting aside and walked over to the tea cart. She'd fixed a cup of tea and

245

served it to Ruth.

Ruth nodded her thanks. "Well, it must have been someone else. Nick Sutton. Or maybe someone who was just jealous of her."

"Maybe." Lucy nibbled on a cookie. Maggie could see she didn't believe that. She thought there was something more going on. Maggie did, too.

She wondered if they'd worn out their welcome. She didn't want to make Ruth tired and their questions were not yielding much information.

"The detectives seem to think your friend is guilty. But I can see you really believe she's not." Ruth paused and shook her head. "I don't know what to believe. My daughter always spoke well of you, Maggie. She always enjoyed spending time in your shop."

"I enjoyed her company. Very much. She had a wonderful way with people. Very warm and charming." Maggie was not able to praise Liza this way when Suzanne was in earshot. But she meant the words sincerely. She knew it wasn't much, but maybe some small comfort to her mother. "I'm sure you miss her very much."

"I do. She came here often. We'd sit and knit together. She'd usually bring Emma, to give Kira a rest and some time to paint. It was nice company for me."

"Did she have plans to visit the night she died?" Lucy asked.

"Yes, she did. But she called around seven o'clock and said she couldn't make it. She said that she was caught up in something at the office and had to stay late, until it was finished."

Poor Liza. She had no idea that *she'd* be finished by the end of the night. "Did you hear anyone in the background?" Maggie asked.

"Not a sound. I assumed she was alone." Ruth paused. "It makes me so sad to realize that was our last conversation." She sighed and sipped her tea. "Early that morning, she'd sent some photos of yarn she'd picked out for me. I needed a dark blue merino to trim a sweater I've been working on. She wasn't sure it was the right color and said she'd change it at your shop if the shade was not right. She wanted to make sure I got the photos, and reminded me to save them, until I saw her. I did wonder about that."

"I remember her buying some blue yarn. Why did the request seem odd to you?" Maggie asked.

"Well, the next time she stopped by, she

247

could bring the skein of yarn with her, couldn't she? I didn't need the photos to check the weight and color."

The logic made sense to Maggie.

"Do you still have the pictures?" Lucy asked.

"I do. I think I can find them. . . . I'll try."

Ruth turned and picked up her phone, then frowned down at it a few moments, pressing her finger to the screen. "So many pictures of Emma on here. It's hard to find anything else."

She finally found the photos and passed the phone to Maggie. Lucy was quickly peering over her shoulder.

The pictures were just as Ruth had described. A strand of blue yarn, stretched across what appeared to be a desktop, in Liza's office, Maggie assumed.

There were some papers on the desk, under the yarn, a spreadsheet with what looked like accounting information. There were several photos of the yarn, many close up and some from a distance. Maggie didn't think the task required so many pictures, but maybe she had done some with a flash and some without, to show the color better?

Maggie glanced at Lucy, but didn't say anything. Lucy handed the phone back to Ruth. "Did you show the photos to the police?"

Ruth shrugged. "They didn't think much of it. I'm not sure if they even took copies."

"Would you send me the photos?" Lucy asked politely. Ruth handed her back the phone. "You'll have to do that yourself. My skills in that area are limited," she said with a small smile.

"I hear you." Maggie didn't see how photos of yarn could help, but Lucy was smart to get copies. One never really knew how the pieces might eventually fit.

Maggie didn't have any more questions and wondered if they were really helping Suzanne, or just causing Ruth more distress.

Lucy had served Maggie a cup of tea, too, and she took a sip, then set it down. "I'm sorry for all these questions. I don't mean to bring you more sadness. Honestly. You must think it was very duplicitous of me to come here today."

Ruth's expression was half hidden by her cup. "Now that you mention it . . . I suppose I do."

"I apologize for that. Sincerely."

"You promised to knit with me. And so we did," Ruth acknowledged. "That wasn't a lie."

"Yes, but . . . all the questions . . . For a good cause," she added.

"I understand." Ruth set her cup down on the side table. "I could be angry at you. But I also want the *real* killer to be caught, as you say. The detectives seem to think your friend is guilty. If she is innocent, as you claim, it will be proven in court. Hopefully. But by then, the real killer may get away." Maggie felt relieved that Ruth saw their point. "Trouble is, I doubt anything I've said has furthered your cause."

"We can't say yet. You may have helped a lot," Lucy replied.

"I've heard around town that you and your friends have solved a few cases for the police."

"Oh, I wouldn't go that far. We've helped a bit." Maggie shook her head, wondering what Charles would think if he ever heard that. Did people really say that about them?

"The police will never admit it," Lucy added.

"I'm sure they wouldn't. If I were in your shoes, I'd be doing the same. We need to protect the ones we love. I feel so frustrated, wondering if there was something I could have done for my daughter. Some way I could have helped, or protected her from this tragedy." Ruth shook her head, looking as if she might cry again. "Now I'm stuck in this chair and there's so little I can do about anything."

Maggie reached over and covered her hand. "There, there . . . We didn't mean to upset you."

Ruth wiped her eyes again and sat up straight. "To be honest, I'm glad you came. I want to help find the awful person who killed Liza. Now I'm wondering, too, if the police overlooked something. Or someone. I know how competitive my daughter was. Always pushing herself to be the best. But she'd never kill someone over it. Your friend probably wouldn't either. I find the motive weak, even if the police are sold on it. But what could the reason be? Maybe we'll never know."

Ruth sighed. She pushed the brake off her chair, hit a button on the armrest, and it started rolling toward the front door.

Maggie thought Ruth was abruptly showing them out. She stood up quickly and grabbed her belongings. So did Lucy. They glanced at each other, not knowing what to do.

But Ruth bypassed the door and ended up at an antique secretary. She opened a small drawer below the pigeonhole compartments and took out a key on a metal ring, then turned toward them.

"This is the key to my house. Liza's

bedroom and study are on the second floor. Maybe if you look around, you'll find something the police missed. That's all I can think of doing to help you."

Maggie took the key and stared down at it. Technically, Ruth still owned the property and was giving them permission to go inside. But her daughters had been living there for some time and such a visit would be an invasion of privacy.

"I appreciate that you want to help, Ruth. I really do. But I'm not sure I feel comfortable taking your key. What about Kira? Maybe we should just stop by and ask her to let us look around. You could give her a heads-up and smooth the way?"

"Kira isn't home. She took Emma up to Maine for a few days to visit friends. It's been a very stressful time for her. She needed a rest."

Maggie glanced at Lucy. That was convenient. And made the offer all the more tempting.

"She's very private, just like her sister. I doubt she'd ever speak to you about this — or let you look around," Ruth added.

Maggie still didn't know what to do. But Lucy did. She leaned over and took the key, then slipped it in her pocket.

"Thank you so much. This could help a

lot. Maybe you can let Kira know you said it was all right for us to go in for a few minutes?"

The solution seemed reasonable to Maggie. Well, not entirely. But at least Kira would know that strangers had been snooping around her residence.

"Don't worry, I'll smooth things over for you. It's still my house," Ruth reminded them.

Maggie and Lucy gathered their belongings, and Ruth followed them to the door. "Thank you again for hearing us out. Someone else would have shown us the door," Maggie said.

"I was tempted. But I don't get many visitors who will sit and knit. For that pleasure, I'll put up with a lot."

Maggie was surprised by the humorous reply. "I'll come again. Very soon. Under better circumstances. And without a hidden agenda."

"I hope so, too," Ruth said.

Maggie didn't say more until she and Lucy were in her car. She clipped her seat belt, but didn't turn the engine on.

"I hope we didn't stay too long. Once I was there, I wondered if we'd done the right thing, asking her to help us."

"I did too," Lucy admitted. "But she

seemed persuaded that Suzanne is not the killer. At least, she's willing to entertain the possibility that it might be someone else."

"It was good of her to answer all our questions and give us that key."

"I feel like it's burning a hole in my pocket."

"I smell the smoke from here," Maggie murmured. "Do you think we should really go there? It seems like crossing a line of some kind."

"I know what you mean. But it is Ruth's house, at least technically, and she gave us permission. It's not as if we're breaking and entering."

"Not really, but . . . that term reminds me of Charles, and he'd have a fit if he knew I even entertained the idea."

Lucy touched her arm. "I took the key. You had qualms. I can go there tomorrow. I'll ask Dana or Suzanne to come with me."

Maggie considered the plan. "By tomorrow, Kira might be home. And Ruth gave *us* permission to go inside. Not Dana or Suzanne. And if the police ever caught Suzanne there . . ."

"Good point," Lucy conceded. "What now?"

Maggie started the engine and turned her head to back out of the space. "Let's go to

254

Hickory Hill and get it over with. We won't stay long. In for a penny, in for a pound?"

"I had a feeling you'd say that. And who's going to tell Charles? You know I never would."

Maggie offered Lucy a small smile. She had plenty of misgivings but felt she couldn't give up now. If Suzanne was convicted of this crime and she could have done more to vindicate her friend, Maggie knew that she'd never forgive herself. She knew that Lucy felt the same.

Night had fallen by the time they returned to the village and reached the Devereaux home. Maggie parked on the street, though the driveway was empty. She didn't feel she should take that much liberty. She got out of the car and pushed up the collar of her thick sweater jacket. It was going to be a cold night, maybe the first frost. A brisk wind blew white, wispy clouds across the dark blue sky.

The house was a grand Victorian, three stories high, with big bay windows, two turrets, and several chimneys reaching up from the peeked roof. Maggie could see why Ruth's voice was tinged with pride when she referred to the house and also, why it had sat months on the market without selling to a new owner. It was a beautiful old home, but not the type young families were looking for these days.

With dried leaves blowing around Maggie's feet and bare branches swaying in the wind, the dark, empty house seemed ominous.

As they headed toward the gate, a slinky gray cat darted out of the shrubs and ran across the lawn. Startled, Maggie grabbed Lucy's arm. Then laughed at her reaction.

"Sorry. I didn't expect that."

"Not a big fan of felines, as you know," Lucy replied. "They usually sneak up on me."

Maggie did like cats. But this one seemed like a bad omen. Or a warning of some kind? She pushed the silly notion aside and kept walking.

"This house is awesome," Lucy said in a hushed tone.

"What we can see of it. Watch your step. We don't want to break anything out here. That wouldn't serve our cause at all."

"Good point." Lucy took her phone out and turned on the flashlight. "This should help."

Maggie did the same, helping to guide their path up the steps, toward the front door, where Lucy took the key out of the front pocket of her jeans.

She glanced up at Maggie. "What if Liza and Kira changed the locks and we can't get in?"

"I'll be greatly relieved and will enjoy the sleep of the just."

Lucy slipped the key in the lock and turned it. The door easily opened. "Sorry to dash your last hope, Mag. There's still time to go back to the car. I won't be offended."

Maggie gave the offer some thought. "Since I made it this far, I am curious."

They stepped inside and Lucy found a light switch. A beautiful crystal fixture that hung from the foyer ceiling filled the space with light. Maggie looked down to see classic black and white tile on the floor and ornate white molding on the pale yellow walls and even on the ceiling.

Lucy walked through the foyer and peered into the entrance of the living room, which was framed by large white columns. Maggie looked in the room, too. The shadowy outlines of furniture looked like large sleeping animals.

"Where should we start? This place looks immense."

"We can't stay all night. I think our best bet is to look around Liza's personal space, her bedroom and study, as Ruth suggested."

"That makes sense to me." Lucy turned and started up the long staircase, which had a landing and balcony in the middle, where it curved around toward the second floor.

Paintings on the walls caught Lucy's attention, and Maggie saw her stop to appraise them. "Lucy, please. It's not a museum tour. Let's keep up the pace."

"Right." Lucy turned and took the last steps with more focus. "Let's try this way," she said at the top of the stairs. She turned to the right and Maggie followed. Lucy began peering into doorways all along the hall as she came to them.

"Guest room . . . library . . . some sort of art studio?"

"Kira paints, remember?" Maggie said.

"Oh right. Must be her work space . . . And this must be Kira's bedroom." Lucy stepped aside and Maggie saw a rather messy room, decorated with wall hangings of painted fabric they'd seen in the studio and large paintings in the same style on the walls.

Small tables held an abundance of random objects, seashells, feathers, rocks, African carvings, candles, incense burners, and abstract pottery. The bed was covered with a canopy of more painted fabric and the mattress covered by a tapestry quilt and multicolored pillows.

"Definitely not Liza's space. Keep going."

"Here's Emma's room." Maggie glanced in the next doorway and saw a small bedroom decorated with pink and yellow flowers on the walls, a shelf that held big fluffy toys, and more plastic toys and puzzles on the floor. Against one wall stood a small white bed with rails on each side.

Lucy opened the next door. "Here we are, this one must be Liza's." Maggie followed her in, quickly surrounded by a sophisticated, spare decor, the color scheme shades of blue, gray, and white.

The cream-colored dresser tops and bedside table were knickknack free, except for a few family pictures, a lamp, and a crystal jewelry tray.

Maggie's gaze came to rest on two stuffed animals that sat near the pillows, a large white bear and a smaller one. Totally out of synch with the rest of the decorating.

She glanced at Lucy. "We can look through the dresser drawers. But that seems so . . ."

"I know what you mean. Let's skip that for now." Lucy turned. "There's her study. Let's check the desk. That could be helpful."

Maggie saw a small, adjoining room,

where a desk and bookshelves were arranged under an eave-slanting ceiling.

Lucy was already at the desk and Maggie browsed the bookshelves. "She liked novels and poetry, literary stuff. I thought we'd find a lot of books filled with tips for being a super saleswoman," Maggie said.

"Liza had hidden depths, that's for sure."

"Oh, here's one, *Mover, Shaker, Deal-Maker.* I stand corrected."

Lucy was crouched down, next to a drawer filled with files. She was rifling through the pages and didn't look up. Maggie stepped over to help, but not before noticing a bottom shelf filled with child care titles. *What to Expect When You're Expecting,* followed by what to expect at various stages a child would go through. All the way to college.

"A lot of child care books here, too," Maggie murmured.

"Must be Kira's."

"Yes, must be," Maggie agreed. She stood by the desk and picked up a photo. It looked like it had been taken the past summer, at the beach. It was either Kira or Liza, who sat in the sand with the little girl, surrounded by plastic shovels and buckets. Emma wore a red bathing suit and held her sand-covered hands toward the camera, looking very pleased with herself.

"She is cute. She has the same blue eyes as Kira and Liza. Did you notice?"

"Runs in the family. Lucky girls." Lucy stood up and brushed off her hands. "It's just a lot of bills from the house, utilities and plumbing. Some records from her mother's move to Brookside. There's a file that says 'Emma.' " Lucy took it out and leafed through. "Medical records in here, mostly."

Maggie looked over her shoulder at the papers. "Why does Liza have her niece's medical records?"

"Maybe Kira doesn't have insurance and Liza paid the medical bills. Didn't Suzanne hear that Liza was supporting her sister and niece?" Lucy replied.

"Yes, that's right. I forgot," Maggie said.

"And maybe Kira is just plain bad at record keeping. If her bedroom is any indication of her organizational skills, I'd go with that guess. Liza must have kept track of things for the family. She also has all the papers from their mother's move to Brookside and Ruth's medical records, too."

"That makes sense," Maggie agreed. "She was obviously the responsible one. Should we look through the files and see if there's anything that jumps out? Her bank statements, for instance. Follow the money and

261

all that?"

"Maybe." Lucy didn't seem keen on that idea. The task of sifting through all of Liza's papers was daunting and they couldn't stay here all night. A neighbor was likely to see lights on and know that Kira was away.

Lucy looked up at her. "The problem is, there aren't any bank records here or even credit card bills. Most people do all that online these days. We can't follow the money if there's no paper trail."

"Right. Hadn't thought of that. I'm still in the Dark Ages with invoices, envelopes, and the US Postal Service," Maggie admitted.

Lucy laughed. "It's a long buggy ride into town to mail your bills. But it's only once a month, right?"

"Right . . . Well, what should we do now? I'm starting to think this wasn't a good idea. How would you feel if some stranger came into your bedroom and started sifting through your private papers?"

Lucy frowned. "It is sort of creepy."

"Exactly. We aren't creeps, are we?"

"I try not to be. If I can help it." Lucy took the photo Maggie was holding, glanced at it a moment, and set it on the desk. Then leaned over and pushed the heavy drawer of files closed. "It's stuck, blast."

Lucy gave the drawer a harder shove and

the picture of Emma at the beach flew off the desk and fell to the floor.

"Oh dear." Maggie watched as Lucy gathered up the pieces.

"The frame burst apart. But I don't think anything is broken. Let me see if I can fix it."

"I hope you can." Maggie watched over her shoulder.

Lucy placed the pieces on the desk — the frame, backing, the square of glass and the photo.

"What's this?" She picked up a piece of folded paper from the collection and a small brown envelope.

Maggie thought the paper might have been stuck behind the photo to fill in space. But the envelope definitely looked suspicious.

Lucy carefully unfolded the sheet, handling it by the edges. Her eyes widened.

"Look at this." She showed it to Maggie.

Maggie read the letter aloud, "Keep your mouth shut or you'll be sorry. Think of Emma." She looked up at Lucy. "Someone was threatening Liza."

"Looks like it." Lucy carefully set the note on the desktop. She fished through her knapsack and came up with a plastic bag. "I don't think we should handle it. Finger-prints."

"Yes, right," Maggie said.

Covering her fingers with the plastic, she folded the paper again and put it in the bag. She turned the page over to the blank side. "Look at that."

Maggie wasn't sure she saw anything except for a thin black smudge along the crease of the note. "Someone stepped on it?"

"It was under a windshield wiper. I'm almost sure of it."

Maggie smiled. "Clever girl."

"Not really. I get a lot of parking tickets." Lucy looked up at her. "Maybe this note was left when her car was vandalized. That's what upset her. The threat, not the dam-age."

"Whether it was on the car, or she got it at some other time, she was definitely threatened. Why didn't she tell the police?"

"Maybe she did but the police didn't tell Suzanne?"

Maggie considered the possibility. "I doubt that. I think they assume Suzanne vandalized the car. What's in the envelope?"

"Let's see." Lucy opened the brown enve-lope and took out a small brass key, etched with the number twenty-three. "Looks like a key to a safety deposit box? Or a box at the post office?"

"My money is on a bank. She probably has something important stored there. Something she wanted to preserve in case anything happened to her."

Lucy nodded. "I agree. But how can we find out what that is? We can't just waltz into every bank in town and pretend to be Liza Devereaux."

"No, you can't. Thank goodness for small favors."

They both heard the voice at once. Maggie nearly jumped out of her skin and caught herself from shrieking, just in time. She turned to find Kira standing in the doorway. She held Emma in her arms in a protective embrace.

"What in the world are you doing here? Who let you in? This is just . . . outrageous."

Maggie cleared her throat and tried to stand tall. "I'm sorry we scared you. Your mother gave us the key. She said you were away."

"I came back."

"She promised to let you know we were coming over," Lucy said.

"I haven't heard a word from her. Why would she let you come here in the first place? Looking through my sisters things?

Isn't it enough that someone killed her? That woman, from her office. The zaftig one with the dark hair . . . your friend. I saw you together at the church. And I know the police took her away right after."

Maggie cringed for Suzanne's sake. She'd hate to be called zaftig even more than being thought a murderer. Maggie stepped forward, willing to take some heat.

"Suzanne is our friend. But she didn't kill your sister. We were hoping to find some small clue or shred of evidence that will prove that to the police."

"Or at least, make them look in a new direction." Lucy held out the key. "She hid this behind a photo. It looks like the key to a safety deposit box."

"We thought it might hold a clue to her murder," Maggie added. "There must be a good reason why she hid it."

Kira stared at the key. Emma was squirming and she let her down on Liza's bed. "Liza was secretive. I'm not surprised she hid a key. She had a lot of jewelry. That's what she probably kept at the bank."

Maggie thought that might be true. Just because they hoped for some breakthrough hidden in the box, it didn't necessarily mean it was there.

Across the room, Maggie saw Emma had

crawled toward the pillows and grabbed the stuffed bears, making them talk to each other. Or maybe the big bear was taking care of the little one? Cuddling it?

Lucy seemed about to say something more. But Kira stepped to the door and pulled it open as wide as it would go. "Get out of here. Before I call the police."

That was enough for Maggie. More than enough. "We're leaving. Absolutely. Right this minute."

She started out of the room, glancing back to make sure Lucy had followed. "We truly meant no harm."

"We probably shouldn't have come, but your mother wanted to help us. She suggested it," Lucy insisted as she started down the stairs behind Maggie.

"My mother's not well. The illness affects her mind. You took advantage of her, a grief-struck old woman. I think I'll call the police anyway. You should expect a visit from them."

Maggie didn't answer. She knew nothing she could say would help and part of her didn't even blame Kira for being angry.

Lucy was more optimistic. "Well, good night. Sorry again . . . By the way, your artwork is very interesting."

"Get out of here! Now!" Kira had followed them to the landing and shouted over the balcony.

Maggie thought she heard the crystals in the light fixture quiver but she didn't wait to find out for sure.

"And you'd better leave that key!"

"It's on the side table in the foyer. We had no intention of keeping it," Maggie called back as she headed out the front door. Lucy followed close behind and quickly slammed the door shut.

They hustled off the porch, down the path, and climbed in Maggie's car.

Maggie didn't pause to clip her seat belt or even take a breath. She started the car and pulled down the street, tires screeching, afraid that they would soon hear sirens and never make it home tonight.

"Maggie, slow down. No one's chasing us."

"Not yet." Maggie turned to Lucy. "She was very upset. I think she will call the police."

"Maybe she'll call her mother first, to check our story, and Ruth will talk her out of it. It's still Ruth's house and it was her idea for us to go there."

"Kira obviously doesn't see it that way."

"Obviously. But she would have never

268

known about that key if we hadn't found it."

"Don't expect a thank you card. I wonder what she'll find in the box. Just jewelry?"

"She'll never tell us. But maybe Ruth will?"

Maggie hadn't thought about that. "Wait . . . you never showed her the note."

"Oh blast. I forgot. All that yelling. She distracted me."

Maggie had been distracted, too. "We can't just give it to the police. They'll ask where we found it."

"I know. But the police should know someone was harassing Liza." Lucy turned to Maggie. "Let's think about it. Maybe Dana or Suzanne will have an idea."

CHAPTER 9

Suzanne had not left the house except for dire emergencies, like picking up Ryan after his fight at school Monday morning. Two days housebound would not bother most people. But Suzanne was used to being in constant motion, moving from one task to the next on her to-do list. She felt trapped in the house, hiding out from reporters who lingered, hoping to catch an interview or a photo. And trapped by her own reluctance to show her face in the village, knowing that everyone was talking about her.

By Wednesday, she was not only restless but nearly screamed after Kevin replaced a few blown lightbulbs in the bathroom fixture, and she saw the true and unsightly state of her hair. Not to mention her eyebrows. But she had learned from bitter experience — never, *ever* pluck during times of distress. A foolproof formula for disaster.

Put the tweezer down and step away from the mirror, Suzanne. No one will get hurt.

But professional eyebrow aid right now would be tricky. There was always a long wait at Sonya's Brow Bar. She didn't want to run into a crowd there. Hair was the priority. She needed a cut and blow out, immediately.

She normally visited the salon at least once a week, convinced that the cost was a valid business expense. Though the accountant who did her taxes did not agree. She couldn't see why not; she definitely sold more houses when she looked and felt her best. No question about that.

Fearful of reporters, Suzanne planned her escape carefully. Her hairdresser, Jillian, was able to fit her in for a red-eye appointment at half past seven. The salon was just down the street from Maggie's shop and her friends planned to meet there at nine.

Maggie and Lucy had been so cryptic in their messages last night, Suzanne couldn't tell what had gone on during their visit with Ruth Devereaux. She was dying to hear if Ruth had told them anything that would help her sticky situation. But she'd have to wait a little longer to find out.

Suzanne slipped into the salon right on time, relieved to see it was practically empty,

271

except for Jillian and the girl at the shampoo sink. After a quick wash, she sat back in the big chair at Jillian's station, feeling cozy under the black silky drape as the chair was pumped up. Jillian had been her hairstylist for nearly ten years. Suzanne thought of her as a friend and practically a therapist. One who got to the point quickly.

Jillian glided a big comb through Suzanne's wet hair. "I can't believe what you've been going through. The police in this town are totally nuts. Give me a break, okay?"

"It's been rough," Suzanne admitted. "I feel so bad for my family. Especially the kids."

"I'll bet. It's awful about Liza Devereaux. Don't get me wrong. What a way to go. She used to come in here once in a while. I never did her hair but I knew who she was. But for the police to say that you did it? That's just insane."

"Thanks, Jillian. The last few days have been a nightmare."

"You poor thing. Do you have a good lawyer?"

"Helen Forbes. She's great." *But even the sharpest lawyer in the world can't make evidence disappear,* Suzanne wanted to say. *Or make the police leave you alone if they're intent on pinning you for a crime.*

"Good for you. That's the whole game." Jillian pinned up a chunk of hair and began to snip. "What are we doing today? Just a trim?"

"At least an inch. Nice blunt cut."

"You got it." Suzanne watched her in the mirror, her intent game face as she handled the scissors.

"Thanks for seeing me so early."

"No problem." Jillian shrugged, her gaze fixed on Suzanne's hair. "I don't mind the early shift. I get out at two and save on sitters."

"Nice." Suzanne saw the photos of Jillian's children, a girl and a boy, elementary school age, tucked in the rim of the mirror. She was about to ask about them, when Jillian turned sharply toward the door.

Suzanne followed her gaze. It was Beth Birney, from her office.

"I didn't know Beth Birney comes here. Is she your client?"

"I thought she was. A real regular. Until she went MIA and I caught her walking out of Hair Spa. I hear she's there every day for a wash and blow out."

Hair Spa was a new, hip salon down the street that touted cutting edge, organic products and sleek, high-tech equipment.

Suzanne had heard the hair dryers merely hummed, and their specialty, a hot coconut oil hair wrap, reportedly left your hair smooth and silky for weeks.

Beth's hair had been looking extra shiny and coiffed lately. No wonder.

"Every day at Hair Spa? There's a pricey routine," Suzanne said. "But she did tell me she's trying to . . . socialize more."

"Good for her. But that place is a rip-off. Hot air is hot air. And I can smash a coconut on your head, if that makes you feel better."

Suzanne smiled. "That's okay. I had some fruit with breakfast."

Jillian shrugged. "I guess the Spa is booked and we're sloppy seconds. I hope she isn't scheduled with me. She's a really cheap tipper. I am so done with that, know what I mean?"

Suzanne didn't know what to say. She liked Beth but didn't doubt the bookkeeper was sparing with gratuities. Gossip was always part of the beauty treatment at Jillian's station.

"You don't have to answer if you don't want to. . . . Have people been talking about me, Jillian?" she asked in a small voice.

The hairdresser met her gaze in the mirror. She'd finished the cut and smoothed a lotion over Suzanne's damp strands.

"Not really." Suzanne could tell she wasn't being entirely honest. "There are always a few who love to get nasty. Who cares? By next week, people will be talking about someone else — a face-lift or a divorce. You'll be old news in no time."

Suzanne tried to take some comfort in the reply. Old news because the police had found out who really killed Liza, she hoped.

"The best revenge is looking good. We've got that covered," Jillian promised.

"Absolutely." Suzanne's reply was drowned out in the hair dryer's mighty roar.

When Suzanne's hair was finished, Jillian spun the chair to show her the style from every angle.

"You're an artist. I'm a new woman." Suzanne slipped an extra generous tip under the brush on the countertop. "Thanks so much. See you soon."

Jillian leaned over and gave her a hug. The pleasant scent of hair products filled Suzanne's head. "Hang in there. This is all going to work out for you. I know it."

"Thanks. I know it will, too." Suzanne was determined not to voice any doubt.

She headed to the front desk to settle her bill, passing Beth, who was already in a chair, discussing her hair needs with a stylist.

Suzanne smiled and offered a small wave, hoping to scoot by without conversation. But Beth jumped up from her seat, the black salon covering flapping as she ran over and smothered Suzanne in a hug.

"Suzanne . . . you poor thing. How are you holding up? How's everyone at home?"

Suzanne's body stiffened, startled by the greeting. She wasn't sure if she felt grateful for the exuberant concern. Or insulted by all the sympathy. Beth had to think she was guilty — or at least, in very deep trouble — if she felt that bad. Did everyone in the office feel that way?

"I'm good. We're all fine." Suzanne forced a bright smile. "Keeping busy. Harry told me to work from home."

"I know. We discussed it. You need to be with your family now. This is a challenging time."

"It is," Suzanne conceded.

"It will all be over soon." Beth patted her hand but didn't smile. Suzanne thought she could have. In a quieter voice, she added, "You'll get your usual check this week. Don't worry."

Suzanne had hoped that would be the case when Harry told her to stay home, but she'd been too stressed to ask.

"That's good news, thanks."

"I told Harry, 'It's the right thing to do.' " Beth gave her a meaningful look and Suzanne knew the office manager had been her champion. Then Beth said, "Innocent until proven guilty, right?"

Suzanne's smile froze. "That's what they tell me." She pulled away from Beth's cloying grasp. "Nice to see you, Beth. Have a good hairdo."

"You take care. I'll be in touch." Beth squeezed Suzanne's arm again, then trotted back to her hairdresser. Suzanne paid her bill and grabbed her coat off the rack.

She buttoned the black trench coat to her chin and flipped up the collar, but stuck the baseball cap in her purse. The dark glasses would have to suffice. No sense ruining her hairstyle, which had not come cheap.

She looked through the salon's glass door and checked the street twice, in both directions. No signs of stalking reporters or TV news vans. Suzanne didn't entirely trust that was true, but decided to make a run for it. She swung open the door and did a speed walk down the street, her head ducked down, her gaze constantly scanning.

She reached the knitting shop and pulled the door open, then jumped inside and let out a long, relieved breath.

Maggie and Phoebe stood behind the counter. Lucy sat on the love seat nearby, already knitting. "Hey, Suzanne . . . Are you okay?"

Maggie looked concerned, too. "Was someone chasing you again?"

"Let's put it this way: just because you can't see them, it doesn't mean they're not there. Trust me on this." She knew she sounded crazy, but it was true.

"You didn't have to trouble yourself. We would have come to your place again," Maggie reminded her.

"That's all right. I had to get out. House arrest was getting to me."

And, sitting there all day alone, imagining how much worse it would be if I was in jail for real. The worst case scenario was never far from her thoughts lately, hovering like a dark cloud, but Suzanne forced a smile. She didn't want to start the visit on that note.

She slipped off her raincoat and took a seat in an armchair next to Lucy.

"It was worth the risk. Your hair looks great," Phoebe gave her a thumbs up, the magenta streak in her own dark hair catching the light.

"Thanks. Looking good is the best revenge. My hairdresser told me that."

"It's true." Lucy was almost done with the yellow baby jacket. Suzanne knew she could have been knitting while sitting at home the past few days. It would have done her good to feel productive, and even relieved some stress. She had tried but hadn't been able to concentrate.

"I hope it's some revenge. Even if it isn't the absolute best. I was just totally dissed by a coworker. Beth Birney, the office manager. She's usually so nice. She acted all sympathetic and supportive. But I'm sure she thinks I did it. I bet they all do."

"That's not right. Sounds to me like any one of them could have been framed with Liza's murder, instead of you," Lucy insisted.

"That's true, Lucy. Too bad for me I was the lucky winner." Before Suzanne could say more, the door swung open and Dana came in. "Sorry I'm late. Did I miss anything?"

"Suzanne just got here. People in her office think she's guilty," Maggie said.

"I'm not surprised. People are so quick to judge," Dana said. "It's up to us to show them that they're wrong."

Suzanne smiled a thank-you. Dana wore a maize-colored shawl she'd knit for herself last fall and pushed it aside as she sat next to Lucy on the love seat. Suzanne had always admired the shawl, though she would have chosen a brighter color than the mild wheat color, which seemed to be Dana's signature.

"Let's show them all. The sooner the better." Suzanne turned to Maggie. "Did Ruth tell you anything that would help me? I hope, I hope?"

She wanted to hear the whole story, but needed the punch line first.

"A mixed bag, I'd have to say," Maggie replied. "She hates Nick Sutton. We already knew that. She said he pulled Liza down, ruined her opportunities. She said he was desperate for money and made a claim for Liza's estate as soon as she died. That's why she was so enraged to see him at the memorial."

"He had some nerve to go there, all things considered," Dana said as she took out her knitting and put on her reading glasses.

"We suspected that. But it was good to hear Ruth confirm it," Lucy pointed out. "I've been thinking, what if there was some way to prove he came to the office to ask her for money last week and she refused? The police would have to admit he had clear motive to kill her."

"I found out something about him, too."

Dana had taken out her knitting but hadn't started working yet. "Jack asked around about Sutton for us. Turns out, in addition to being a gambler, he's recently gotten into loan sharking. Helping his down and out gambler friends, I guess. At less than friendly interest rates."

"I don't get it. Why does he need money if he's got enough to loan it out?" Suzanne was confused.

"Good question," Lucy replied. "I didn't get it at first either. But you have to figure that even a compulsive gambler like Sutton is winning some of the time. Instead of using his extra cash to pay his debts to bookies and the like, he's using it to make even more money by handing out short-term loans at sky-high interest rates. Probably hoping he can make enough from the loans to pay his debts down faster. Before the shady types he's dealing with lose patience with him."

"That's right, Lucy. That's pretty much his scheme, and his sideline worked for a while. But Jack says that the real professionals in that business don't like freelancers. They not only closed his shop, but must be pressing him for the profits he stole from their business."

"Scary," Phoebe said. "That's like serious

281

organized crime you see in the movies."

"Serious enough to leave him with one arm in a sling and walking with a cane at the memorial service," Dana pointed out.

"When I saw him at our office last week, he was bandage free," Suzanne recalled.

"How do Jack's police friends know all this?" Lucy asked.

"They talk. Someone who works in Sutton's restaurant was brought in for using stolen credit cards, so he traded information about Sutton for a lesser charge."

"So now the police are after Sutton, too, for loan-sharking?" Maggie asked.

"They could be. But it's hard to prove. His customers are reluctant to come forward and make formal complaints." Dana spread her knitting across her lap.

"Understandably." Suzanne wondered how this information could help her. She looked at Lucy, gazing into space, her knitting hanging slack in her hands. Suzanne could practically hear the wheels turning.

"So, desperate to save his skin, Sutton went to Liza for help, but she wasn't in the office," Lucy began. "Maybe he eventually found her, but she refused to help him. So he can't pay his debt and gets beat up, as a warning. He thinks his goose is cooked, but he figures out how to kill Liza and blame

Suzanne. By Friday morning, Liza is dead. They're not officially divorced, so he makes a claim on her estate, thinking he's saved."

"Wow, Lucy. That was impressive." Suzanne sat up and nearly clapped.

"When was Liza's car vandalized? Do you remember, Suzanne?" Maggie had come out from behind the counter and stood by Suzanne's chair. "Ruth talked about it and said Liza was unduly upset, and we think we know why."

Suzanne thought back. "I think it was Thursday morning, the day she died. The police would love to tie me to that car damage. But that's one piece of their argument that doesn't fit. Her car was vandalized sometime between eight-thirty and ten. I didn't get back to town until one."

"This might help, too." Lucy reached into her knitting bag. "We found it last night. It's a note that may have been on her car. I think it's from Sutton."

Lucy handed Suzanne the plastic bag and she read the letter out loud. " 'Keep your mouth shut or you'll be sorry. Think of Emma.' " Suzanne looked up. "What did he want her to keep her mouth shut about?"

Lucy shrugged. "Maybe he threatened her about giving him money and she was going to tell the police? Or maybe he told her the real reason he needed the money but knew if she told anyone, he'd be in even more hot water."

"So you think Sutton vandalized her car to scare her into helping him?"

"I think it fits." Lucy nodded. "When she still wouldn't give in, he put Plan B into action."

"Kill Liza and frame me," Suzanne said.

"That part was trickier," Dana conceded. "He could have known about the allergy and even the office rivalry. And could have gained access somehow to plant the drink. He knows people with questionable skill sets."

"But how about the computer files? I can't see him going that far into the weeds. Though he could have hired someone to do that for him." Maggie had set up her yarn swift on the table and fitted a skein of yarn on the contraption. Suzanne could tell that Maggie wasn't convinced.

Phoebe was still behind the counter, working on her laptop. Suzanne wasn't even sure she'd been listening. Phoebe suddenly looked up and glanced around at her friends.

"I know Sutton is totally shady and pathetic, and he would probably kill his own granny for five bucks. But something about this theory doesn't work for me, sadly."

Lucy turned to her. "What is that, Phoebe?"

"Well . . . last I heard, Mafia hit men don't go around poisoning people with diet drinks. They have more direct methods."

Lucy seemed unhappy that her theory had been challenged. "Wait a second. A Soviet spy was killed not too long ago with a piece of poisoned sushi. It was all over the news. You can't be more professional than the KGB."

Suzanne was unhappy to see a hole poked in Lucy's theory, too, but Phoebe had a point. "Sorry, Lucy. As much as we want to believe Sutton did it, it doesn't quite fit. Like those thousand-dollar designer shoes that are half price, and then another twenty per cent off with a coupon. But when you try them on, your toes fold in half? You want to buy them so bad, but you've got to leave them."

Phoebe leaned over the counter. "You'd really pay four hundred dollars for a pair of shoes?"

"Nice math, Phoebe. But what if Sutton had help. Maybe even someone in the office," Dana said.

Suzanne had wondered about that, too, and was about to speculate aloud about his possible inside man . . . or woman, when Lucy waved the plastic bag that contained the note.

"I still think the police need to see this. Maybe Sutton didn't leave it. Maybe Liza was being threatened by someone else, who isn't even on our radar. But a note like this could lead to her murderer."

Suzanne tried not to bite on the tempting nugget of optimism. She didn't want to get hopeful again and disappointed later. "Where did you get it? Ruth Devereaux?"

Maggie and Lucy exchanged glances. "Not exactly," Maggie said. Suzanne could see she felt self-conscious about explaining how it had all come about. "We were talking to her for a while, about how we were sure that you're innocent. She said she wanted to help find the real killer. So she gave us a key to her house, where Liza and Kira have been living. She told us we were free to go there and look around, in case the police missed something."

"It was all her idea, honestly," Lucy added quickly.

"It was?" Dana blinked with surprise. "And you went there last night?"

Lucy nodded, her stitching speeding up a bit, Suzanne noticed. "It seemed a wild goose chase and we were about to leave.

But we found that note and a key to a safety deposit box hidden behind a picture frame."

Maggie fitted another skein on the wooden arms and tightened the apparatus to the table. "Kira was supposed to be in Maine. Or we would have never gone inside. But she came home earlier than Ruth expected and had a fit when she found us there. Not that I blame her one bit."

"The house is still in Ruth's name." Lucy sounded as if someone was arguing with her. "It's her property and she gave us permission. Kira didn't see it that way."

Dana still looked shocked by the story. "You're lucky she didn't call the police when she saw the lights on and knew someone was inside."

"We are lucky. But she must have realized burglars usually don't drive around in a dumpy Subaru with a bumper sticker that says, 'I'd rather be knitting,' " Lucy pointed out.

Suzanne was surprised by the story, too, and felt genuinely grateful. "Wow, you guys really go the limit. I can't believe you went to all that trouble for me. What did Kira say about the note? Did she have any idea who wrote it?"

Lucy winced. "I forgot to show it to her. She was making such a fuss, all we could think of was getting out of there."

Dana started knitting again. "Maybe that was for the best. She might have held on to it. It sounds like she thinks Suzanne is guilty and she may not want the police to look further."

"Good point. I didn't think of that." Suzanne turned to Maggie. "Can you pass it to Charles?"

"I'm sorry, Suzanne, but I doubt that would work out." Maggie's gaze was fixed on the yarn swift.

Suzanne didn't like the sound of her reply. "I hope you didn't have a fight with him about my . . . situation. I know it's nothing personal. He's just doing his job. Though, he could do it a little differently, from my perspective."

Maggie looked up but didn't answer.

"I think you should give it to your attorney," Dana said. "Let her bring it to the police. She can say it's from a source who wants to remain anonymous right now, for their own safety. The threat is enough to raise questions. Reasonable doubt and all that?"

"Good idea, Dana. But please don't use any courtroom talk. I'm not ready for that. And I'd look like a pumpkin in an orange jumpsuit."

Dana looked sorry for the slip. "It will never come to that. Please don't worry."

Maggie was gathering up the balls of yarn she'd rolled with the swift. Suzanne guessed a class was starting soon. "I agree. Don't fret. It will never come to orange outfits. Give that note to your attorney. She'll know what to do. Tell her we'll sign a statement if she wants our word on how and where we found it."

"I'm good with that plan, too. Though happy to remain an anonymous source for now." Lucy handed her the note and Suzanne slipped the plastic bag into her purse.

Was this slip of paper her golden ticket? Was it enough to send the police looking in a new direction?

Two women walked into the shop, both in their thirties and dressed in leggings and big tunic tops that stretched to cover pregnant bellies. Maggie greeted them cheerfully. She stood up, holding the basket filled with pastel balls of yarn.

"I'm almost ready. Please take a seat at the table in the back. I'll be with you in a moment."

"What to Knit When You're Expecting?" Lucy asked, naming a popular class.

"That's right. The project is a simple hat, but I'm going to tell them about our charity goal and see if anyone wants to help." She started toward the back of the shop. "I think they'll be sympathetic to the cause."

Suzanne had to agree. Motherhood was definitely a wide and level playing field. Once you were a member you felt a bond with mothers of all kinds, no matter how different the women were from you.

As Maggie got busy with her class, her friends headed off to start their workday. Suzanne wished she was going to her office, too. She promised herself she wouldn't procrastinate, or worry, but would do some real work once she got home.

She walked outside with Lucy and Dana, accepting their hugs and words of encouragement as they were about to part.

Lucy's dogs had been waiting on the porch and she held the leashes short once she untied them, to keep the friendly canines from shedding on everyone's clothes. "When are you going to talk to Helen about the note?" she asked.

"I'm going to her office right now. This could be important."

"Good luck, Suzanne. I hope it shakes the police up a bit. They know you have a solid alibi for the car vandalism." Dana met her gaze with a serious expression.

Suzanne felt excited and anxious, too. She

didn't want to get her hopes up, but the note was a new development. Maybe Helen could spin it just the right way? Pushing the police to look for new leads?

She drove down Main Street toward Helen's office, which was near the harbor, taking deep breaths to settle her nerves. A white car pulled out from a space without warning and Suzanne hit the brakes just in time. She glanced at the license plate and a lump jumped into her throat.

It was Liza's car. Suzanne could tell from the license plates. AMEYMOXI. The car suddenly slowed and pulled into a parking spot. Suzanne glanced into the car as she passed by. She saw Kira behind the wheel and Emma in back, in a big car seat.

The sight of Kira at the wheel of Liza's car was totally unnerving. The only difference between them was the way they dressed and Kira's shaggy haircut. But today Liza's twin wore a plain tan raincoat and had tied her hair back, as Liza often did. Suzanne felt as if she'd just seen a ghost.

Maggie called Charles around noon, but he didn't call her back. It was not a good sign. Even if he was totally overwhelmed with a case, he always managed to send a text or two.

291

She didn't feel good about his silence, and a few times during the day, considered trying again.

But by closing time, she had not made another call to him or even sent a text message. As she straightened up the shop and closed out the cash register, she thought of him again and felt sad and uneasy. But there didn't seem to be anything she could do. Or should do. If he wanted to keep his distance during this investigation, maybe that was the best route right now. She'd live with it and try to sort things out later — when Liza's real killer was found and Suzanne's name was cleared.

A heavy knock on the shop door broke the spell of her rambling thoughts. She'd already turned the sign to SORRY, RESTING OUR NEEDLES. COME BACK SOON! But it could have been a customer. Some got very desperate when they'd planned a night of knitting and had run out of the yarn they needed.

"Coming, one minute," she called out.

Her expression set in what her friends called her "shopkeeper's face," Maggie opened the door to find Charles. She felt a catch in her breath.

"It's you. Come in. I'm glad you stopped by. I called you this morning. Maybe you didn't get the message."

Already giving him excuses? He's the one who should be explaining, she reminded herself.

"Hello, Maggie. I saw the light on. I need to talk to you."

Charles walked in, his hands jammed into the pockets of his long, loose raincoat. He wore a hat with a brim, a brown canvas fedora with a leather band, the type men seldom wore these days. She called it his detective's hat, though never out loud. It made his features look sharper and his expression even more serious. His dark eyes peered out at her from under the brim.

Being well mannered, a trait Maggie valued, he always took his hat off indoors. But tonight, he kept it on. That did not bode well.

He stared down at her. "You and Lucy broke into the Devereaux house? What in the world were you thinking?!"

He wasn't yelling. Exactly. But his words had the same effect. Maggie took a step back, alarmed. "It was Ruth Devereaux's suggestion. Her name is still on the deed. She gave us the key and permission to go inside."

She nearly added, ". . . and look around."

But caught herself. The detail would not help.

"Ruth Devereaux is an old, possibly senile woman in a nursing home. Overcome by the loss of her daughter. Do you really believe she's capable of a rational decision about such a thing?"

"She is grieving," Maggie conceded. "But she seemed very sharp otherwise. And it's assisted living. Not a nursing home. That's very different."

Charles pulled off his hat and tossed it on the counter. A gesture of frustration more than etiquette, she realized.

"Don't quibble with me, Maggie. That is not the point and you know it."

She bowed her head and nodded. "I do. And I get your point, honestly. But we didn't feel as if we were trespassing." Maybe a little, she thought, recalling her pangs of conscience. But he didn't need to know that. "We certainly didn't break in. I don't know who told you that."

"Kira Devereaux. She made a full report. You and your pal came this close to being picked up and charged with breaking and entering." He formed his index finger and thumb into a tiny pinch of space. "A lot of crooks get their hands on house keys. That doesn't make it all right, or lawful, to enter private property."

She hadn't thought of that. It was probably true. She persisted pleading her case. "Ruth promised to call Kira and let her know. And she told us that Kira was away. We thought the house was empty. We would have never gone in otherwise."

He stared at her a moment. Then looked down and shook his head. When he looked up again, he was yelling. "I don't know why you went in at all — No, I do know. That's what makes me so frustrated. After I've asked you time and again to stay out of police business. You just won't respect my wishes."

Wishes? More like orders, she wanted to say. But knew that was the wrong direction to take.

"I do consider your feelings, Charles. I don't mean to disrespect you, honestly. But this time is different. It's about Suzanne, and I'm so torn, weighing one priority against the other."

He didn't answer for a moment. She hoped her honest admission had softened his anger, just a bit?

Then he said, "I can see where I come in. Second place, at best. I just don't know, Maggie. I just don't know —"

"What don't you know?" she cut in.

"I would take myself off this case, the way you asked me to. But I can see now you still wouldn't let it go. You and your friends would keep snooping around and compromising the investigation. I'd be the dupe, sitting it out on the sidelines."

Maggie wanted to tell him he was wrong. That's not how it would go. But the words wouldn't come. She knew in her heart he was right. She and her friends wouldn't give up until the real culprit was found and Suzanne was shown to be innocent.

"It's hard not to help Suzanne. I've never seen her like this. She's so upset. Ashamed to even show her face in town."

She could tell from his reaction her bid for sympathy had backfired. "That's how guilty people act, Maggie. Apparently you don't know as much about this business as you think you do."

His cold comment made her angry. Not the slight to her. That didn't matter. But the insinuation about Suzanne. That was the part she could not abide.

"Suzanne is totally and completely innocent. I know enough to guarantee that the police department will be very embarrassed when it turns out that the professional investigators on this case didn't even entertain the theory that she's been framed by bits and pieces of circumstantial evidence."

She could see her words had stung, and she felt sorry. But she had to be honest. She had to say what she knew in her heart was true.

He pulled on his hat and stepped back, his expression blank and hard. "I knew you'd argue with me. It was foolish to come here. I guess there's nothing more for us to talk about." He turned and headed for the door. "Good-bye, Maggie," he called over his shoulder.

Maggie was stunned. She couldn't reply. She couldn't say good-bye to him. Not in such a final-sounding way.

CHAPTER 10

After visiting her attorney, Suzanne had done her best to carry on a normal day — a quick, surreptitious stop at the supermarket, some work for the office at home, chauffeuring the kids to sports practice and music lessons, then picking everyone up again, and cooking dinner.

All the while, one eye was on her phone, checking for a message from Helen Forbes. The lawyer had promised to let Suzanne know the minute she heard if the police were taking any action on the newly discovered note.

It had been a challenge not to reveal Maggie's and Lucy's identities. Suzanne had simply said the note was passed to her by "people on my side" and assured Helen they would come forward if needed.

"It's the real thing. I swear. It was found in Liza's belongings."

She thought Helen was going to ask more

questions, or maybe even balk about handing it in. But to Suzanne's great relief, she accepted the bit of evidence, and promised she would do what she could.

"I can't guarantee the police will take this seriously. But if we ever go to trial — and I'm not saying this will go that far, so don't get that terrified expression on your face — but if we do, we can always say that the investigation neglected to explore all possible leads, and that would poke a nice hole in the prosecution's argument."

More legal jargon and courtroom scenarios. Suzanne felt a rash coming on. Talk about strange allergies.

"I understand, Helen. How will you know if they follow through?"

"I'll know, don't worry." Helen offered her calm, confident smile and Suzanne felt reassured. At least at that moment.

As the hours passed with no word from the attorney, Suzanne started to worry. She'd pinned her hopes on this new clue, but what if it didn't make any difference at all?

Then where will I be? She didn't want her thoughts to go in that direction. She moved through her day in fear that the police might be at her doorstep again at any moment, announcing some new bit of damning evidence they had discovered.

That evening, she sat next to Kevin, her knitting in her lap as she blindly stared at the TV. She suddenly realized that a basketball game was on and she hadn't even noticed.

"I'm watching sports with you. How did that happen?"

He glanced at her. "I thought it was strange. But I didn't want to say anything. Are you all right?"

She shrugged. "It was hard to be in town today. I feel like everyone's talking about me. I met Beth Birney in the hair salon. You know what she had the nerve to say?" Suzanne paused. " 'Innocent until proven guilty.' I know she thought she was being nice. But I'm sure she thinks I'm guilty and it's just a matter of time before I'm locked up forever."

Kevin's gaze had been fixed on the players stomping up and down the court. He suddenly turned to her.

"Don't even say that, honey. Don't even say those words out loud. And don't pay any attention to people like that. What does she know?" He put his arm around her shoulder and pulled her close. "Nothing like that is ever going to happen. We just have to grit our teeth and get through this."

She nodded and took a breath, trying not to cry. "I know. Guess I'll just stick around the house a little longer until it's over. I don't know what else to do."

"That note your friends found is going to be something big. I have a good feeling."

"I hope so." She leaned her head on Kevin's chest and sighed.

Her husband was such an optimist. He always made her see the positive side when life looked bleak.

"You're such a good person, Suzanne. So sweet and loving and nice to everybody. Such a great mom and a terrific wife. You are not going to be arrested. It's just not going to happen."

Suzanne was touched. "That's so sweet, Kev. I love you so much."

"I love you, too. You know I do." They sat quietly a moment. Suzanne took some calming breaths, feeling a bit better about things. Then he said, very quietly, "Would you make me some popcorn for the second half?"

She pulled away and stared at him. Talk about killing the mood. "Did you really just say that? Really?"

He stared back sheepishly. Her phone buzzed with a text, saving him from a stronger scolding. Suzanne was surprised to see the message was from Dana.

Jack heard Sutton was just brought in for questioning. Good news for our team.

Suzanne sat back, her eyes squeezed closed. "Thank you. Thank you. Thank you," she murmured to some mysterious power above. When she opened them again, Kevin was watching her.

"Good news?"

"Liza's sleazy, not-quite-former husband is being questioned by the police."

"Sounds good to me."

"Fingers crossed." She showed him her crossed fingers as she jumped off the couch. "I do think we need some popcorn for the second half."

Kevin went to bed right after the game. Suzanne stayed up, trolling the multiple listings on her laptop, looking for properties that might appeal to a few hard to please clients. Some of them just loved looking . . . and looking. But she had to act as if they would buy something eventually. *If I ever get back to work again.*

She was really waiting for further word from Helen or Dana, about the fate of Nick Sutton. Finally, at nearly one AM, another text came through. This time, from her attorney:

Sorry, Suzanne. Sutton was released.

Highly unlikely he was able to plant the drink, unless he had help.

Forensics say now the toxins would break down within twenty-four hours and not be potent enough to kill. That's our new timeline. Will explain more tomorrow. Call me.

Suzanne wanted to scream and throw her phone across the room. But she held tight to her temper. She was too tired for an explosion and could not afford a new phone right now. No way.

She dragged herself up to her room and crawled under the quilt. On the other side of the bed, Kevin slept peacefully. She lay back, tears squeezing out the corners of her eyes. She knew she wasn't going to sleep a wink.

Maggie set out early Thursday morning, before she would be needed in the shop. The low clouds and nickel-colored sky matched her mood perfectly. She passed through the big iron gates and slowly drove down the gravel drive, under the tall trees, heading for the far section of headstones.

It was an old cemetery, established when the area was first settled, over two hundred years ago. The granite markers near the entrance were covered with moss, cracked and crumbling around the edges, the inscriptions faded, as if the stones had lost their power to remember, like old people do. Leaning to one side, struggling against the weight of time passing.

The timing was uncanny. What were the chances she and Charles would have such an awful falling out the day before the anniversary of her husband Bill's passing? On this day, Maggie always visited the cemetery and left flowers on the grave, every year since, without fail.

She had brought a few garden tools, a watering can, and three small pots of mums, dark red, burnt orange, and yellow. Bill had loved to work in the garden almost as much as she did. She had taken for granted the long afternoons they'd toiled side by side, weeding and planting. A satisfying pastime that didn't feel like hard work, though it often was. Afterward, she'd cook a good dinner and they'd relax at home, too tired to go anywhere.

Charles was a sailor, not a gardener. She never thought she would enjoy being out on the water all day, but the long, sunny afternoons and warm, breezy evenings, where the sky and sea seemed one, had opened up a whole new world. She'd taken their time together for granted, too, she realized. Now consigned to the memory box, along with the rest.

She found the grave easily. She knew the way by now. She knelt down, pulled on garden gloves, and picked up the hand rake. Then tugged at weeds and dead vegetation of some former offering. Geraniums on his birthday?

Once the patch in front of the headstone was clear, she dug three holes, filled them with water, and carefully planted the mums. Then she sat back and brushed the stone with her gloved hand. William James Messina. The date he was born and the date he'd died, etched in her heart.

She closed her eyes and said a prayer. Then with her eyes open, she spoke to him. Not out loud, but inside, though she was sure he could hear her.

Bill . . . I need your help. What have I done? Is there something wrong with me? Do I want to be alone forever, living on your memory? I know that you, of all people, would want me to be happy. To have companionship. To have love. But I messed things up. Big time. Maybe I did it on purpose. Maybe I secretly prefer to be a solitary creature and I've purposely sabotaged things with Charles. Maybe I'm afraid of being hurt again, of losing someone I love. So I pushed him away, to get it over with.

It's positively pathological. Who else will ever put up with me? The odds were slim enough before he showed up. Next to nothing now, I'd say.

Maybe you even sent Charles my way, if such a thing is possible. And now you must be as frustrated with me as he is.

Please tell me what to do? You always had such sound advice.

She knew that Bill would not answer. Not in the conventional way. But she closed her eyes and pictured him, his gentle smile and soft eyes, amused at her foibles. Most of the time.

After a long moment, Maggie took a breath and came to her feet. She still didn't know what to do, but she did feel a certain peace. The right choice would come to her.

She gathered her things and headed for her car. As she placed the gardening supplies in the hatch, she noticed a woman standing alone at a graveside only a few rows away.

Instead of the traditional headstone, Maggie saw a statue of an angel marking the spot. The woman looked forlorn, her eyes closed and shoulders sagging. She whisked a strand of hair, or maybe a tear, off her cheek, then crouched to drop a bouquet of pink roses on the ground.

306

As the mourner turned away from the statue, Maggie recognized her — Claire Prentiss, the wife of Suzanne's boss at the realty company. Claire walked toward a parked car, climbed in, and drove away.

Maggie got behind the wheel of her car and headed for the gates. She had to pass the statue and paused to read the inscription: CHELSEA JANE PRENTISS. The date she was born, about fifteen years ago. The year she died, only two years more. Maggie felt a pang. The ultimate tragedy, to lose a child so young. She didn't know much about the couple, but they had endured a great heartbreak, one powerful enough to break up even the strongest marriage.

She wondered if Suzanne knew about this sad page in Harry's history. Perhaps this was the real reason he had not left his wife for Liza Devereaux.

Suzanne didn't feel much better when she woke up Thursday morning, but was quickly swept up in the daily rush of making breakfast, packing lunches, finding lost loose-leaf binders and lacrosse sticks.

When she'd told Kevin that Sutton was released without charges, she could see that he was disappointed, too. But he quickly rallied, offering her a comforting hug as he headed off to work.

"Don't worry, babe. Maybe they can't pin it on Sutton. But that note made the police take a second look at things, right? They must see someone else is involved."

Suzanne wasn't so sure. Maybe the police thought the car vandalism and murder were separate situations. Or maybe they now thought she had some reason to tell Liza to keep her mouth shut and had left the note at some other time and location.

But she nodded anyway. "Sure . . . they must be taking a new look at things. Helen says they have to now."

She clung to that slim hope as she kissed her husband good-bye, drove the kids to school, and pretended for their sake it was just an ordinary day.

All the while, she heard a clock ticking and wondered if the police were tightening their net. Coming for her soon.

After the drop-off, Suzanne swung through the village. She decided to stop at the knitting shop, even though her friends were gathering that night for their meeting.

When they heard Sutton was let go, Maggie and Phoebe would give her a dose of sympathy and another cup of coffee. She needed that.

She pulled into a space near the shop and

suddenly noticed the familiar white Mercedes parked in the driveway of Maggie's shop. Kira stood at the back and took a brown carton out of the hatch. She slammed the back shut, then opened the rear passenger side door and leaned in toward Emma's car seat.

Suzanne grabbed her purse, got out of her car, and quickly walked up the drive. Her boots made a crunching sound on the gravel that startled Kira.

"Listen . . . I know you hate me. I know you don't even want to talk to me. . . ."

Kira's eyes widened and she took a quick step back.

"Yes, I hate you. You killed my sister! Get away from us. I'll call the police."

Her words stopped Suzanne in her tracks. Kira looked so much like Liza. The resemblance at close range was unnerving.

"I'm surprised you aren't locked up already. I don't know why it's taking so long."

Suzanne was surprised, too, but didn't dare admit it. And she didn't care if Kira did call the police. She was desperate.

"I swear on my children, I never harmed your sister. We exchanged harsh words, plenty of times. I'm sorry for that. I can see now she was not the person I thought."

Kira rolled her eyes. "Give me a break.

Do you think I have a drop of sympathy for you?"

"I'm sure you don't. But I'm willing to beg. I'm fighting for my life. Just the way your sister did, the night she died. I'm not the one, Kira. Please just open your mind to the possibility?"

When she didn't answer, Suzanne said, "Did you know that someone left a note? 'Keep your mouth shut or you'll be sorry.' They probably put it on her car, when it was vandalized."

"I heard about that mysterious message." She crossed her arms over her chest. "Convenient for it to pop up now. Turned in by an anonymous source?"

Suzanne felt the blood rush to her cheeks. "Was someone threatening your sister? She must have mentioned it."

"I'll tell you exactly what I told the police. I think your friends cooked that note up, but it's not going to save you."

Suzanne swallowed hard. She couldn't lose her temper. This was too important. "I just need to know one thing. The safety deposit box . . . There might be something in there that can help me. That can help the police figure out who really did this."

Kira's expression turned smug. "You heard about that from your snooping friends, too, I guess. There was nothing in it that would help your case. Thank goodness."

Suzanne's hopes fell. But she persisted. "Please, just tell me what you found. I'll leave you alone. I promise."

"I doubt it." Kira's tone was sharp. She didn't answer. She leaned in the car and handed Emma a toy that had dropped on the seat. Finally she said, "It was jewelry, as I'd suspected. And some papers — copies of bank statements. From the realty office. I have no idea why she put them there."

Suzanne had no idea either. Why would Liza keep statements from Prestige Properties under lock and key? Was she helping Beth and Harry with the accounts? Why all the secrecy?

Emma was fussing. Squirming in her seat and reaching out her little arms. "K-k! . . . K-k!"

Kira's expression softened. "Just a second, baby." She looked back at Suzanne. "I think we're done here."

Suzanne nodded bleakly. "Thank you. I mean that."

The information hadn't been the lifeline Suzanne had hoped. But she knew it had been hard for Kira to even face her. No less carry on this brief conversation.

"Now you can do me a favor." Kira glanced at the carton. Suzanne could see it was full of knitted baby clothes. "My mother asked me to drop this off at your friend's shop. She and Liza made them. Your friend is putting together some sort of donation in my sister's name."

"That's right." Suzanne picked up the box and stepped back. "Tell your Mom we said thank you."

Kira had no response. She got behind the wheel and quickly backed the car into the street.

Suzanne saw Emma's little face through the passenger side window. She held up a stuffed dog and waved it.

Suzanne watched the car disappear down Main Street.

AMEYMOXI. What in the world did that mean? *The answer to that question has probably died with Liza,* Suzanne thought. *Like so many answers to so many questions. Including the one that can save me.*

Maggie was not in the shop and Phoebe was busy with a customer. Suzanne waved to her and left the box behind the counter with a note. She headed home, wondering how she'd make it through the hours before the knitting group met without jumping out of her skin.

312

Extreme cleaning. Her go-to, mind-numbing activity whenever she was over the top, crazy stressed. Scrub the bathroom tile? Wash windows? Rent a machine at the hardware store and shampoo the rugs?

She sighed, wondering where she'd left the plastic bucket and rubber gloves.

Might as well have a clean house when they drag me off to jail. . . .

It was the only time Suzanne could recall being early for the meeting. Except, when it had been held at her own house. She helped Maggie and Phoebe set up for dinner.

"I've been so busy this week, I wasn't able to cook. I ordered a big tray of sushi. I hope that works for everyone," Maggie said.

"If they don't like it, I brought a chocolate cake. Definitely a crowd pleaser," Suzanne said.

Maggie already looked pleased. "I was wondering what was in that cake holder, but I didn't want to peek. When did you manage to bake that, on top of everything else going on?"

"I'm not really sure. In the middle of my cleaning frenzy. It's all a blur."

Maggie offered a sympathetic look as Suzanne set plates and napkins at each place on the long table. "I'm sorry I wasn't here this morning when you dropped off Ruth's donation. Did you really speak to Kira?"

"It wasn't a long conversation. But we exchanged a few meaningful words. She knew about the note."

"What did she think? Did she know that someone was threatening her sister?"

"She didn't put much stock in it. She said, 'Your friends cooked that note up, but it's not going to save you.'"

Maggie frowned. "That is harsh, but she's in a great deal of pain."

"I know that." Suzanne nodded. "I have lost hope about that note. I don't think it's going to save me," Suzanne admitted. "I did ask her what was in the safe deposit box and actually got an answer."

Maggie was filling small white bowls with soy sauce. "You did? Brave girl. What did she say?"

"She told me it was just some copies of bank statements, from Prestige Properties. She had no idea why Liza was holding on to them and frankly, neither do I."

Maggie looked puzzled, too, Suzanne noticed. Then she smiled and patted Suzanne's shoulder. "Let's wait until the others come. Maybe together we can sort this out."

A short time later, the rest of her friends

had gathered around the table, sharing the huge tray of sushi and various appetizers Maggie had ordered. She'd even warmed some saki, though Suzanne still preferred good old Chardonnay.

"A cold dinner was a good idea. Keeps the wits sharp." Lucy guided a piece of flying tiger roll toward her mouth and chewed thoughtfully. "I was so annoyed to hear they let Sutton go. Did they rule him out for good?"

Suzanne dipped a slice of spicy tuna roll in soy sauce, careful not to drop it. "Annoying is not the word. Here's the thing . . . Helen said the forensics lab figured out that the drink was only potent enough to kill Liza for about twenty-four hours after it was mixed. Beyond that, the chemicals would have broken down and would not be strong enough to cause such a deadly reaction."

"So whoever killed her must have mixed and planted the drink by say . . . Wednesday night?" Lucy calculated.

Suzanne's mouth was full and she could only nod. "Uh-huh."

"But Sutton came to your office Tuesday. And that was too early," Dana worked out. "If he didn't have help, I mean."

"That's right. Unfortunately, his alibi for Wednesday and Wednesday night is solid.

315

He had an early business meeting from his unhappy personal bankers and was in the hospital, overnight, after that."

"I guess that leaves out the car and the note on Thursday morning," Suzanne said. "Unless he limped over to do the damage?"

It sounded far-fetched, even to her own ears.

Maggie frowned, her spoon poised above a bowl of miso soup. "Let's not go round in circles. Let's forget about the car for now. And the drink. What about the computer files? The same person has to be responsible for both."

Dana reached over for more sushi, then sat back. "Maggie's right. If we can figure that out, we should know who's behind the rest. Who's in charge of the network?"

Suzanne wasn't sure this would get them anywhere, but she was willing to try. "It was installed by a professional computer company. But Beth Birney oversees it. She's the one we complain to if anything goes wrong. But I'm not sure how much she knows about it. All she does is call up the IT company."

"She has all the passwords?" Lucy asked, clearly more savvy about these things than Suzanne was.

"She must," Suzanne replied. "I guess

Harry has them, too."

Dana seemed to perk up at the mention of the realty broker. "Of course he does. Or at least, would know where to find them. What about Liza? Did she know how to navigate the network?"

"I'm not sure." Suzanne had never really thought about it. "It's possible. She was smart that way. Do you think she killed herself and framed me? Just to get the last shot in? As much as Liza disliked me, getting me fired would have been probably enough for her."

Her friends were trying not to laugh at her dark humor, but mostly, gave in. "Suzanne, come on. We're being serious here," Maggie scolded.

"So am I." Suzanne eyed the sushi slices collected on her plate, but had suddenly lost her appetite.

Lucy abruptly picked up her phone and started scrolling through the photos. "Look at this . . . What do you think she had on her desk the night she died? It looks like printouts from a computer to me."

She handed the phone to Suzanne. All she saw was the picture of a strand of yarn, stretched out on a desk. "Liza was a pretty lame photographer," she murmured. "One thing she wasn't perfect at."

Suddenly she realized the yarn was not the subject of the photo. It was the background, the printout.

"Okay . . . I get it. She was sending her mother a picture of these printouts. For safekeeping or something?"

"That's what I think," Lucy said. "Can you read what they say? Can you figure out why she'd want to save them?"

Before she could answer, Phoebe handed over her laptop. "E-mail them to me, Lucy. I'll blow them up on the computer."

"Brilliant." Suzanne was pleased by that idea.

"Okay, here we go. Here's the first photo, Suzanne. I enlarged it as much as I could."

Phoebe turned the screen around so Suzanne could read it. It looked like a spreadsheet, the kind accountants and bookkeepers create to calculate profit and loss. She knew enough to recognize that much.

"Looks like monthly accounts," Suzanne said. "I recognize the companies we do business with — utilities, the water cooler guy, the cleaners . . . nothing strange here. Sorry."

She sensed the disappointment of her friends, though no one said a word.

She paused and took a closer look. Then felt goose bumps break out on her skin.

318

"Wait. Maybe there is something off. Let me see the other photos."

Phoebe quickly brought them up. Suzanne studied the other spreadsheets, each covering a different period of time. "There's something off here. There are lots of names on these sheets I've never heard of." She looked up at her friends. "Today, when I asked Kira about the safety deposit box, she told me Liza had socked away statements from the corporate bank account." She glanced around at her friends. "Get it? Liza figured out that someone is skimming the accounts. That's why she was working so late Thursday night. She was looking for proof."

"And that's why she was warned to keep her mouth shut," Lucy added.

"But someone decided to shut it for her," Suzanne cut in. "And figured out how to blame me."

She sat back, the truth sinking it. "I can't believe it. It's like I've been looking at one of those optical illusion drawings and only seeing the pretty girl's profile."

"And now you see the creepy old lady?" Phoebe asked.

"I do . . . And she's not that creepy looking, actually . . . because she can afford to go to Hair Spa every single day. Online dating, my foot, okay?"

Suzanne felt incredibly angry. And completely elated at the same time. And as if the top of her head might blow off.

She suddenly realized her friends were staring at her, totally confused.

"Who is it? What are you ranting about?" Maggie asked in a small, cautious voice.

"Beth Birney. Mild-mannered, ever helpful Beth. Our 'Office Mom.' It's got to be. She's the only one who could have pulled this all off so easily. Stealing my bottle of diet shake and putting in the Botox, dumping those files in my computer. She must have known Liza was on her trail, so she messed up the Mercedes and left that note."

Lucy sat back, her eyes wide. "Of course. That's it. Why didn't we see it sooner?"

Dana looked surprised, too. "Why didn't Harry Prentiss see that he was being robbed is the question. Why didn't he notice someone was stealing from him?"

"That one is easy." Suzanne waved her chopsticks, feeling practically weightless with relief. "Harry loves the limelight, but despises sweating the details. Monthly accounts and payroll and figuring out what he's spending on paper towels is all grunt work to him. He's very lazy that way and he trusts Beth implicitly. She does seem so honest and trustworthy. So loyal to the company."

"Liza had an MBA and did all the bookkeeping for her husband's restaurant, before they broke up. Her mother told us that," Maggie recalled. "She probably knew her way around a spreadsheet better than Beth does. She must have noticed something amiss."

Suzanne nodded. "So she dug around a little. I guess she didn't want to tell Harry until she had proof."

"Do you think that's why she wanted to talk to him after the staff meeting?" Lucy asked. "Not to convince him to have you fired?"

"Maybe." Suzanne had not considered that. "But Beth's scheme got her first." The realization made Suzanne sad.

"You need to call Helen. Right away." Dana's tone was so insistent, Suzanne froze. A piece of sushi that was halfway to her mouth dangled from her chopsticks. "Lucy can send her the photos, and if Kira didn't give the police the bank statements she found, they'll soon catch up with them."

"Just call Helen," Maggie echoed. "This whole ordeal can be over in a few hours."

"Not soon enough for me." Suzanne picked up her phone and headed for the front of the shop, so she could speak with her attorney without distraction. She was smiling so widely, her cheeks hurt.

She returned to the soothing sound of needles clicking. After talking to Helen, she called Kevin and quickly told him the good news. He was so excited, she was sure his whoop of glee had been heard in the next room. But when she joined her friends again, she could see their peace had not been broken. Everyone stopped stitching at the same moment and looked up at her.

"How did it go?" Dana asked.

"She wouldn't really say one way or the other. But I could tell from her questions, she agrees that all the pieces fit." Suzanne didn't want to count her chickens too soon again, but couldn't help the bright note in her voice.

"Will she bring this to the police tonight, or wait until tomorrow?" Lucy sounded worried. "If Beth is smart enough to skim the accounts and frame you for murder, she must know someone will figure her out. She may try to get away."

"Helen thought of that. She's going to speak to Charles and Detective Oliver right away."

"I bet that Beth has about ten bank accounts and five fake passports . . . and a shelf full of wigs in her closet," Phoebe said.

"I bet you're right. Let's hope she doesn't get to use any of them." Suzanne was too happy to entertain the possibility of Beth escaping apprehension.

"The police will call in forensics accountants to check the books at your office, Suzanne. I'm not sure how long that will take," Dana said.

Suzanne didn't like hearing that. "Not too long, I hope. Maybe they can verify enough from what we gave them to bring her in for questioning."

"I think it's enough." Dana's reply made her feel better. Suzanne hoped she wasn't just saying that to placate her.

"There's such a thing as forensic accountants?" Phoebe made a face, as if she didn't believe her.

"Oh yes," Maggie replied quickly. "Charles told me all about their role. You'd be surprised how many cases they work on. And they are called to testify in court, too."

Phoebe considered the idea. "Sounds sort of geeky . . . but cool. So, what do we do now? Just wait?"

"And knit." Lucy picked up her needles.

"And eat chocolate cake." Suzanne headed to the shop's kitchen, where she had stored the treat. "I whipped up a beauty with coconut icing that's impossible to resist. I made it to console myself about Sutton going free. Little did I realize, we'd be celebrating."

"As well we should be," Maggie commended.

Suzanne's friends smiled at her, and at each other, and Suzanne trotted off to fetch the cake. She felt her world, so shaken and shattered the past week, falling back into place.

By noon on Friday, Suzanne wondered if she'd celebrated too soon. Beth Birney had not been picked up by the police and she couldn't stand the suspense as she waited for some word. And there was nothing left in her house to clean.

Barkly caught her eye, as he snoozed on his huge dog bed in the kitchen. Suzanne approached quietly and gave him a pat. He yawned and wagged his tail, offering a doggy smile and his big stomach for a scratch. Clearly, the big, sweet mutt had no idea that she'd decided it was bath time.

It would be a challenge; he was eighty-five pounds and not partial to water. But the job would be distracting enough.

"Here, boy. Look! I have biscuits," she cooed, trailing the treats up the stairs, toward the bathroom.

Just as they reached the top of the steps, Suzanne heard her phone ring. Maggie's name was on the screen and she quickly answered.

"Turn on channel five. The police brought Beth in for questioning."

"Amen. I've been waiting all day." Suzanne ran to the nearest TV, in the guest room, and quickly turned it on just in time to see a video of Beth, flanked by two uniformed officers as she was escorted into the station.

Instead of the elation she expected, Suzanne felt only sympathy. The sight of Beth's bowed head and public drama brought back fresh memories of her own walk on that path just a few days ago. She knew firsthand the humiliation and fear Beth was experiencing.

"There she goes," Maggie said on the other side of the phone. "I think this was taped earlier. The police must know everything by now."

"If she confessed quickly," Suzanne replied.

"I don't think it will take long. She might deny diverting funds from Prestige Properties, but her trail must be obvious if even you could see it."

"Uh . . . thanks, pal. I think."

"You know what I mean. And she must have stashed the money she stole somewhere. They can look up financial information like that very easily. The murder will be harder to prove," Maggie mused. "But if Liza had discovered Beth's scheme, Beth's motive was strong. Stronger than the one the police tried to assign to you."

Maggie had to go. A customer needed attention. Suzanne ended the call, feeling calmed by her friend's words. Beth was in custody. The ordeal was not officially over. *But it will be. Very soon,* she promised herself.

Another call came in and she expected to see Lucy or Dana's name on the screen. But it was a client. A closing date had finally been set on a waterfront property, located on Beach Road. The meeting would be Tuesday; Suzanne needed to gather some paperwork at the office and check the property, which was vacant, before the buyer's walk-through on Monday. Tasks she was happy to carry out, and promptly. She'd been waiting for this closing to come through. It was the only house she'd sold in weeks but would yield a large commission.

She lifted her chin and practically skipped across the guest room. The dog had followed her and now stared up with a curious expression. "Sorry, we have to reschedule your bubble bath," she told Barkly. "I guess you lucked out today, too, pal."

She tossed the dog another biscuit and headed to her bedroom, to change out of her house clothes. She considered the choices in her closet with care. She wanted to look sleek and stylish, but as if she hadn't tried that hard. And she definitely didn't want to look as if she'd been hiding out, cleaning her house all week.

She smiled into the bathroom mirror and fluffed her hair. "Watch out world . . . *I am back!*"

CHAPTER 11

Suzanne had a few minutes to spare when she arrived in town and cruised by Maggie's shop. She saw Lucy's car out front and couldn't resist stopping by. She had some news to share about Beth Birney and knew her friends would be eager to hear it.

Lucy sat in the big, blue wing chair, knitting. She looked up, surprised to see her. "Nice power outfit. It's working for you."

"I have to show face at the office. I made some extra effort, since I've been in sweats all week." The black leather blazer, pencil pants, and short black boots had been a good choice. A gray satin blouse and a string of pearls, in Liza's honor, was the finishing touch.

"She's roaring back. That's the spirit." Maggie stood behind the counter, sorting through button cards with a customer.

"What can I say? I clean up well." Suzanne offered a casual shrug.

"I saw Beth Birney on the news," Lucy said. "Have you heard anything more from Helen?"

"She called on my way into town. Beth has confessed to skimming the accounts, and even vandalizing Liza's car. She wouldn't own up to the note, but the police found her fingerprints all over it. And just as you guessed, Lucy, they were able to determine it had been on the car, stuck under the windshield."

"So that nails the threat. One tiny step to the actual deed," Lucy pointed out.

"So far, she claims she didn't do it." Suzanne's tone was not quite as cheerful.

"Give it time. The police have a lot to charge her with. She's not going anywhere." Lucy turned her knitting over and began another row. The baby jacket was almost done. Suzanne was impressed.

"Maybe the DA will bargain with her, to get her to admit to the murder." Her customer had left and Maggie came over and sat next to Lucy. She carried the carton of knitted baby items from Ruth.

"I hope they persuade her to confess. Bargains or not," Suzanne said.

"Everyone in your office must be upset. Another front page story. Right on top of Liza's murder last week." Lucy shook her head. "Probably not very good for business."

"People say, any publicity is good publicity. But I'm not so sure about that. I guess I'll find out when I go over there. Everyone liked Beth. Everyone trusted her."

"Especially Harry. Obviously," Maggie said.

"He was so played." Suzanne shook her head. "At least he'll get back most of the money. Helen said she had about seven bank accounts."

"I guessed ten. But that was pretty close," Phoebe said. "What about the passports? Any wigs?"

"Helen didn't go into detail. But I'll check for you," Suzanne promised.

The pile of baby clothes on the low table was building. "Are those the items Ruth sent?" Lucy asked.

"Yes, they are. I wanted to sort them out and count them. I haven't had a minute." Suzanne watched Maggie take out each of the hand-knitted baby items — hats, sweaters, sets of booties, and leggings.

"Nice work." Maggie spread a white sweater with a detailed border along the hem and button line.

"It is," Suzanne agreed. "I was wondering why the note said, 'Think about Emma.'

Isn't that odd?"

Lucy shrugged. "Just trying to push Liza's buttons. She lived with her niece. She was very close to her. You can tell from the pictures we saw in her bedroom. Beth was playing on Liza's loyalty to her family."

"I guess." Suzanne considered the explanation as she watched Maggie unpack more sweaters.

"My, my. They were a productive duo. I think the donation will cover half of our goal," Maggie remarked.

"Liza learned to knit in Maine. I guess there isn't much to do up there," Suzanne said. "I saw Kira again on my way over. Just the car. What are the chances? Gives me the chills every time I see her behind the wheel. I get a Liza flashback." She pulled her leather-bound notebook from her work tote and wrote in block letters, then turned the page toward her friends. "Now that we know who killed Liza, what the heck do you think this means? Please tell me, somebody, and I'll be able to sleep tonight. A-M-E-Y-M-O-X-I."

She held up the pad where she'd written the letters from the personal license plates.

Maggie stared at the page. "I have no idea. Sounds like medicine. Something the doctor would prescribe for stomach trouble?"

"More like cat medicine," Phoebe chimed in. She flopped on the love seat next to Lucy. "But you'd have to call it 'Meow-ski.' "

Lucy and Maggie laughed.

"I'm serious. It's the letters of Liza's license plate. It drives me crazy every time I see it."

Lucy looked back at her knitting. "Let's see . . . *OX* might mean kisses, or love? But most people write in the other order, *XO*."

"I didn't even think of that. I was trying to make out a word."

"I don't think it's a word. I think it's an abbreviation of some sort. If the *XO* is backward, maybe the rest is, too." Lucy put her knitting aside, took the pad, and wrote the letters in reverse. "Let's see . . . IXO-MYEMA."

It still didn't mean anything to Suzanne. "That looks even more confusing."

Lucy was concentrating. She didn't seem to hear her. "How about this? I XO MY EMA?"

Suzanne stared down at the page for a moment. A lightbulb went off in her brain. "Or, I love my Emma."

"By George, I think she's got it." Lucy put on her very bad English accent.

Suzanne sat up even straighter. "I've got

332

something better than that. When I was with Kira the other day, Emma kept calling her 'K-k.' Not 'Mommy' or 'Mama.' " She paused, her mouth growing dry. "I know she's very young, but most babies do manage to say 'Mama' or just 'Ma.' But Kira is not Emma's mother. Liza was. And that's why Liza went to Maine. To have a baby . . . And that's why she came back."

"Because Harry Prentiss is the father?" Lucy finished for her. She glanced at Maggie, whose eyes had grown wide. Maggie pushed the piles of baby clothes aside.

"Exactly. Who else could it be?" Suzanne replied.

"Heavy stuff," Phoebe said quietly. "I think you nailed it, Suzanne."

Lucy leaned forward, looked at Maggie. "All the child care books in Liza's bedroom, remember? And the stuffed bears on her bed. They seemed so out of place with the decor, but Emma seemed so familiar with them. And the room looked so stark. But it wasn't minimalist decorating. It was child proofed."

"Even that photo," Maggie said. "I assumed it was Kira and Emma at the beach. But it could have been Liza. It must have been, if she had it sitting on her desk in a special frame. And hid her secret belongings there."

"The way a mother does," Suzanne concluded. This was a real game changer. Heavy stuff, indeed.

"Do you think it has an impact on our theory about the murder?" Maggie asked.

"Not really," Lucy said. "I still think Beth killed Liza because she'd uncovered her larceny. But maybe Beth figured out that Liza was Emma's mother, too. Hence the threat having real impact."

"Beth was good at math. Just count the months that Liza lived in Maine and compare that to Emma's age." Suzanne shook her head. "I don't know why I didn't see that before."

"Because the sisters sold the story of Kira being a single mother so well and even Ruth believes it, too. At least, she seems to believe, Kira is Emma's mother. You had no reason to suspect it," Maggie replied.

"I guess not." Suzanne shrugged and picked a tiny thread off her black slacks. "The truth is, I never saw Liza as the motherly type, playing on her bed with her little girl. That sort of thing." She felt an unexpected wave of sadness. "Poor Emma. She's lost her mother so young."

"That is true." Maggie's voice was somber. "At least she has Kira. She seems very responsible and loving."

"Liza must have left Emma all her money. In trust or something?" Lucy said.

"Ruth told us that, according to Kira, the estate is protected, and Kira wasn't worried about Sutton's legal claims," Maggie recalled. "That must be why."

"I'm not surprised. She was smart that way." Suzanne's head was spinning. "I wonder if Harry knows. He must, right?"

"I wouldn't be too sure, Suzanne. Are you going to be the one to tell him?" Lucy asked.

"Me? I'd never do something like that."

Phoebe started laughing. She had the nerve to slap her knee. "Good one."

Suzanne glared at her. "Besides, we're just speculating. Though it is a pretty good guess."

"If Harry is the father, it would be interesting to know if he's aware of that. Did you know that he and his wife lost a child?" Maggie had begun putting the baby clothes back in the box, handling them carefully.

Suzanne thought she must be mistaken. "Harry and Claire? Are you sure? Who told you that?"

"I saw Claire at the cemetery yesterday morning. I was planting some mums at Bill's grave. And she was putting flowers near a statue. When I passed in my car, I took a look. It was a memorial statue for a child, Chelsea Jane Prentiss. I read the dates. Barely two years old when she died."

"Wow, that's so sad," Phoebe said.

"It is. The ultimate loss." Suzanne was silent a moment. She didn't dare imagine it. "No wonder she's devoted her life to teaching toddlers."

Lucy continued knitting, her expression thoughtful. "It must help her feel she's doing worthwhile work that's somehow connected to the child she lost. I hear the reputation of her school is growing. There was an article about it in the *Boston Globe*. They say her teaching theories are groundbreaking."

"She's a real brainiac. I don't know how she and Harry ever got together. Another mystery, ladies. I'm going to save that one for a rainy day." Suzanne stood up and smoothed down her blazer. "Got to run. It was enlightening."

"As always." Maggie met her gaze and smiled. "Keep us posted if you hear anything more about Beth Birney."

"Don't worry, I will." Suzanne blew kisses to her pals, grabbed her big bag, and headed out to her car.

It was a short drive to her office and Suzanne found a parking space in front. It

336

threw her off a little when she realized it was the same space she'd parked in the night she'd found Liza.

Sweeping anxieties aside, she lifted her chin and sailed through the glass door. *Life isn't for sissies, Suzanne. Buck up and put your game face on.*

As usual, Janine sat at the reception desk. She was talking on the phone but quickly ended the call as Suzanne approached. Her pretty face lit up with a smile. "Suzanne . . . you're back. You look great. How's it going?"

"Can't complain." Especially since the police took Beth in for questioning. "I have a closing Tuesday. The Neubauer house on Beach Road. I needed to pick up some keys to check the property."

"I'll get them for you. You heard about Beth, right? It was all over the news today."

"Oh yes. I definitely did." If Janine had any idea that Suzanne and her friends had been instrumental in unmasking the office manager, she didn't show it.

"Isn't that wild? I can't believe it. I said there must be some mistake. It can't be our Beth Birney. It must be someone else. Weren't you shocked?"

"I was surprised at first," Suzanne said honestly.

"She was always so nice to everyone. So helpful. Like if I needed a long lunch, or had to leave early, she never minded covering the desk. 'Take your time,' she'd say. And she'd bake everyone a cake on their birthday, remember?"

"Right. Those cakes, decorated with your hobby." Suzanne had forgotten about that.

Last spring Beth had presented Suzanne with one that had a ball of yarn made out of blue icing, and knitting needles made out of chopsticks. Everyone had oohed and ahhed, though it was easily the ugliest cake Suzanne had ever seen. But Suzanne had been impressed by the time and effort, and touched by the thoughtfulness. Now, those thoughtful gestures seemed tainted, probably all a big act.

"She told me her dream was to win a baking contest on TV. I guess that will never happen." Janine's tone was wistful, as if Beth had passed on. In a way she had, Suzanne realized. The Nice Beth they'd known and worked alongside for years was gone.

"How's Harry? He must be shocked. Again." Suzanne gazed down the corridor, toward his office. The door was closed.

"He's pretty shaken. Not himself. The police were here for hours. They carried out half the office. They just left a few minutes ago. Anita told him to go home but he wanted to stay."

Suzanne guessed the police had been looking through financial records and searching Beth's office, among other places. She saw yellow crime scene tape across the doorway of the room where records were kept and also across Beth's office door, right next to Harry's.

"Anita and Lyle left hours ago. But Harry didn't want to close early." She rolled her eyes. A phone line lit up and she reached for the receiver. "I better get this. Harry wants us to act like it's business as usual."

"He would have done well as the captain of the *Titanic.*"

Janine smiled and nodded as she greeted the caller, but Suzanne could tell she hadn't heard the joke. It was for the best. Janine covered the phone with her hand a moment. "If I'm gone, I'll leave the keys out here for you."

Suzanne thanked her and headed for her cubicle. She quickly found the file she needed, then walked down to Harry's office and knocked on the door.

"Yes? Who is it?"

Suzanne opened the door a crack and poked her head in. "Harry? It's me."

"Suzanne. Come in. Come in . . ." He

339

waved his hand, beckoning her forward.

Suzanne took a few steps into the office but didn't sit down. Harry sat behind his large wooden desk. He looked pale and tired, his expensive, pink, oxford cloth shirt as rumpled as if he'd slept in it, and his hair stuck out in all directions, as if he'd tugged at it in distraction. Suzanne wondered if he'd been drinking. She wasn't close enough to smell liquor, but his greeting had sounded thick and slurred.

Could you blame the man? First he loses the woman he loves and now he finds out his office manager has been stealing him blind.

"Good to see you. Why did you come in? Curious about Beth, I bet."

"A little," she admitted. Though she did not admit she probably knew as much as he did at this point. Maybe more. "You must have been devastated. She seemed so loyal."

"Devastated doesn't come close. I trusted that woman with . . . everything. I should have seen what was going on, right under my nose. I'm a big fool. I deserved it."

He sounded angry and embarrassed. A bad combination.

"Don't be so hard on yourself. She fooled all of us. Maybe she had a split personality?"

"Maybe," he mumbled. "Those stupid cakes she made? The last one she gave me was hideous. It was supposed to be a golf club but it looked like a turkey drumstick. I didn't know what to say."

Suzanne fought to hold back her laughter. She could see he was totally serious.

He sighed and leaned back in the big leather chair. "She didn't fool Liza. Liza was the only one who saw through Beth's act. And Beth killed her to keep her quiet. That's what the police think now."

Suzanne felt relieved to hear him say it. "Yes, I know."

"I'll be honest with you, Suzanne. Nothing can really shock me or hurt me after losing Liza. I'm just . . . numb." He met her gaze. "Do you know what I mean?"

Suzanne nodded. She didn't know what to say. Liza had meant that much to him. That's what he was trying to tell her.

"Some people are like that," she said finally.

"Once in a lifetime. If you're lucky." He covered his eyes with his hand. She thought he might be crying. Finally, he looked at her again. His voice was hoarse. "At least there's little Emma. That's something."

Suzanne's heart skipped a beat. "That's a lot. Because Emma is your daughter."

She didn't ask a question, just stated the fact and watched his reaction. His eyes opened wide for a moment. Then he quickly gained control of his expression. "She is. She's my little girl. Mine and Liza's. How did you know?"

"I put it together." *With a little help from my friends.* "Don't worry. I won't tell anyone. I guess you and Liza had your reasons for keeping it a secret."

"I wanted the three of us to be together. I was trying to work it out." He replied as if Suzanne had been arguing with him. "Liza wasn't ready. She didn't trust me. She wouldn't forgive me for the time I disappointed her. But I thought she'd come around. Sooner or later. She didn't want Emma to grow up without knowing her father."

"So Kira is her only guardian now? You have no claim?"

"Yes, officially. I could go to court, I guess, and straighten it out. I hope it won't come to that. I want to see my daughter grow up. I want to help her, provide for her." Harry squeezed his eyes closed and Suzanne saw tears fall down his cheeks. "I miss Liza so much. If only she were still here. I don't know what to do. Sometimes I think I can't go on. Then I think of Emma. Liza would have wanted me to be here for our girl."

Suzanne thought of another little girl, Chelsea Jane. Harry's daughter with Claire. At least he had another chance.

"What about Claire? Does she know?" Suzanne's voice was almost a whisper. Did he think she'd gone too far asking that question?

"I could never tell Claire. It would be too much. She's a fragile person. She's done remarkably well, considering her challenges," he insisted. "I'm very proud of her."

"Of course you are. She's very accomplished."

Harry wiped his hand over his eyes. "I'm sorry. I can't talk anymore. It's been a long day. Very long," he murmured.

"Sure, Harry. I understand. The Neubauer house on Beach Road is closing Tuesday," she said as she headed to the door. "I'm going there now to make sure everything's in order for the walk-through."

"Good work, Suzanne. You're always so responsible."

"I try." She glanced back as she left the office and closed the door. "So long, Harry. Take care."

"You too, dear. And, Suzanne?" His tone stopped her in her tracks. "I'm glad everything worked out for you. Personally, I

343

thought it was all a big mistake. I told the police that, too."

She wasn't sure if she believed that, but decided to give him the benefit of the doubt.

"Thank you. I appreciate that. Good night, Harry."

She closed his door and headed back to the reception area. Janine had left for the day but the keys for the Neubauer house were on her desk, as she'd promised. Suzanne picked them up and dropped the ring in her purse.

She checked in at home with a quick phone call, to make sure things were under control. Alexis did not report any major calamities but reminded Suzanne that she had to be back at school by six for a basketball game.

Suzanne calculated she had just enough time to check the Neubauer house and pick up a few pizzas. If she hustled. She drove on with focus, not speeding but coming as close as she dared.

All the while, her strange conversation with Harry played back in her head. He mourned Liza deeply and hardly seemed to care that Beth had robbed a fortune from him.

Then again, Harry was an actor. A master manipulator. Was that all a performance for

344

her sake? And if so, why?

Did he kill Liza and try to frame me? she wondered suddenly. Beth had confessed to embezzlement but claimed she didn't murder Liza. *Maybe she's telling the truth. Maybe it's Harry.*

But why? He claimed he loved her. A once in a lifetime relationship, he'd said. But he'd also said she didn't want to be with him, and maybe he couldn't stand the idea of that?

Was it Emma? Did he want the child all to himself? Maybe Liza was not allowing him to have a relationship with their daughter, as Harry claimed.

She had left the village and was whizzing past Lucy's neighborhood, the Marshes. An eclectic mix of quaint cottages and starter houses, for young couples. Or what she called, "end game" properties, for downsizing seniors. Though she never used that term in front of them.

Soon after passing the community beach, the pricey neighborhood began, mini mansions perched on waterfront lots.

The Neubauer house was a few miles down, and Suzanne drove slower on the narrow, sandy road. She came to the house and pulled into the driveway.

A man might think like that, wanting a child

all to himself, she reasoned. *But it's more likely that a woman would.* Suzanne suddenly remembered Claire's interaction with Emma at the memorial service. No, it was not Harry who yearned for Emma. But a mother who had never gotten over a devastating loss.

It was suddenly clear. Claire knew about Emma and wanted her, so that she and Harry could have a second chance.

She knew about the office rivalry, the allergy, and had even stopped in at the Botox party with Harry for a little while. And she knew her way around the computer network, Suzanne recalled. She was always helping Harry and Beth when the system went down.

She came in and out of the office as she pleased. No one really noticed. Suzanne thought back to the day Liza had died. Was Claire around?

Yes, she was. She'd come by during the staff meeting with Harry's tuxedo. She waited in the car while he changed, but she could have easily planted the drink while everyone was in the meeting room.

And she had every reason to want Liza out of the picture. Of that, there could be no doubt.

Suzanne decided to call Lucy or Maggie

as soon as she got on the road again, eager to know what they'd think. Either she'd gone mad, trying to figure it all out, or she was really on to something.

Suzanne could hardly focus long enough to get the key in the door. It was dusk and she switched on the lights to find her way through the empty house. Her footsteps echoed in the spacious center hall as she carefully surveyed the floor, walls, and fixtures. Not too bad, except for a few marks where paintings had been removed from the walls.

She headed for the kitchen next and flipped on the lights. The fixture on the ceiling flickered and went out. Suzanne was annoyed and made a note. Hopefully, just the bulb and not some overlooked electrical repair. She found a switch for low lights above the counters and didn't like what she saw.

Cabinet doors hung open, a few random boxes and cans left here and there. Miscellaneous chipped cups and mismatched glasses. On the counter near the sink, a well-used wok with a few rust spots and a few pot covers. It looked like the owners had moved out in a hurry and left her to clean out their odds and ends. She hated when this happened, but it couldn't be helped.

You'd hate it more if this place doesn't pass inspection by the buyer on Monday, she reminded herself. She found an empty box in the hallway and began cleaning out the cupboards.

Then she decided to check the commercial-size refrigerator, large enough to easily hold a dead body, she thought as she pulled open the door. She hoped there was no old food in there. That was the worst, she thought.

The shelves were surprisingly clean and clear. But she suddenly heard a scuffling sound nearby.

Mice? Really? Give me a break . . .

She closed the fridge and stood very still, waiting for the sound.

She'd been mistaken. It was footsteps. The human kind. Unless the mouse in question was wearing boots with heels. Someone walked quietly into the kitchen; she could only see an outline in the dim light.

"Hello? Who's there?" She slammed the fridge shut and took a few steps backward, surprised at the identity of the visitor.

"It's me. Claire. The door was open."

Suzanne's mouth went dry. She was screaming inside but on the outside, willed herself to remain calm. "Hello, Claire. You scared me," she said with a small laugh.

"That makes us even. You scared me, Suzanne. I heard you talking to Harry."

Suzanne felt a chill, as if a frigid breeze swept through the room. "You did? How's that?"

"He wouldn't answer my calls. So I came by the office, to check on him." Claire stepped forward, her hands jammed in the pockets of a boxy, tweed blazer, her hair in its usual messy bun. "When I came to his door, you were there. Talking business, I thought at first. I didn't want to interrupt. The conversation was so interesting."

"Really? What did I say that scared you?" Suzanne thought back. Harry talked a lot about Liza and how much he'd loved her. That part must have been unpleasant for Claire to overhear.

"You were talking about Emma, and I felt sure it wouldn't be long until you figured out why Liza had to die."

When Suzanne didn't answer, she said, "He is Emma's father. Kira's just her aunt. Any court will grant him custody in a minute. Especially once they hear my credentials. I'll be an outstanding mother. She'll thrive with my care. She'll be a prodigy. Kira is a spoiled, self-centered child herself. She could never love Emma and care for her the way I can. Neither could Liza."

Suzanne was stunned by this confession, and Claire's gossamer thin hold on reality. But she decided the best tack right now was to humor her. "You would be a wonderful mother, Claire. Much better than Liza."

"That's right. You're very clever, Suzanne. Much sharper than I thought." Claire cast Suzanne a warm smile, as if praising one of her genius babies.

Harry had called her "fragile," but Claire is plain crazy. And I'll be lucky if I get out of here alive, Suzanne realized.

She squared her shoulders and checked her watch, as if preparing to head home. "Well, got to go. My own brood is waiting for me." She took a few tiny steps toward the door. "I won't tell a soul, if that's what you're worried about. The police have Beth Birney in custody and can make a good case against her."

"I thought that might work out, too. Until I heard you and Harry talking. I'm sorry, Suzanne. You're just too bright for your own good."

Suzanne didn't answer. She scanned the room for the quickest way out. The only choice was making a mad dash past Claire.

If I hunker over like a football player, maybe

I can knock her down?

Suzanne had just lowered her head like a bull, preparing to stampede, when Claire's right hand emerged from her jacket pocket. Holding a small, shiny gun.

"Not so fast, dear. Don't make any hasty exits." She waved the gun to underscore her warning. "I don't believe firearms should be legal, to be honest with you. But Harry keeps this little pistol in the house, under the bed, and I had a minute to stop home and pick it up on my way. I guess it can come in handy."

Harry's house was not far from this one, she recalled. She had passed it on the way. Suzanne stood up and raised her hands in the air. "You don't want to shoot me, Claire. You really don't."

"Oh, you're right. But you want to shoot yourself. First, you'll send a text to your husband confessing to Liza's murder and tell him that you can't live with the guilt. Where's your phone? Get it out."

Suzanne met her gaze. She couldn't believe this was happening. She fished in her big leather tote for her phone, her hand shaking wildly.

"Hurry up. No funny stuff. Give it here." Claire held out her free hand.

Suzanne finally found the phone and

351

handed it over. Claire stared at the screen.

"Open it, it's locked. What's your code?"

"I-I-I can't remember," she lied. "I just have to do it. By habit. Here, let me have it back. I'll put it in."

Suzanne took the phone back and tapped in some random numbers. Then purposely dropped the phone so that it bounced under a cooking cart.

"You idiot . . . get that phone. Give it here." Claire sounded angry and frustrated, but there was nothing she could really do but wave the pistol around.

Suzanne crouched down on the other side of the cart and grabbed the phone. "Sorry . . . it went way under. I can just about grab it. . . ."

Kneeling on the other side of the cart, Suzanne pretended to be reaching under to grab the phone, while she deftly opened it with her code and somehow managed to send Lucy the shortest text in history.

An emoji of the Edvard Munch screaming face, followed by: 23 Bch Rd.

Was Lucy even home right now, only a mile or so away? Would she remember Suzanne had to come here, to check the house?

She heard Claire walking around to her side of the cart and jumped up. "Here it is. Got it, finally."

Suzanne squeezed the button and the home screen appeared. Claire poked her with the gun and grabbed the phone. "Sit down. And stay there."

Suzanne sat on a stool next to the kitchen island. She felt sweat running down her body. What could she do? What could she say to get out of this?

She stretched out her hand and stroked the countertop. "This is *real* Carrara marble. From Italy. Isn't it gorgeous?"

Suzanne could tell that Claire was trying to find Kevin's number in the contact list. But it wasn't under *K*. Suzanne had it under *H*, for Hubby, and wasn't going to offer that information, either.

"You real estate people. You never give up, do you?" Claire murmured.

"But it's fabulous. A great selling point in this place . . ." Suzanne stroked the marble as if making love to it, then lunged for the wok.

She flung it at Claire, who screamed and put her arm up.

Suzanne heard the gun go off as she dashed across the kitchen, pushing the stool down in her wake to block Claire's path.

Claire stumbled but quickly gained her balance. "Come back here. I'll shoot you, I swear. . . ."

Suzanne had considered that possibility. But it wouldn't look like suicide if she had a bullet in her back and she hoped Claire would not revise her plan.

The front door would not do as an exit strategy. Claire was in the foyer, thinking Suzanne had run up the stairs.

She pressed herself to the hallway wall and wracked her brain, trying to remember the layout. Then she ran down a flight of stairs to the lower level. Claire had lost track of her for a moment, but Suzanne soon heard footsteps following close by.

Suzanne dashed down a narrow hallway that opened to an entertainment area, filled with low couches, huge palm plants, a fire pit, and a long bar on one wall. Large glass windows that opened onto a stone patio and pool were covered by heavy curtains.

Suzanne left the lights off and stumbled around the room, bumping off the couches like a pinball as she finally found the windows. Somewhere along that wall, a door opened to the patio, she was sure of it.

She skittered under the curtain like an insect, searching for the door handle. Her heartbeat was so loud, she was sure Claire would hear it.

She heard Claire's footsteps on the slate floor and froze in place. "I know you're in here. Come out now, and make this easy on yourself."

Crawling as quietly as she could, Suzanne made her way to the bar and slipped behind it. Claire was crazy but she wasn't dumb. Suzanne knew it was only a matter of moments before the hiding place would be discovered.

"Some lights will help." Suzanne heard switches click and lights flashed on. She had tucked herself behind the bar just in time but felt sure she was doomed.

She looked around the back of the bar, desperate for something to use to defend herself, and suddenly grateful the departed owners had been so sloppy. A corkscrew? A martini glass? There was an ice pick, but it was no protection against a gun.

Then she saw a blender and two bottles, bloody Mary mix with sriracha and a heavy square bottle of quality gin.

She heard Claire's foosteps on the far side of the room and then the sound of the curtain yanked open with one hard pull. "You're under here, aren't you?"

Suzanne huddled down and set the gin near her side, then poured the mix into the blender as fast as the bottle would empty. There was a glug, glug sound and she was sure Claire had heard it.

She checked the blender plug and held her breath, not daring to move a muscle as the footsteps came closer.

"Suzanne . . . please. This is a silly game. I'm getting very tired. And annoyed."

Claire peered around the edge of the bar. She smiled and pointed the gun at Suzanne.

"There you are. Naughty girl. Looks like I won."

Suzanne sprang up and turned on the blender. Eyes squeezed closed, she pointed the whirring machine at her adversary while bloody Mary mix flew in all directions. Claire screamed and staggered backward, pressing her hands to her face as the spicy mixture seeped into her eyes.

Gin bottle in hand, Suzanne struck Claire squarely over the head, and with a surprised groan Claire dropped to the ground, then just lay there.

Suzanne was breathless. She turned off the blender and stared at Claire's immobile body. What should she do next? Call the police? Tie her hands before she woke? And where the heck was that gun?

She heard Lucy call out as she ran into the room. "Suzanne . . . what happened? Are you shot?"

Suzanne looked down at her clothes and laughed. "Just tomato juice, honest. But what a waste of a perfectly good batch of cocktails."

CHAPTER 12

Maggie had not heard all the details, but enough from Lucy to be assured that Suzanne had finally unmasked Liza's real murderer and their dear friend had been proven innocent, once and for all.

It was after six, but she lingered in the shop, straightening out displays and then preparing for a children's class she taught on Saturdays, Little Knitters. They were going to start knitted animal hats that could serve as masks for Halloween. Maggie stood at the back table and counted out the simple patterns and sets of supplies.

The notion of masks brought Claire Prentiss to mind again. Hers was a sad story, truly, Maggie thought. Her mind had been twisted by grief and loss. Maggie felt bad for her, though she'd had no right to take a life and certainly no right to make Suzanne pay for her crime.

Maggie did wonder what Charles was

thinking, and his dour partner on this case, Frank Oliver, faced with this surprising turn and forced to see now that they'd been wrong all along about Suzanne. *Just as I told him.*

The thought gave her some satisfaction. But not as much as she'd expected.

The shop door swung open. A late customer, she guessed. "Be with you in a minute," she called over her shoulder.

"Take your time. I didn't think you'd still be here."

She turned to find Charles, standing by the counter. Hat in hand, she noticed.

She'd expected to hear from him, sooner or later, now that the case was solved. But not this soon. Why wasn't he at the station, filling out reports and all the other paperwork?

She set aside the knitting supplies and walked toward him.

"I'm sure you heard already. It was Claire Prentiss." Charles shook his head. "I didn't see that coming."

"I did hear . . . and it's big of you to admit it."

He shrugged. "I never really thought it was Suzanne. You know that."

"Yes, I guess I do. That's why it's been so hard for me to figure out these past few days why you stormed out of my house last weekend."

"I didn't storm. I walked out very calmly. I don't want to argue with you, Maggie. But I've been doing some thinking and I want to talk things out."

His serious expression set off alarms. Maggie braced herself. Of course, he'd never be the type of man to just disappear, without offering some closure. He was far too mature for that. Nonetheless, this was not going to be an easy conversation.

She crossed her arms over her chest. "All right. What have you been thinking about, Charles?"

He cleared his throat and lifted his chin. "It's hard for me to say this, but we can't keep going around in the same circle. Having the same argument, over and over. You know how I feel about you. But something has to give, Maggie."

She was right. He was trying to break up with her. Maggie felt tears well up behind her eyes but blinked them back. "I agree," she said in the most forceful voice she could summon. "I can't be happy that way either and . . ."

He held up his hand and met her glance. "Just let me finish, okay? Before you sign the death certificate?"

Maggie laughed at the dark humor and took a deep breath. He was determined to dump her first. And wouldn't let her beat him to the punch, would he? All right, he was the one who started the conversation.

"Sorry, Charles. Please continue. Say what you have to say."

And then please go, and leave me alone to cry my eyes out.

He cleared his throat again. "I want you to know that I've decided to retire. I've fought the good fight and landed a few good punches, I'd say. But this is a young man's game. I've done my part. I can't keep up this pace and the long hours on a case like this one."

Maggie was so stunned she could not speak. She knew she was staring at him bug-eyed but couldn't help it. "Retire? You never mentioned you were even considering it."

"I didn't think I was either. But it's been brewing, on a back burner, I guess. As I searched for an answer for the problem between you and me, it suddenly seemed like the perfect solution. The only solution," he added.

He'd been thinking so hard about their relationship? Maggie had never expected that either.

"I can't keep your nose out of police business, Maggie, so I'll just stop being a police officer. I think that would solve it. Don't you?"

Maggie took a few steps closer. Had she really heard him right? "You're giving up your job for me? For our relationship?"

Charles finally smiled at her. "Let's say it's a combination of factors. But you're at the top of the list. I don't want to be at odds with you. Not if I can help it."

Maggie's heart melted. No one had ever offered her such a tribute. "And I don't want to fight with you," she rushed to assure him. "I was looking forward to you moving in with me, so much," she confessed. "I've been very upset, but I didn't know what to do. I didn't think you even wanted to talk to me again."

"I didn't when I left your house last week. But only for as long as it took to walk to my car. I was feeling awful and nearly called you before I even got home. I haven't been myself since."

His confession was a great consolation to her. "So, you will move in? Very soon, I hope," she said.

He put his arms around her and smiled. "I've been thinking about that, too. You know, we're not kids, Maggie. I'm not sure I feel comfortable with this living together

362

routine."

He had not said that before, but Maggie wasn't surprised. He was so traditional.

"All right. I understand. I'm just happy that . . . well, that we've made up. I've missed you."

"I've missed you, too. A lot. But you still don't understand me. Why just live together? I think we should get married."

Maggie was shocked. She felt Charles hold her tighter as her knees went weak for a moment. She leaned back and stared up at him.

"I thought you came in here to break up with me . . . and now you want to get married? Was that really a proposal, Charles?"

He laughed, a deep warm sound that she'd been aching to hear. "All right, I can do better." He cupped her face with his hands, then stepped back. "I never thought I'd find love again. Then I met you, right in this shop, and I can't imagine my life without you. Will you please marry me and spend the rest of our days together?"

Maggie felt breathless as Charles took her in his arms again. She smiled into his eyes. "I love you, Charles. I'd be thrilled to be your wife."

Before she could say more, Charles kissed her, holding her tight. A long, aching kiss that made up for everything and more.

When they finally parted, she felt almost light-headed.

"Are you happy?" he asked quietly.

"Overjoyed. But it is a lot all at once," she admitted. "How about a long engagement? Would you live together then?" she asked quietly.

He laughed and hugged her close. "All right, I'll take engaged. I knew you'd have a counteroffer."

Maggie smiled, her cheek pressed against his shoulder. He did know her well by now, didn't he? And loved her, quirks and all.

Her friends wanted to meet her at the Schooner for breakfast Sunday morning, but Suzanne invited them to her house for a brunch and a debrief of her narrow escape from Claire Prentiss. In the custody of the police, Claire had confessed quickly to Liza's murder, and how she had framed Suzanne.

Helen Forbes had filled in some of the details, and Suzanne hoped Maggie had heard more from Charles by now. Were they talking again? She certainly hoped so.

As a golden quiche bubbled in the oven and a green salad, with pears, cranberries, and walnuts, chilled in the fridge, Suzanne blended a special cocktail for the celebration.

There were hugs all around when her friends arrived and they soon settled at the large island in Suzanne's kitchen.

"Back in your element, I see. I can't believe with what you went through Friday night, you still cooked this beautiful meal for us." Dana smiled as Suzanne served her some herbal tea, though she'd made strong coffee for everyone else.

"Oh, it's not that much. Just some quiche and salad. And bloody Mary's, of course." She tipped her own glass in the air, a silent toast to her pals, and took a sip. "Happy to be here, free and clear. I was secretly consoling myself with the thought that even Martha Stewart did some jail time."

"We knew it would never come to that," Phoebe insisted. "But how did you ever figure out that Claire Prentiss really did it? Did you know before she cornered you?"

Suzanne had taken out the salad and spooned portions onto the chilled plates as her friends passed them around. "It came to me while I was driving on the Beach Road. Something Harry said triggered the idea. I'm not sure now. I just realized that even though he's Emma's father, it didn't sound as if he planned to fight for full custody, now that Liza is gone. But Claire has such an obvious baby hunger and had never recovered from losing their daughter. I remembered the way she was hovering over Emma at the memorial service. She wanted that little girl for her own so badly. She said as much to me, too."

"Really?" Phoebe had taken a bite of salad and munched quietly. "What did she say exactly?"

"Something like, she would be the perfect mother for Emma. She would turn her into a genius, a prodigy, and even Liza couldn't have loved her more than she would."

"How sad," Maggie said. "She does sound as if she was living in some altered state of reality."

"I'm guessing her attorney will use her mental state to lower the charges," Dana said.

Suzanne had sliced the two quiches and started serving her friends. Maggie held her dish out for the broccoli and cheddar combination. "That's what Charles said, too."

"You're speaking to Charles again? You've worked things out? Kissed and made up?" Suzanne teased, as she served Maggie.

Maggie met her gaze, then looked down at her quiche. "You could say that. I'll tell you all about it, later. He did tell me more about Claire Prentiss and how she framed you."

"I'd like to hear that." Lucy held her dish out for some of the mushroom, bacon, and onion pie.

"It was very much as we guessed. She knew that you and Liza both drank the same diet shake and knew about Liza's allergy. And that you had been at the Botox party, Suzanne. She took a bottle from your package of shakes, used a syringe to add the drug, and relabeled it with Liza's initials." Maggie sipped her bloody Mary. "She didn't know that the mixture would break down, but Liza did drink it within twenty-four hours of her planting it in the office fridge."

"When was that?" Suzanne asked, serving herself a sliver from each quiche since she couldn't decide.

"She'd come to the office a few nights earlier and moved the files, using the computer in Harry's office. She planted the drink during the staff meeting. She had the perfect cover, with the excuse of dropping off Harry's tuxedo for the fund-raiser that night."

"While Liza and Suzanne were having a screaming match in the meeting, she was setting the stage for Liza's murder. With Suzanne framed as the killer?" Lucy asked.

"Exactly. The argument in the meeting was again, a lucky break for her. She planted the vials in the Gertwigs' trash a few days later," Maggie added. "She told Charles and his partner that she had nothing personal against you, Suzanne. But Harry had often told her how you and Liza were always fighting over your sales turf. I think she did cancel the office cleaners, hoping Liza would work past five, to make up for such a long meeting that afternoon. But even if Liza ingested the drink on Friday, it would have had the same effect."

"I heard that from Helen, too." Suzanne wasn't sure if she liked the mushroom or broccoli quiche better. Both had come out pretty good, she thought. "And that Liza didn't carry an EpiPen, because this was her only, very strange, allergy and one she thought totally avoidable. Even if people were around when she had the attack, it's very likely she would have died before help came."

Maggie nodded. She looked a little teary eyed. Suzanne realized it wasn't just sadness over Liza's death again, but the effect of the spicy cocktail. "May I have some ice water?" Maggie asked. "That drink is a bit

368

much for me."

"I did fix some. It's in the fridge." Suzanne quickly fetched the pitcher with ice water and lemon slices. She filled Maggie's tall water glass and noticed her other friends quickly filled their glasses, too.

"Sorry, guys. But I had to celebrate with the cocktail that saved me. If not for sriracha sauce, I would not be here to tell the tale."

"A brilliant strategy. It would never have occurred to me." Dana lifted her glass of ice water to honor Suzanne, before she took a sip.

"It was an inspired solution. And a horrifying scene when I got there. Just for a minute or two," Lucy confessed. "Did Claire tell you when she found out about the affair and that Emma was Harry's child?"

Suzanne shrugged. "I guess I could have asked. But it seemed a better idea to throw a wok at her head and make a run for it."

"That was quick thinking, too," Phoebe noted. "I would have been paralyzed with fear."

Suzanne smiled at her. "I wasn't exactly a cool superagent, Phoebe. You never know how you'll react under that kind of pressure."

"I did hear from Charles that Claire knew about the affair years ago, and knew about Emma soon after Liza returned to town," Maggie said, answering Lucy's questions. "Harry's philandering had killed her love for him, but she believed he could at least get custody of Emma. Especially if Liza was out of the way. She felt he owed her that, to make up for his failings in their marriage. And because he knew how heartbroken she was, losing their own child. But she had Harry believing that she was totally oblivious while she figured out how to get rid of Liza."

Dana helped herself to another small bite of quiche. Suzanne felt gratified to see that; Dana so rarely had seconds of anything. Even celery sticks.

"It was a diabolical plan," Dana said. "But some part of me feels sorry for a woman who was so twisted with pain."

"I agree." Lucy nodded. "I wonder what Ruth and Kira thought when they heard Claire was arrested. Have you been in touch with her at all, Maggie?"

Maggie nodded and set down her glass. She'd drained the water and left only tinkly ice cubes. Suzanne felt sorry now she'd made the drink so spicy. "I don't know about Kira, but Ruth called the shop yesterday. She was relieved to see that Liza's killer was finally apprehended, and that your name was cleared, Suzanne. And proud that she'd helped by giving us that key. She gave all of us credit for being so persistent and sticking by you."

"You sure did. You guys . . ." Suzanne glanced around at her friends, suddenly too emotional to speak, to find the words to express her gratitude.

"Now, now . . . don't get all weepy. You'll make us start, too. This is a celebration, right?" Maggie patted her hand. "Of course we stuck by you."

"We'd do it again in a heartbeat. Though you have the credit for figuring out that it was Claire," Dana reminded her. "And that Emma was Liza's child. Do you think Ruth knew?" she asked Maggie. "Did she say?"

"I wondered about that, too," Suzanne said. Her friends had finished their first course and Suzanne brought over the coffee carafe and a dish of French pastries Lucy had picked up at the bakery — mini eclairs, cream puffs, and Napoleons.

"Ruth told me she did not know all this time. The sisters kept it from her." Maggie fixed her coffee with milk and one sugar. "After Liza moved to Maine, when she was about three or four months pregnant, Ruth

371

guessed, her daughters would switch identities every time they were with her. So that Ruth thought Kira was expecting. Pregnant by accident with a man she didn't really care for, but still wanted the baby. Kira just told her the truth and how they'd tricked her Friday night. After Claire was arrested."

"That must have been a shock." Lucy nibbled on an eclair.

"I'm not so sure of that," Maggie replied. "Ruth said she was surprised at first. But later realized she had suspected it all along, but suppressed the idea. It just seemed too far-fetched, and her daughters were wonderful at acting out their roles of mother and doting aunt whenever the four of them were together." Maggie selected a Napoleon from the platter and set it on her dessert plate. "Ruth said she'd like to come to the shop and knit with us sometime soon, while we're still making the baby sweaters."

"That would be wonderful. She has a very strong spirit, doesn't she?" Dana said.

"Yes, indeed. She does." Maggie glanced at Suzanne, but didn't say more.

"So did her daughter, Liza." When Suzanne said the words out loud, she felt better, somehow, relieved of some burden she'd been carrying. "She was not the conniving, cold-hearted person I thought, not by a long shot. She was competitive and assertive, that's for sure. And a very sharp salesperson. But much more than that. I wasn't fair to her. I can see that now."

Maggie looked the most surprised by her speech, but quietly pleased, Suzanne thought. She met Maggie's glance. "I'm just curious to know why Charles was so forthcoming with all the nitty-gritty info about his case. He's usually so closemouthed. Did you slip some truth serum in your meatballs and tomato sauce Saturday night?"

Maggie laughed. "We went out for dinner Saturday. But I suppose the wine got him talking, and also, maybe he doesn't feel quite so invested. Charles has decided to retire," she announced.

Suzanne was surprised to hear that. "Wow, that's big. Did this case push him over the edge? Or maybe all of our meddling in his work finally drove him out of the police force?"

Suzanne had been joking and was surprised to see Maggie nod in reply.

"You might say that. My meddling, in particular," she added. "It wasn't the only reason, but he decided that we were going around in circles, always arguing about the same thing, and if he retired, we could move to the next level."

"The next level? That sounds promising." Phoebe was on her second cream puff, but paused to stare at Maggie. "Come on, tell us more."

Suzanne could see the color rise in Maggie's cheeks. How rare was that? She had a sudden intuition Maggie had news to share. "Are you two finally moving in together? Is that the plan?"

Maggie sat back and smiled. "Yes, we've made plans. We are moving in together. Charles has asked me to marry him, and I've accepted."

Suzanne was so surprised, she nearly fell off her chair. She steadied herself while her friends gasped and laughed. They hugged and congratulated Maggie.

"How did that happen? I thought you were on the verge of breaking up," Lucy managed between her happy laughter.

"So did I. Especially when he stopped by Friday night with such a serious look on his face. I said, 'Oh no. This is it.' "

"And it was. But not the 'it' you expected," Dana teased her.

"No . . . not in the least." Maggie smiled in a certain way that made Suzanne sigh. She looked so happy and very much in love.

"Another wedding, and so soon," Lucy said eagerly. "Did you talk about a date?"

Maggie's contented expression quickly melted. "We'll get to that. Eventually. I'm fine being engaged a while."

"No rush," Dana said. "Every couple needs to do these things at their own pace."

Dana and Phoebe had already taken out their knitting. Suzanne saw Maggie and Lucy were about to do the same.

"I agree, no rush," Suzanne said. "It's a big step."

"Yes, it is," Maggie said, slipping a strand of yarn around a slim needle to start a new row. "You know me. I like to look before I leap."

"We do know that about you, Mag. It's okay. All sheep do," Suzanne teased.

Suzanne and her friends laughed while Maggie looked flustered a moment. Then she smiled and continued knitting. "Very true," she said. "We do."

FROM THE BLACK SHEEP & COMPANY BULLETIN BOARD

Dear Knitting Friends,
I want to thank everyone who contributed to our donation of hand knit outwear for children in need. These beautiful garments will keep so many babies and toddlers warm this winter — extra warm, because they were made with love. My knitting group's ambitious goal was one hundred items, but with the help of such generous customers, and garments made by Ruth Devereaux and her late daughter, Liza, we sent a donation that nearly doubled that number. To paraphrase the famous anthropologist Margaret Mead, never doubt that a small group of thoughtful, committed knitters can change the world.

As many of you know, the donation was made in honor of Liza Devereaux, and sent to one of her favorite charities. Liza was a frequent and favorite customer at this shop. We shall miss her and hold her dear in memory.

If you missed the fun, it's certainly not too late to knit and donate. Here's a link to a great collection of over 18 patterns for babies and toddlers, all designed in the simple and speedy garter stitch. From booties and blankets, to hooded sweaters and cuddly toys, most of the patterns are free. Maybe baby clothes just aren't your thing? There are so many charities looking for volunteer knitters and all kinds of knitted creations. I've also posted a link below to a list of ten such organizations.

The main thing is, let's share the joy of knitting!

Maggie

intheloopknitting.com/garter-stitch-little-one-knitting-patterns/

http://mentalfloss.com/article/73330/10-charities-looking-yarn-crafters

Hi Everyone!

I know you've all been gossiping about me. It's okay, I get it. How often is someone you know personally accused of murder? Frankly, if the designer shoe had been on the other foot, I'd have done the same.

If you haven't heard by now, I'm totally and completely, without a doubt, innocent. I even apprehended the real culprit — poor, deranged soul. Yes, she was pointing a loaded gun at me. But I was armed with a high-speed blender. No match, apparently.

I learned my lesson. From here on in, I will do my best to keep a lid on my temper and zip up my lip. And not to judge people so harshly, even if I don't get along with them. Nobody's perfect, including yours truly, and you never really know what other people are going through. I certainly didn't have a clue about Liza Devereaux.

Enough pearls of wisdom. Or should I say, "purls"? Time to share the recipe for my famous Celebration Chocolate Cake with Coconut Icing, which looks as good as it tastes. I certainly have a lot to celebrate. Things are looking up without a murder trial on my calendar.

As for my future plans, I have no idea what will become of Prestige Properties. No telling until the dust has settled. My heart goes out to Harry and Claire Prentiss for all they're dealing with right now.

But this unexpected turn has given me the bug to finally pursue a broker's license and open a real estate office of my own. A goal I've put off while my children were growing. How does Cavanaugh Realty sound?

In the meantime, my advice is, think twice before you speak. (Three times is better in my case.) And celebrate whenever and wherever possible. You can't go wrong with that philosophy.

Love & hugs,
Suzanne

SUZANNE'S CELEBRATION CHOCOLATE CAKE — WITH COCONUT ICING

Ingredients for the Cake:

1 3/4 cups all purpose flour
1 3/4 cups granulated sugar
1 1/2 teaspoons baking soda
1 1/2 teaspoons baking powder
3/4 cup unsweetened, Dutch Processed Cocoa
1 rounded teaspoon instant espresso powder (optional)
2 eggs
1 cup milk
1/2 cup vegetable oil
1 tablespoon vanilla extract
1 cup boiling water

Have all ingredients at room temperature.

Heat oven to 350 degrees.

Prepare two 9-inch round cake pans, greased and floured, with wax paper or parchment paper on the bottom.

In a large bowl, sift together dry ingredients: flour, sugar, baking soda, baking powder. Mix in cocoa (and espresso powder, if desired).

In a medium size bowl, beat eggs, mix in milk, oil and vanilla. Gradually pour into dry ingredients with mixer on medium speed. Mix for about two minutes until ingredients are blended. (Not too much longer or cake will be tough.)

Stir in boiling water. Pour the batter, which will be thin, into the cake pans.

Bake 30 to 35 minutes, until a thin knife blade or toothpick inserted in the middle of the cake comes out clean and the edges spring back if touched.

Cool the cakes in pans 10 minutes and then

carefully remove them from the pans and cool on a cake rack, with paper peeled off.

Cool cakes completely before frosting.

CELEBRATION COCONUT FROSTING

Ingredients:
1 cup granulated sugar
3 cups shredded, sweetened coconut
3 cups frozen, whipped topping — thawed
1 pint (16 ounces) sour cream

In a medium sized bowl, combine the sugar, sour cream and 2–2 1/2 cups coconut.

(Reserve 1/2 cup or more to sprinkle on top and sides of the cake.)

Fold in the whipped topping.

Fill and cover a two layer cake.

Sprinkle the remaining coconut on the top and sides of the cake.

ABOUT THE AUTHOR

Anne Canadeo is the bestselling author of more than thirty books, including her popular Black Sheep Knitting Club Mystery series and the Cope Light series, written as Katherine Spencer. She lives in Northport, New York, with her husband, daughter, and canine office assistant. You can contact her at anne@annecanadeo.com or follow her on Facebook.